MOON RISING

JERRY KACZMAROWSKI

Cover design by Visual Quill
Space elevator image by Adrian Mann

DEDICATION

To my wife and kids.

ACKNOWLEDGMENT AND AUTHOR'S NOTE

Moon Rising is not intended to be a science fiction novel. I intentionally selected technologies that are in the press on a daily basis to build the fictional world in which Moon Rising is set.

China is pushing hard to build a space program that rivals the United States' efforts. While they are behind, they appear to have a national will that is currently lacking in the United States. They regularly announce to the world that they are going to the moon to harvest helium-3. While much of this is propaganda from what is still a communist state, at least they are talking about it.

Likewise, the space elevator concept is one that has been around for a number of decades. Early designs were straight science fiction. They had conceptual merit, but no real research was being done. The materials didn't exist to practically build something tens of thousands of miles long. Much of this has changed since the creation of carbon fiber technology. A number of companies and academic institutions in countries like the United States and Japan are actively doing applied research to see if they can build a space elevator.

In the spirit of writing a story that was based on a realistic extrapolation of current research trends, there were two books that sat at my right hand throughout the writing of Moon Rising. The first was Leaving the Planet by Space Elevator by Bradley C. Edwards and Philip Ragan. While there is a metric ton of information on space elevators on the Internet, this book does a phenomenal job pulling everything together into a single location.

In addition, Return to the Moon by Harrison Schmitt was incredibly valuable in outlining some of the technical and economic challenges of setting up early moon bases. It contains a wealth of technical and business information that made it possible for me to conceptualize some of the challenges the first businesses will face on the moon.

Please visit my website www.jerrykaczmarowski.com for additional information on the real-world technology at the heart of Moon Rising.

Chapter 1

Arizona Desert, Yuma Proving Ground, 2035

The only thing Frank Sawyer liked more than building things was blowing them up. Today, he would get to do both. He wiped the sweat from his eyes and continued to type on his laptop. After several days of one-hundred-plus-degree highs, he questioned the reality of such a thing as a dry heat. He appreciated the smell of the desert sage and dust, but it was too hot even for someone raised in Texas. Like every other day in the field, he wore his traditional outfit of jeans, cowboy boots, and a canvas work shirt. The well-worn, dust-smudged cap of his beloved Army Black Knights shielded him from the morning sun as the temperature climbed into the low hundreds. Traditional garb for him when heads down on complex technical problems, but perhaps not standard attire for other wealthy industrialists of his prominence.

He sat on a folding field chair, oblivious to the audience as he labored. His gray eyes scanned code and three-dimensional models of the surrounding landscape. The fevered pitch with which he typed contrasted with his placid demeanor as he finalized his sales pitch. Benjamin Whitman, Frank's longtime friend and the handpicked CEO of Frank's company, was anything but relaxed. He pulled away from the crowd of military officers to speak to Frank privately.

"How's it coming? The VP is a few minutes out. I hate it when you change the play at the last minute." This, a reference to the time they had spent playing on West Point's football team so many years in the past. Frank had been the team captain and Benjamin the star running back who had taken them to victory over three seasons.

Frank leaned back and stroked the head of the German shepherd lying at his feet. Patton was Frank's good-luck charm and was a constant companion at any of his product demonstrations. His military clients allowed the idiosyncrasy due to his technical wizardry.

"Relax," Frank said with the slightest hint of a drawl from his native Texas. "I know it's your job to worry, but I've got this. My finale felt weak. I want to keep the army boys on their toes. Anyway, why is the Veep joining us? Shouldn't he be at a fundraiser or kissing a baby while some uncomfortable mother looks on?"

Benjamin ignored the jab at the VP. "You've had this locked down for two months, and you're changing things now?"

Frank gave Benjamin a quick wink and a lopsided grin. He had a playful gleam in his eye.

"Keep it simple. No last-minute surprises for a change. We need this contract. You've been funneling our profits into your skunk works projects at a frightening pace."

Frank glanced at the pale moon in the bright Arizona sky. "I want to win this one as much as you do. I know we need it."

Benjamin bent down and rubbed the dog's head. He pushed his water bowl closer, encouraging him to drink. Patton stared straight ahead, refusing to acknowledge Benjamin's affection. "The vice president will pull on any thread he can find," Benjamin said. He looked down at the dog. "What's wrong with Patton?"

"If you had a fur coat in this heat, you wouldn't want to socialize either. And don't worry about the VP."

As Benjamin headed back to glad-hand the general, a dust cloud rose on the horizon. A flotilla of black Suburbans and a stretch limousine hurtled down the dirt road. The general inquired, "Is everything OK? It's time to start."

Benjamin took one more look back at Frank and said, "General, we're set. Frank's doing some last-minute preparation to ensure things go smoothly." He marched toward the arriving convoy of black vehicles.

Two Secret Service agents in black suits and mirrored sunglasses exited the lead Suburban and opened the door of the limousine. Thomas Gladwell, the vice president of the United States, stepped out of the car. The general extended her hand to greet the VP. "Welcome, Mr. Vice President. We're not used to having someone of your stature join us for a simple weapons test. We're honored that you can be here."

Benjamin's large black hand swallowed the vice president's delicate, manicured fingers. "Welcome, sir."

Gladwell squinted his eyes in the blinding sun. He paused for a moment to glance at Frank hunched over his laptop. Nodding in Frank's direction, Gladwell ignored the pleasantries. "General, I've heard that the project is behind schedule. I'm not surprised to see Mr. Sawyer isn't ready to proceed. My contacts in the defense industry indicate that the project is speculative in the extreme. As an elected official of the people of the United States, I want to make sure their money isn't being squandered."

At this, Frank paused at his keyboard. He unwrapped his tall frame from the narrow confines of the folding chair and stood to give the vice president a wry smile. "That wouldn't be contacts at Defense Mechanics would it? Your brother-in-law's company? Our competition for this contract?"

Benjamin gave Frank a withering glance. "Vice President Gladwell, we're excited to show you just how ready we are. You will be impressed by today's demonstration. As you know, Automated Technologies is already familiar with the battlefield through our work on automating armored vehicles. We want to bring the same devastating firepower to our infantry units to keep our troops safe. If I can take you to your seat, we'll get started." Benjamin nodded to Frank.

"Ladies and gentlemen, thanks for the opportunity to show you how we have been spending your money for the last two years. While I know most of you are well aware of our design goals, let me reiterate the basics. Modern war is small skirmishes against guerilla infantries. It's been decades since we've seen enemy tanks squared up against U.S. armor.

"Modern war is Vietnam, Afghanistan, Libya, and Syria. Our enemies are guerillas who know their own country and have time on their side. They know the American people have limited patience with young boys and girls coming back in body bags from wars that last decades. Our enemies don't beat us in straight-up combat, but they can outlast us. They kill our troops with a combination of stealth, terrorism, and numbers. When we fight these insurgents on their terms, too many American kids die.

"Automated Technologies aims to change that. You're all familiar with the AutoDrive systems that are at the core of all modern cars. We did that. You are familiar with the battlefield versions that we've put in U.S. tanks. We did that, too.

"However, to date, our company hasn't benefited our infantry units. The army asks small groups of soldiers to go deep into the heart of enemy territory. They are isolated from their bases. This puts them in situations where large groups of enemy combatants can swarm and overwhelm them. This is how America will swarm back."

Frank pulled two objects out of silver briefcases and set them on the viewing table in front of the audience. "Meet the Dogs of War." The first looked to be a medium-sized stuffed dog that would make an ideal companion for a small child. The second was the same size, but it looked more like a robot out of a science fiction movie. It had titanium teeth, razor-sharp claws, and a shiny metal sphere where the stomach would be. It had a single large camera that formed a red, unblinking eye.

"It's no accident that these models look like their organic counterparts. Nature offers excellent design patterns for building swarms of ground-based combat drones. We can also disguise these weapons as animals when appropriate to provide easier stealth movement. Imagine a flea-bitten mongrel providing surveillance in the streets of Somalia."

At this, the VP scoffed. "You've spent taxpayer money on a fleet of Chihuahuas. What's the cost of these remote-control dogs? Your chief competitor is modifying five-hundred-dollar remote-control cars that provide the same capability."

Frank's eyes narrowed. His already sunburned face turned redder. "This isn't remote-control technology, as you well know." Frank turned to the Secret Service agent who drove the limousine. "Did someone remote control your vehicle to get the vice president here? Or did you tell it where to go, and it got here by itself over miles of paved highways and dusty dirt roads?" The agent opened his mouth to answer, but he shut it at a sharp glance from Gladwell.

Frank continued, "You bet your ass these cost more than five hundred dollars. Remote control. What do you do if the radio frequency is lost or blocked? Does your toy car just stop? Are you going to have an operator per car? How is that a swarm? How is that a force magnifier? I'll be running every unit here today myself by providing only high-level instructions."

Benjamin took over from Frank. "Beyond the obvious attacking capability of the teeth and spikes, each of the stomach bladders can carry an explosive device. Like grenades, they can generate explosive shrapnel, incendiary explosions, or nonlethal gas. You have options. You can subdue an enemy by biting off a hand, or you can kill twenty hostiles at once with an explosion."

Benjamin pointed to a holographic screen showing a satellite overlay of the proving ground. "We'll be demonstrating this system against a trained team of Army Rangers. They're familiar with the technology as they've been part of the project. The Rangers are entrenched in a mountaintop bunker. They're defending their position with claymore mines, machine guns, and snipers. They know the attack is coming. Overall, these odds are decidedly different than fighting an unsuspecting enemy. We've intentionally stacked the odds against ourselves."

Frank picked up a radio from his podium. "Captain, are you and your team ready?"

"Yes, sir. We've been ready. Let's see if the Dogs of War have what it takes to beat U.S. Army Rangers. Hooah."

Frank smiled at the kid's enthusiasm and tapped a key.

***

Captain Stephen Clark signaled his team to get ready. They had trained hard to develop effective countermeasures against Frank's mechanical dogs. Soldiers would have to live with these weapons in the field. They did not want unproven toys from Santa's workshop. That said, they had come to see the promise of these weapons during the last several months.

The team consisted of ten combat-hardened veterans. Captain Clark had handpicked the best gunners and snipers to test this new technology. They had fought the machines off in the past using a combination of explosive devices, flamethrowers and good old-fashioned lead. On their best day, they had beaten ten of the dogs. "Game on, gentlemen. Weapons ready."

They could see the first dogs coming online at the base of the hill. One of the snipers took aim and let loose a .300 round from his M-24. The dog exploded in a blast of metal and red paint. The sniper pivoted to aim at the next dog, but it accelerated to full speed. He missed, took aim at another, and killed it. The dogs were coming en masse now. Thirty of the dogs ran up the hill simultaneously, dust clouds flying off their clawed feet.

They broke into three separate packs. They reached speeds of thirty miles an hour even climbing the steep hill. One of the rangers shouted, "Fire in the hole." One pack of ten exploded as a claymore lit up the hillside with a bright flash. A brilliant crimson smear covered the lower part of the hill. The remaining packs broke left and right, evading gunfire while they raced up the incline.

Captain Clark shouted, "Take the shot if you have it." He fired his own weapon. Dogs exploded in red here and there, but they continued their steady race up the mountainside. In a flash of metal, the dogs were upon them. Paint exploded from the stomach bladders of two of the dogs, covering the soldiers. Five dogs stood intact in the bunker. The red paint only served to make them look more fearsome.

Captain Clark leaned back in his bunker and slammed his fist into the dirt. "Cease fire. Secure weapons." His men had trained with a maximum of twenty dogs. As he watched, another thirty dogs sauntered into view on their whisper-quiet legs from the other side of the hill. Three of the thirty lined up. They were each wearing small dog T-shirts with paw prints and a single world emblazoned on each of their sides: Bang...Yur...Ded. Stephen hated to lose, but he chuckled at Frank's humor nonetheless. "Command... the exercise is complete here. The testing ground is secure. Other than bruised egos, we're fine. I hope the project has budget for new fatigues."

***

Back at the officers' pavilion, the audience sat in stunned silence. A trained combat team of Rangers familiar with the technology and aware of the incoming attack had been overwhelmed in minutes.

Benjamin nodded his head in appreciation and whispered to Frank, "Nice touch on the finale. The extra dogs did a great job emphasizing the swarming capabilities. I didn't know you had that many out of production."

Frank winked at him. "We're not done yet."

Patton came out of his reverie and jumped ten feet in the air. He let out a growl that sounded more like a grizzly than a dog. He advanced on the audience pavilion. An overzealous Secret Service agent drew his gun and put his finger on the trigger. Before he could shoot, Patton's stomach exploded and strips of army-green confetti flew into the air.

The audience gasped while Gladwell made a high-pitched yelp. Frank snorted at him. He noted the vice president's scowl and was thankful that the man wasn't the ultimate decision maker on the vendor-selection process.

"Son, you can put away your gun," Frank said. "The demonstration is over." He went over to Patton and gave him a light push on the shoulder. The automated dog toppled over like a department-store mannequin.

The general brushed confetti off her uniform. "Impressive, gentlemen. We weren't expecting to see the clandestine capabilities today."

"Always better to show a client how something works than tell them about it," Frank said.

"Point taken. We would all be dead if this was a real attack."

"What would've happened if I'd shot the dog?" asked the agent.

"With that pistol? Nothing. It's armor-plated. The confetti bomb would still have gone off."

The audience's heads jerked toward the vice president as he clapped his hands. "Bravo, gentlemen. I'm impressed. This is orders of magnitude beyond what I've seen from your competitor." The general nodded her head in enthusiastic agreement.

While the military leadership clustered around Frank to ask technical questions, the vice president took the opportunity to pull Benjamin aside. "I'm impressed, as you said I would be."

Benjamin noted that one-on-one the vice president's slight Brahmin accent was more pronounced. He supposed Gladwell masked it when speaking in public to avoid sounding haughty when politicking. "Thank you, sir. Sorry about Frank. His desire to put on a good show can overwhelm his good judgment."

"Consider it forgotten. I wanted to talk to you alone. We speak the same language. You have more of an appreciation for the current political environment."

Benjamin nodded his head but narrowed his eyes.

Gladwell continued, "I would love to present what I've seen here today to the president directly. My recommendation would go a long way. As Frank pointed out, it would be particularly valuable since my brother-in-law's company has a competing bid."

"Thank you, Mr. Vice President. I'd be happy to give you more details."

"Actually, I wanted to discuss a different matter. I would love the support of Automated Tech in the upcoming elections. I don't have a strong reputation with the business or military communities. Public support from a man like Frank would help."

Frank's lack of support was an understatement. Gladwell made a living playing unions and government employees against the interests of the business community. He took every opportunity to divert money from the military to his political cronies.

The vice president continued. "Perhaps Automated Technologies wants to participate in my upcoming campaign in a more material way. There could be a cabinet position in my new administration for you or Frank. At a minimum, I will guarantee more contracts like this in the future."

This felt more like bribery than a request for political support. Benjamin, always serene on the outside, replied, "I'll discuss it with Frank, and we'll let you know." Without this lucrative contract, Frank wouldn't have the money he needed to fund his research. The company would be fine, but Frank's side project would have to end. Benjamin knew how much Frank valued his research. He could also guess Frank's reaction to Gladwell's shakedown.

Chapter 2

Austin, Automated Technologies Labs

Samantha Sawyer had the kind of beauty that didn't depend on makeup. That was good, because she hadn't left her lab at Automated Technologies headquarters for forty-eight hours. She gulped another drink of her now-cold coffee and rubbed her aching eyes. She briefly considered going home to shower, but instead pulled her blonde hair into a ponytail. After three years, they were close. Damn close.

Despite her youth, her father had put her in charge of the Automated Technologies fusion energy program four years ago. Industry followers wondered why Frank Sawyer would waste the talent of such a promising young leader on such an esoteric line of inquiry. To Sam, the reason was simple. Her father was betting the company on this technology, and her technical skills were second only to his.

They shared a passion for the nuts-and-bolts aspects of Automated Technologies products. While other children played with dolls, she walked the production lines with her father. She grew up sitting in the corner of boardrooms learning how to run a multinational company from her father and Benjamin.

Within weeks of her project's initiation, her father delivered a thick package to her desk. It consisted of a series of photocopied handwritten notes and a large-capacity memory card. His only comment, "Get someone you can trust to translate these for you. They're in Chinese. For now, no one knows about this other than you, Benjamin, and me."

The packages arrived every few weeks thereafter. The data within was a treasure trove of scientific knowledge. Sam and her small team completed in months what should have taken years. However, the information was spotty. She needed more to hit the aggressive deadlines set by her father.

While the clandestine research helped, it was useless without a steady stream of helium-3. Helium-3 was forty times more valuable than gold. It existed in a natural state in minute quantities on earth. The only way to get even small quantities of the material was as a natural product from the decay of tritium. While helium-3 itself was not radioactive, the only countries with ready access to large quantities of tritium were those with a nuclear weapon arsenal. These governments controlled the distribution of the resulting helium-3 through a closely monitored international bidding process. This ensured that no agency or company received helium-3 in a disproportionate amount.

The problem was that Sam needed helium-3 in disproportionate amounts. This is where Benjamin worked his magic. Without letting anything show up in the books, he used a series of shell companies to purchase enough helium-3 to meet her needs... barely.

Sam took another large swallow of coffee and put her hand on her lead engineer's shoulder. "How's it going?"

He turned from his bank of computer monitors. "We've increased the energy yield, and it's still stable."

Sam's face grew determined. "Double the output again."

"Are you sure, Dr. Sawyer? Perhaps a more measured pace?" The engineer's caution was understandable. Their early prototype tests consumed small quantities of helium-3 as they studied the basics of the fusion process. Now they were focused on proving out the scalability of the process. This meant risking larger amounts of helium-3. A mistake today would waste ten million dollars. However, caution meant they might fall even farther behind their Chinese competitors.

"Let's go for it," she said. "I'm confident we have it this time." Her father expected her to take calculated risks. Their timelines were tight. The engineer tapped on his keyboard. The power output spiked for five seconds, then ten, then thirty.

She slapped her engineer on the back and said, "It's working. Increase the output by five percent." He made the necessary adjustments.

The process shut down, and the power output dropped to zero. Sam clenched her fists. Another failure, and their supplies of helium-3 were running out.

Chapter 3

Shanghai, Chinese House Church

Dr. Jing Yang typed the last lines of code into his workstation, checked it for errors, and executed the program. He stood and stretched to get the kinks out of his neck. He had arrived at his office at Shanghai Nuclear Engineering Research and Design Institute at 5 a.m. He needed to leave early to attend a church meeting later that night.

The Mao Tse-tung 1970s-era building was claustrophobic with its block concrete and tight spaces, but Dr. Yang loved his work. His job as a senior researcher on the project was fascinating. It also provided a good middle-class life for his small family. For the hundredth time, he wished he could share the work he was doing with the international scientific community. Because China had benefited immensely from the research of nuclear engineers around the globe, he wished he could reciprocate. However, a combination of loyalty and fear ensured that he was never too tempted to share any of his data.

He rubbed his eyes and rechecked his watch. He and his wife, Li, were members at one of the many Shanghai house churches. In addition to regular Sunday worship services, they met with their church friends once a week to study scripture and support each other. Dr. Yang and his wife had big news for their small group tonight.

As he stood to go, the project director blocked his doorway. "I need you to stay late and finish up those tests. You are behind schedule."

"Director Lu, I cannot. I have a church meeting this evening. My wife would not forgive me if I skipped it. I will come in early in the morning to ensure everything is complete."

The director sucked air in through his teeth. "This is not good. You should quit the church and get more involved in the party. Your research is good, but your lack of party affiliation is holding you back. You know the party does not trust Christians in senior leadership positions. Your church is stifling your career."

"I apologize, but I must attend. My tests will be done before you arrive tomorrow morning," Dr. Yang said. The director left, shaking his head.

As Dr. Yang locked his office door and walked into the crowded Shanghai streets, he was troubled. He and Li had discussed at length whether they should share their news with the congregation tonight. As a house church, they had to register with the Communist government. To do otherwise, their congregation risked shutdown and imprisonment. They loved their church, but one never knew whether the government monitored the services. Perhaps the Communist Party had bugged the house. He chided himself for being paranoid. Even with their wide reach, the party couldn't monitor the thousands of house churches in Shanghai.

He entered the apartment. He glanced at the peeling replica painting of the Last Supper and the battered folding chairs. A meager plate of spring rolls and noodles sat on a small side table. While the surroundings were humble, the presence of close friends always made it feel like a second home.

The group was already talking. Li had saved him a seat. He sat next to her and gave her a quick hug. Her apprehensive smile mirrored his concern over sharing their news this evening.

He listened as the conversation went around the room. People shared intimate details of their personal lives. They gave thanks for exciting news like new job opportunities or asked for prayers for aging parents or sick children.

The leader turned to Dr. Yang and his wife. "Brother Jing, Sister Li, do you have anything to share?"

Jing glanced sideways at Li. "We do." The rest of the congregation smiled at them encouragingly. Li gripped his knee. She looked sick.

"Li is pregnant." The congregation shifted in their seats but said nothing. Everyone looked away and avoided eye contact. They all knew the Yang's young son. They had been part of his life since he was born. The toddler already showed signs of his father's intelligence. They also knew the consequences of violating China's one-child policy. The Communist Party had little patience for anyone who violated the rule. Forced abortions were the norm.

Li broke down and sobbed. "We don't know what to do. Our faith teaches us that abortion is wrong. We just want our baby."

One of the congregants asked, "What will you do?"

Dr. Yang answered. "We're not sure. We don't have enough money to bribe party officials. While that would be wrong, I would do it if it was an option."

The congregation nodded in agreement. The greater good was saving the child, but the money required to bribe the host of minor party officials was exorbitant.

"We may send Li to the countryside with her parents to raise the baby. We would have to split up the family," Dr. Yang said.

"You could lose your job. You could be imprisoned," one of the congregants said.

Dr. Yang nodded. "We wanted to share our situation with you. Please pray for our family."

They closed the evening with prayer, lifting their concerns to God, including the Yang's plight. After saying good night, the couples departed.

As the Yangs started down the dark streets toward their humble apartment, one of the congregants caught up with them. "I was touched by your plight. You should be able to celebrate this new child, not fear for your family."

"Thank you. Just keep us in your prayers. It's all we can ask."

"Of course, but I can do more. One of my customers at our factory is an American businessman. He also shares your faith. He has aided other families in similar situations. I can introduce you." Dr. Yang felt his wife's hand on his arm.

"How can an American possibly help?"

"He has money to bribe officials to turn a blind eye. I trust him. He is a fair and ethical man."

His wife's grip on his arm tightened. She looked up at him with hope in her eyes for the first time in weeks. He answered, "I admit it worries me. But if you say he can be trusted, I will meet with him. Thank you, brother."

Chapter 4

Washington, DC, Washington Monument

Tim Sawyer parked his BMW M6 at the Mandarin Oriental three blocks away from the Washington Monument. He flipped the keys to the valet. His studied nonchalance in dress was in sharp contrast to his vehicle. The faded jeans and worn sports coat made him feel a bit more accessible to his coworkers at the Washington Gazette. He had to prove his liberal credentials with the name Sawyer hanging around his neck like an albatross. His friends excused the M6 and his expansive Georgetown apartments, because he always emphasized that he was sticking it to his old man.

As he turned onto Jefferson Drive, the noise from the protest was already audible. It was a good turnout today. He captured some quick video footage with his phone to get a sense of the rally's size. His Canon hung around his neck so that he could get professional shots later. Although he was a print journalist, he had taken several photojournalism classes when he got his master's at Columbia's School of Journalism.

As he reached the barriers near the edge of the rally, he flashed his press credentials to the police at the cordon. They would have passed him through anyway, but showing the credentials made him feel important.

As he entered the edge of the throng, he prominently displayed his pass as he moved through the crowd. Despite the chaos, people made room when they saw the camera and the

Washington Gazette credentials. It smelled like a blend of patchouli and marijuana. While the patchouli was an unfortunate affectation of the young progressive crowd, the marijuana made him wistful for his own drug of choice. He rubbed his raw nose and patted his jacket pocket. Hopefully, the rally would be quick. Afterward, he could swing by the bathroom in one of the fashionable DC bars on the way out. Maybe also grab a few drinks.

He was close enough to make out the words from the speaker at the front of the crowd. A guy with dreadlocks said something about war crimes and Defense Mechanics. At least they weren't slamming Automated Tech. While his father's businesses disgusted him, hearing the criticism from others always put him in a defensive mindset. *Why should I have to justify myself for my father's activities?*

He snapped pictures of the crowd. The usual protest signs abounded ranging from the thoughtful to the ridiculous. "Iran didn't bomb Hiroshima!" and "Mossad = 9/11!" The crowd was outraged about U.S. saber rattling against Iran. Now that Iran had the bomb, they were increasingly belligerent. From Tim's perspective, any thoughtful student of history should know Iran was bluffing. The only country aggressive enough to use nukes was the U.S. to this day.

As he snapped pictures of the crowd through his viewfinder, he pulled his head back from the camera. *Who is that?* A dark-haired beauty stood out in the crowd thirty feet away. She nodded her head in agreement with the rest of the crowd. She seemed as passionate about the cause as anyone else at the rally. Even better, her tight Armani jeans were a sharp contrast against the hemp skirts and ragged t-shirts. Her salon-styled hair was the perfect balance between high fashion and I don't give a damn. Tim prided himself on being able to fit in with the protest crowd, but he liked to do it with a bit of class. This was a woman after his own heart.

He held up his camera and snapped several quick pictures of her. He studied the results in his camera's screen and frowned. He refocused and brought his camera up to snap a few more pictures. She was staring right at him… busted. He slid the camera down and looked at her. She had a quizzical expression on her face. Great, now he felt like a stalker snapping pictures of pretty girls. He held up his press pass in a defensive gesture. Her frozen expression softened as she laughed and motioned him over. He flashed a "who me" expression and felt like a fool. She waved him over again.

He worked his way over to her. "Hey, aren't you Tim Sawyer? Frank Sawyer's son?" she said. This was not off to a good start. He readied his standard excuses to distance himself from his dad, but she spared him the discomfort by continuing. "I'm friends with Ansley Westerton. You guys knew each other from journalism school at Columbia." She smiled and held out her hand. "I'm Lucy Lee."

"You got me. How do you know Ansley?" He remembered his brief fling with Ansley back in school. The breakup was amicable, but they hadn't kept in touch. One of those relationships where you weren't sure who dumped whom. Old girlfriends didn't seem like a good conversation starter. He pushed his head closer to Lucy's to hear her response as the chanting got louder. Her hair smelled great, much better than the patchouli.

"We went to prep school together on the East Coast, and we've always stayed in touch. I've seen pictures of you and her on online. She said you were a great guy—she was sad when you guys broke up."

This was encouraging. "Ansley's great. We had a good time together, but we kind of went our separate ways."

Lucy rewarded him with another smile. "What are you doing after the rally? A bunch of my friends and I are grabbing drinks. Do you want to join us?" She had to shout as the crowd was really getting into it.

"Yes, I—"

A wave moved through the crowd ten feet to their left. An old man held up a sign that said, "My son died for your right to protest. Support our troops!" *This old hick stumbled into the wrong protest*, Tim thought. Two young guys and a girl with pink bands on their arms were shaking their fists in the old guy's face. The man gazed straight ahead, not moving. Tim grabbed his camera and snapped some quick photos.

The crowd around the old man was getting unruly. One of the protestors shouted something and punched the old man hard in the face. Tim held up the camera again and snapped more pictures. Blood gushed from the man's crushed nose. His expression was unfocused and his mouth slack as he stumbled to the ground. As he fell, the makeshift sign came apart. Through no fault of his own, the sharp end of the stick put a deep scratch in a girl's cheek, narrowly missing her eye. The crowd erupted. The man hit the ground, and the peace protestors jumped into the fray, kicking him in the ribs and face.

Tim held his camera high overheard and held down the button. The high-speed camera shutter made a satisfying staccato sound. He shook his head one more time at the man and mumbled under his breath, "Dumb redneck." He turned to Lucy. "Let's get out of here."

They pushed their way toward the outer ring of the protest. They swam upstream as more of the protestors ringed the old man to join the action. They were almost out when the momentum turned. The fighting spread, and now people wanted out. As they clawed their way toward the surrounding street, police poured into the crowd.

Lucy tripped and fell. Tim struggled to lift her as a cop bulldozed through the crowd. She tripped again and fell into the cop, almost knocking him over. The cop shouted, "Hippy Bitch!" and hit her with his baton. She went down again.

Tim stood with his hands up and said, "Hey, man, you can't do that. I'm with the press, and I'll have your ba—." The cop clubbed him in the stomach before he could complete his tirade. He hit the ground hard.

The cop shouted at him, "Stay down!" Despite the order, Tim climbed to one knee. He fought to regain his air, but only a garbled sentence came out. "Do you know who I am? Do you know who my Dad—" The cop hit him again, this time in the head. Tim went down a second time.

The cop shoved Tim's face into the ground and cuffed him with zip ties. Tim's vision blurred. The last thing he remembered was one of the damn protestors stealing his phone from his back pocket.

Chapter 5

Beijing, Pine Valley Golf Club

"That is not the right club," said General Secretary Feng to his son.

Colonel Fei Feng ignored him and swung with all his might. The force caused the ball to hook right before it landed thirty yards short of the hole. He winced.

"Ha, the hero of the Chinese space program, indeed. Perhaps you should play from the forward tees." Secretary Feng chose a club two lower than his son, and his ball landed with a solid thunk on the green.

"Nice shot, Father."

"We have much to discuss. Let us walk." Even in his advanced years, Secretary Feng was fit enough to walk the eighteen holes. It helped that no one was pressing them. He had ordered the course shut down while he and his son played.

Secretary Feng pondered the irony of his current fixation on his low golf score. It was a sharp contrast from the concerns of his early years in the Communist Party when political failure meant a prison camp or death.

"Our fusion experiments are complete. Your efforts to collect adequate helium-3 from the moon's surface made it possible."

"Perhaps we can finally celebrate the success of the program," Colonel Feng said.

Secretary Feng frowned at his son. "The ruse was necessary." The initial trip to the moon five years ago was viewed both internationally and at home as a waste of money.

The colonel pressed the issue. "It would be good to get public credit for a mission that did exactly what is was supposed to do."

The general secretary slammed his club into the manicured grass leaving a deep gash. The colonel retreated a half step. "It was critical that others view the investment as a waste. We could not risk a space race. We could not risk a fusion race." He knew his mercurial temperament was part of his success, but he tried to restrain himself with his son. He took a deep breath and relaxed.

Secretary Feng continued. "It is a testament to the innovative spirit of the Chinese Communist Party that we are the first to commercialize fusion. No longer will the West be able to accuse us of copying and stealing their technologies. This accomplishment belongs to China alone. This will be the second Chinese Revolution."

"Yes, of course."

"Your team will return to the moon. I want China's manufacturing base powered by helium-3 within a year. Within three, China will provide fusion-generated power to the world."

"I will begin immediately."

"In the meantime, I will codify our lead into international law. We will nullify the 1967 Space Treaty. We will claim all helium-3 mining rights on the moon. In return, the world will have cheap, clean power. All of it provided by China."

"I understand why our allies will buy power from us. But what about the Western democracies? What of America?"

"They have sold their souls to their green parties and their welfare programs. They will be happy to give up their economic freedom for cheap, abundant energy. Perhaps we will create a sham organization under the auspices of the UN to give them a sense of control."

"We will be the greatest country in the world."

Secretary Feng's good mood returned, and he clapped his hands again. "We will announce our plans to the world in a month. You must be ready to back it up with action."

He swung his driver, and his ball careened into the trees. He put another ball on the tee, and it sailed down the middle of the fairway. The leader of the most powerful country in the world did not need to ask permission to take a mulligan.

Chapter 6
Shanghai, Noodle House

Stephen Clark was beginning to get comfortable in a suit and tie. After so many years in the military, the new job in the corporate world still felt unnatural at times. This was his first major mission for Frank. Frank had gleaned some minimal information about the Chinese energy program so far. However, despite his best efforts, the Chinese lead on Frank's fusion program widened. Dr. Yang could change all that.

Stephen sat with his back to the wall so he could keep a close eye on the patrons and the doorway. The other diners were used to seeing him conduct business meetings here. As always, he made sure no one followed him. There were so many expats in Shanghai at this point that the chances were low. However, various patent infringement lawsuits caused constant strain between Automated Technologies and the Chinese government. Stephen scanned the restaurant one more time to be safe.

He spotted Dr. Yang in the doorway and nodded to get his attention. Dr. Yang looked around the restaurant and wiped his sweaty brow. Stephen spoke first. "Relax."

"Yes, sorry. Our mutual friend said you could be trusted."

"We've done this before many times."

Dr. Yang conjured up a half smile but again glanced left and right at the other patrons. "I must say your Chinese is exceptional."

"Thank you. I was born in California, but my mom immigrated to the United States from China. She insisted that I learn Chinese when I was growing up. I didn't like it at the time, but it has been useful over the years. But tell me more about your situation."

Dr. Yang lowered his voice. "I'm sure my friend told you we are expecting our second child. A girl."

"Yes, congratulations."

"China's one-child policy complicates things."

Stephen frowned and shook his head in disgust. "It's an appalling law."

"It is difficult for Christians in particular. We didn't set out to flaunt the law, but my wife is pregnant anyway. It's hard to know whether to view the child as a blessing or a curse. It will cause grave difficulties for our family."

"No doubt. I might be able to help. It's no secret that my employer is a strong supporter of the Christian movement in China."

"Yes, our church uses Chinese Bibles distributed by his wife's organization."

"Frank's motivations truly come from a good place, but he also likes to antagonize the Communist Party." Stephen grinned.

Dr. Yang returned the smile. "Yes, the tension between your employer and the Chinese government is frequently headline news. I'm surprised that he continues to do business here."

"He sees the business advantages in using China's manufacturing base, but he now avoids building things here that have a high intellectual-property component. He likes the Chinese people, but he struggles with their government."

Stephen continued, "But let's discuss you. He has helped others in your family's situation. We know which officials will accept bribes and how to handle the delicate discussions. At your request, we can make the problem go away."

Dr. Yang's eyes narrowed. "That is quite generous, but why would Mr. Sawyer do this for us? I know he's wealthy, but why my family in particular?"

"First and foremost, he views it as a moral duty. He knows the difficulty the law places on the Chinese Christian community."

"And he expects nothing in return?"

"Usually nothing. In special cases, he'll ask for favors if he feels someone is in a position to help him."

"Is my situation special?"

"Your situation is very special. Your research is of interest to us."

"How so? I'm a low-level researcher working out ways to increase the safety of our fission reactors. I know Mr. Sawyer is involved in many things, including military hardware production. However, none of my research is military in nature."

"We must be honest with each other if this is going to work." Stephen leaned back from the table and folded his arms.

"I don't understand," Dr. Yang replied.

Stephen shook his head slowly back and forth. "The only thing you said that was true is that you are not doing military research."

Dr. Yang mirrored Stephen by also leaning back from the table. He glanced at the doorway as if he was ready to leave.

Stephen felt the conversation slipping and leaned forward. "Your energy research has nothing to do with fission, and you are no low-level researcher. The public propaganda shared by your government regarding failed attempts to commercialize fusion is a lie. You are much closer than you let on."

"What do you want from me?" Dr. Yang whispered as he again scanned the faces of the other patrons.

Stephen held up his hands, gesturing for Dr. Yang to relax. "Just information. We need data on your research. What's working, what's not. In return, your family gets to stay together and you get to have a second child." He knew the doctor had no good options: forced abortion, splitting up his family, perhaps losing his job.

"You ask me to betray my country."

"Do you honestly feel the research you are doing should be controlled by a single government? A government that would kill your unborn child?"

"If I am caught, I will lose everything."

Stephen weighed his response carefully. "Are you ready to tell your wife that you are too scared for yourself to save her baby girl?" Stephen resisted the urge to look away. He felt dirty.

Dr. Yang's face was expressionless as he stared back at Stephen. A full minute went by. Stephen guessed he had overplayed his hand. He should not have called the man a coward.

"I will do as you ask," Dr. Yang said.

"That's wonderful news, sir. This is a good decision for your family."

"Please do not tell me again what is good for my family. What must I do?"

"Take this memory card and gather the appropriate information from work. This satellite phone has a matching memory slot in it. It looks no different than any other telephone, but it will periodically synchronize data through our satellites. Do not attempt to communicate with us any other way. As you know, the government monitors the Internet too closely for it to be safe." Stephen slid the phone under a napkin and pushed it across the table.

Dr. Yang nodded his head once. "I understand." He reached under the napkin and nearly dropped it onto the floor. He recovered and slipped it into his pants pocket.

"You and I will likely not meet again. Someone will be in touch with you soon to tell you when your situation is fixed. I wish you and your family the best."

Dr. Yang walked out of the noodle house. Stephen stayed to finish his lunch. As he reflected on today's efforts, he was proud of the results. This would close the gap between the Chinese and American programs. Stephen was not a strongly religious man, but he was happy to assist the Yangs. He would do his best to make sure Dr. Yang remained safe and undetected. His first attempt at espionage was a success.

Chapter 7
Austin, Automated Technology Labs

Frank arrived at the Automated Technologies lab in Austin at five a.m. He rose early on those rare days when he was able to do real work. Benjamin did a wonderful job isolating him from many of the day-to-day activities necessary for running his mammoth company. Even with that, Frank never spent as much time working on the technical challenges he loved so much.

Today Frank was checking final progress on the carbon fiber manufacturing efforts. Most of his technical expertise lay in the automated systems that had made him so wealthy. The material science project was a refreshing change of pace. Ten years ago when he started the project, he knew little about the topic. After a decade of research, he guessed he knew more about advanced carbon fiber design and manufacture than anyone in the world.

More than any other line of engineering inquiry at Automated Technologies, this was now Frank's baby. He effectively served as the lead engineer on the project. To keep the project secret, he doled the work out to various third party contractors and other Automated Technologies facilities. Outside of a handful of engineers on Frank's team, only Benjamin and Sam knew the overall scope and scale of the project.

As he walked across the bright, spotless factory floor, he smelled the faintest odor of polyacrylonitrile. The chemical was the primary ingredient used in carbon fiber. He made a mental note to work with his operation engineers to boost the airflow in the lab.

He knew he was well within the safety guidelines required by the government, but the health of his engineers was paramount to him. They were like family.

Several engineers welcomed him enthusiastically as he walked onto the main floor. He spared no expense on the engineering side of the business. Frank's labs were a playground for engineers who had a passion for pushing technical boundaries. Frank's office lacked the expensive artwork of other wealthy executives, but the lab area always had the latest technology.

"How's my carbon fiber coming?" he asked.

They crowded around him vying for attention and walked him over to the far end of the floor. A huge roll of carbon fiber towered above their heads.

Frank grinned from ear to ear and turned to his lead material scientist. He felt the cool, smooth surface of the carbon fiber and smiled. "Tensile strength?"

"It's able to hold up to two tons plus its own weight," she replied.

"I ask for one ton, and you give me two. I love it." He turned to the industrial engineer in charge of producing the huge roll. "How many runs did it take to get the roll?"

The engineer didn't meet Frank's eyes. "Ten. We had to burn through tons of carbon fiber to get the consistency high enough to generate something of this length."

Frank frowned. "We need better than that. Carbon is cheap, but time is precious. We're going to need a lot more of these, and that failure rate is too high." The engineer's expression soured, so Frank changed tactics. He slapped the engineer on the back and said, "I know you have this. You're the best industrial engineer in the world. That's why I hired you."

The man met Frank's eyes and stood straighter. "Nothing has ever been engineered that can circle the earth one and a half times until now," the engineer said.

"This will be the greatest engineering achievement since the dawn of mankind. You will be proud to tell your children and your grandchildren that you were part of this team." Frank gave them a big grin. "Good progress, but get us back on schedule."

Chapter 8

Washington, DC, City Jail

Tim's head throbbed. He woke up in the back of the police van with a number of other protestors. When he arrived at the DC jail, the police dumped him in the tank with the rest of the scum. Worse, the cops found his drugs when they booked him. His employers would support him with regard to police abuse. He was after all part of the vaunted fourth estate. The cocaine might be more difficult to explain.

He could call his lawyer, but the police were struggling to process the mass of protestors. While he would typically push his way to the front of the line, a drug charge complicated things. He needed to stay in the police's good graces. He also didn't need to call attention to his family name. The peace protestors would turn violent if they knew Frank Sawyer's son was in the cell with them.

A uniformed officer walked up to the jail door. "Timothy Sawyer, front and center."

Tim stepped forward avoiding eye contact with the other protestors.

He heard one of the other inmates call out, "Hey, that's Frank Sawyer's son."

Tim scowled in a feeble attempt to look tough as he pushed his way to the jail door, but one guy spit on him. Someone pushed him, and he fell to his knees on the concrete floor.

"Knock it off," the guard shouted. He opened the jail door and pulled Tim out into the corridor by the back of his shirt. Tim glared at the guard for the rough extraction, and the man appeared suddenly worried. He dusted Tim off. "Sir, you've been bailed out. Please come with me."

Tim's thoughts raced. *Did the Gazette hear I was tossed in jail?* He wanted to handle this without them knowing. At least he was getting out. He trailed behind the officer and gathered his belongings, minus the drugs.

At the front of the jail, he was met by a police lieutenant and Lucy Lee from the rally. The lieutenant said, "Your friend here informed us of your family connections and your press credentials. It might be best for all concerned to let things slide in this case. If you and your family can overlook the incarceration, any other charges can be dropped." The lieutenant shifted his feet and looked away.

Tim took advantage of the officer's distress. "You guys hit my girlfriend for no reason and probably gave me a concussion. I'm a member of the damn press. We both know my lawyer can make 'any other charges' go away. I'm tempted to sue the department and turn this into a front-page story."

Lucy rested a hand on Tim's shoulder and leaned closer to him. She said, "The police at the rally made a mistake, but they apologized. I'm fine, so let's drop it. I want to get out of here."

It would be more fun spending the day with her than going round and round with the police. He glared one more time at the officer, but nodded his head. "OK, let's go." The young lieutenant's shoulders relaxed, and he walked them to the exit. He disappeared back into the station.

At his departure, Lucy turned to Tim and arched an eyebrow in mock irritation. "Girlfriend? Seems a bit sudden considering we just met."

Tim's cheeks flushed. "Sorry. I figured it would make more of an impression on the cop. You know, scare him a bit."

She laughed. "Fair enough. Forgiven for now. By the way, I rescued your phone." She handed it back to him.

As they walked out of the station, a photographer at the bottom of the stairs whirled and snapped several pictures. "Is it true that you were held overnight for disturbing the peace and cocaine possession? Can you comment?"

One of the cops must have tipped off the tabloid for a couple of extra bucks. "No comment," Tim said. He hailed a nearby cab.

"This wouldn't be the first time," the reported pressed. "Did your father pull some strings?"

Tim spun and faced the man with a savage expression on his face.

"That's right, smile for the camera." The man snapped more pictures. Tim balled his fist and stepped toward the man, but he was met with the steady clicking of a high speed camera shutter.

Lucy grabbed his shoulder less gently this time. "Let's get in the cab."

Tim took one more look at the grinning photographer and jumped into the waiting car with Lucy.

Chapter 9

Beijing, Office of the Chinese General Secretary

General Secretary Feng straightened his hand-tailored suit as he waited for the makeup artist to finish. The days of senior party leaders in Mao suits were thankfully gone. His hair was impeccable, as always. Feng had earned his role as China's preeminent leader, and he liked to look the part.

The camera countdown started. He looked to his translators to confirm they were ready. He spoke fluent, unaccented English, but he would share the news with the world in Chinese. It would serve to emphasize China's changing role in the world.

The camera's red light blinked on. "Ladies and gentlemen of the community of nations. The People's Republic of China has wonderful news to share with you today." He paused to allow the translators to catch up.

"China has long been criticized for emphasizing economic progress over the environment. While we make no apologies for lifting our people out of poverty, it has come at a cost."

"Our own cities are polluted, and our huge manufacturing base has contributed disproportionately to mankind's carbon footprint." China's cities were indeed the most toxic on the planet. However, the planet's temperature had not increased a single degree in the last thirty years. Still, the message played well with the green parties of the West.

"Today, China will begin the process of powering the city of Shanghai using clean-burning fusion from our stocks of helium-3. Mere pounds of the helium isotope will provide power to the citizens of Shanghai for over a year.

"While I am excited to share this new technology with our citizens, I am even more pleased to share this great leap forward with the world." He opened his arms in an expansive welcoming gesture.

"To that end, China will establish a permanent, large-scale helium-3 mining operation on the moon. Hundreds, then thousands of Chinese citizens will move to this permanent lunar base to create cheap, green energy for all people.

"China will work with any large industrialized nation to retrofit their existing energy production networks to leverage helium-3 fusion. These plants will provide boundless energy to the citizens of the world. We will cut energy costs to a fraction of their current levels while reducing pollution to almost nothing." He sliced his arm diagonally across his body.

"I will work personally with the United Nations to ensure that all mankind benefits from these advances in technology. China is one of the few nations on earth with the technological skill to harvest helium-3. However, we will ensure that those countries unable to make this kind of national investment will still benefit.

"We must ensure the economic viability of this mammoth undertaking. Therefore, we will propose changes in rules to intellectual property laws and ownership of lunar real estate. We also propose the creation of a Fusion Energy Security Council in the United Nations. China will head this council, but we will work with those members of the world community that we view as responsible."

Secretary Feng outlined his plans for green fusion for another ten minutes. He concluded by turning to the Taiwanese ambassador behind him on the stage. "As part of these changes, Taiwan has expressed interest in receiving fusion energy for free for their manufacturing base and their consumer needs. We have generously agreed to Taiwan's proposal that they rejoin China as our twenty-fourth province."

"In addition, in secret one-on-one negotiations, North Korea has finally agreed to give up their nuclear weapons program effective immediately. As part of this agreement, we will supply their energy needs as well. They will become the sixth of China's Autonomous Regions joining arms with Tibet and Inner Mongolia. We welcome them to the larger People's Republic of China."

The secretary uncharacteristically answered questions for another twenty minutes from a stunned world community. Feng smiled to himself. China would lead the world in the next century. And the Feng family would lead China.

***

Frank and Benjamin sat in Frank's office at his ranch, drinking beer and going over various work items. The army's Black Knights played in the background. They weren't getting much work done, but Frank was all right with this. As they watched the Knights drive the ball down the field, a breaking news story interrupted the game.

Frank leaned back from his desk and steepled his fingers as the Chinese general secretary loomed on the screen. Frank absorbed the information without moving. He expected this, but not so soon. He turned to Benjamin. "Can you move up our meeting with the president?"

Chapter 10

Washington, DC, Washington Gazette Headquarters

Tim entered his boss's office with his story ready. He expected a minor hand slap. He knew how to handle the aging political editor of the Washington Gazette. He needed to keep his cool and let the man play the concerned father figure.

His boss frowned and motioned for Tim to take a seat. He loosened his already-loose tie and pushed his rolled-up sleeves even higher on his arms.

"I was disappointed to see you on the front pages in the checkout line at the grocery store," he said.

"I know. I shouldn't have let myself get caught in that situation."

"And what situation is that?"

"I was detained by the police unlawfully. I was doing my job as a member of the press. The police had nothing on me or they would've charged me. The tabloid shouldn't have run that story. I may sue."

"That's bullshit. I may sit on the political desk, but my peers have connections back to the police department. The only reason you weren't charged is because the police didn't want to mess with Frank Sawyer's son."

"The important thing is that I wasn't charged. No one is going to take the tabloid seriously."

His boss peered over his glasses and down his nose at Tim. "In other words, the important thing is that you weren't caught? You miss my point. You have a drug problem. You're consistently late, you look like shit, and your work has been suffering for months."

"The story isn't true. You can't possibly take the word of a tabloid over me."

The man shook his head in disgust. "You go through great pains to distance yourself from the Sawyer name. A real self-made man. Well, I'm going to treat you like I would anyone else. You're fired."

"You can't do that."

"Get your stuff and clear out. You have the makings of a good reporter, but I don't need a junkie on my staff. "

***

When Tim arrived at the bar, Lucy was already there. She sipped a club soda. He wanted something stronger. He ordered a Manhattan, but she held up her hand and motioned for a second club soda instead.

"It's been a long day," Tim said making no effort to mask his annoyance.

"I know you liked the job at the Gazette. I know the termination seems unfair, but it's not."

Tim pushed back from the bar and turned to face her. "You're taking the side of the paper? I wasn't even charged."

"I was there. We gamed the system. Anyone else would still be in jail."

"I expected more support from you, at least. This is the kind of crap I would expect to hear from my father."

She put her hand on his and looked into his eyes. "I like you. But you have to dial it back. You're not a kid."

Tim looked at her long, slender fingers. *Why am I so attracted to her?* She was beautiful, but Tim's girlfriends were always attractive. A wealthy family offered many perquisites.

Lucy continued to push. "I talked to some friends, and they gave me the name of a good substance-abuse clinic out in

California. They deal with high-profile clients where discretion is important."

"I don't need this."

"You lost your job today." She pulled her arm off his shoulder. "I don't want to hang out with an unemployed cokehead. I'm at the point in my life where I'm looking for more."

And that was it. Because she thought long-term, she wouldn't put up with his crap. All the other girls he had dated had accepted or even encouraged his irresponsible behavior as long as they could date someone from the wealthy Sawyer family.

"So now you're showing me the door too?"

"No. I'm telling you to grow up and get help. I don't want to date someone who's self-destructing."

Tim rolled his eyes and shook his head, but said, "Give me the number. I'll check it out."

She locked her stunning almond eyes on his and kissed him passionately. "I know they can help you. I'll fly out for moral support if you want. Now, what's next on the job front?"

"Don't you ever quit?"

The beautiful eyes narrowed.

He threw his hands up. "I was fired three hours ago. I don't have any immediate ideas. I could try independent blogging or freelancing."

"Blogging?" The eyes narrowed even more.

"Just while I get my next thing figured out."

"You're better than that. Why don't you ask your dad for a job?"

"Because I don't want to be a hypocritical sellout."

"Convenient." She wrinkled her nose and looked away.

"What does that mean?"

"Don't let daddy issues get in the way of a smart decision."

"Daddy issues? You want me to join my dad's company and hawk weapons."

"He could get you something in media relations that doesn't deal with the military side of the business. Your dad's an amazing man. You should give him credit for the good things his company has done."

"I don't want to talk about this right now."

"You said your dad is in town later this week. You could talk about it then."

"I was thinking about coming up with an excuse not to meet him."

"Why? That seems mean-spirited."

"Because I don't want to get into it with him over my termination. He'll treat me like a kid and offer me a job like I need a handout."

"Then that should make it an easy topic to broach."

Tim shook his head again and stared at her for several seconds before answering. "If you drop it, I'll meet him for dinner. You could join us. It might keep things more civil."

"I would love to give you air cover, and I would like to meet your dad. Let's get out of here." She kissed him and smiled seductively.

Chapter 11

Washington, DC, 701 Restaurant

Frank sat at the bar sipping an East Coast microbrew. He didn't enjoy either the location or the beer. Half the patrons were politicians. A couple of the more prominent ones introduced themselves. Frank was cordial, but he would have preferred a more private place to catch up with his son.

He checked his watch again. Tim was thirty minutes late as usual. Frank's punctilious nature rebelled at this, but he promised himself he'd let it slide tonight. His relationship with his son was challenging enough without letting the small things get in the way. He reminded himself that he had a part to play in things. He wasn't around as much as he should have been when Tim was young. The demands of his military career and the startup phase of his business were all-consuming. He rectified the situation when Sam was born, but he had lost a decade with Tim that he would never get back.

As he forced himself to calm down, Tim entered with a beautiful Asian woman on his arm. She wore jeans and an expensive, conservative blouse. The outfit reminded him of something his daughter, Sam, would wear.

Tim walked up and nodded a greeting.

"I see you brought a guest." Frank said, nodding at Tim's date.

"This is Lucy Lee."

Lucy blushed and extended her hand. "Sorry we're late. It's my fault. I changed outfits twenty times. Tim told me to relax, but it's not every day that I get to meet one of America's most famous business leaders."

"Tim's correct that I don't do formal. One of the benefits of owning Automated Technologies is that I don't have to wear a suit and tie to impress. Let's grab a table."

The maître d' took Frank's cue and sat them.

"How are things at the Gazette?" Frank said.

"Not great."

Frank was silent. He hated the liberal rag and wished Tim had chosen a different media outlet for employment. However, he also didn't want to spend the evening talking about another of his son's screw-ups.

"It seems one of the tabloids caught wind of a story that I was busted for drugs. The police didn't file any charges, but the Gazette let me go."

"That shouldn't be a surprise. They have a reputation to protect."

"Tabloids are tabloids. Who cares what they write? They take shots at you all the time."

"Your timing is awful. I'm in town to meet with the president tomorrow, and I would've preferred that this not be a conversation topic."

Lucy threw Tim a lifeline. "Mr. Sawyer, I was there. I bailed Tim out after some confusion at a rally that turned violent. Someone from the police department must've tipped off the reporter to the initial charges."

She's here to deflect my anger. Just like Tim to hide behind a girlfriend. What did I do wrong? "It's great that there are no formal charges, but that doesn't mean they weren't valid."

"Tim's signed up in a rehab program out in California. Some of my friends recommended it," Lucy said.

"That's good news. I've been asking Tim to take that step for years."

"They're both effective and discreet," she said.

Frank turned back to Tim. "Any ideas on the job front?"

"I might freelance for a bit." Frank noticed the briefest scowl cross Lucy's face. She moved an almost imperceptible inch away from Tim.

Frank smiled to himself. *Intelligent, beautiful woman meets eligible bachelor with some rough edges. Wants to clean him up and make him presentable before she commits.*

"You need a real job. Why don't you come work at Automated Tech?"

"You and I wouldn't work well together."

"We'll have you work under Ben. He loves you like a son. We always need help managing the press and molding our public image."

"That's because Automated Technologies is always doing something evil. I'm not working for a company that profits from war, destroys the environment, and who knows what else."

"You shouldn't speak to your father that way," Lucy said. "I'm no fan of the military either, but your Dad's company has done great things for society."

"I didn't invite you here to take his side," Tim said.

Lucy changed the subject. "If you don't mind me asking, why are you meeting the president? I'm sure it's not the first time for you, but I'm sure it has to be exciting. I'm a huge fan of President Brown. I voted for her."

"We're meeting to discuss what I would call a green energy initiative."

Lucy laughed and slapped Tim on the knee. "See, I told you Automated Tech did good things. You should consider your dad's offer."

Frank liked this girl more and more. Politics aside, she was better than many of Tim's previous girlfriends.

They ordered and continued their conversation through dinner without further revelations.

At the end of the meal, Frank said, "Tim, are you still going to make it back to Austin for Thanksgiving? The Whitmans will be there, as will your sister."

"Sure, I'll make it down this year." Tim turned to Lucy. "We'll make it down this year?"

"Mr. Sawyer?" Lucy asked.

"You're welcome to join us, but you'll have to call me Frank. It'll be a small, informal affair. You will also have to participate in some of our family traditions."

"Such as?"

"We have an annual skeet-shooting contest. I'm awful, but it's a fun way to ring in the holiday. My wife is much better with a shotgun. If you join us, she can give you some tips. It's guys versus girls."

"I've never shot a gun before. I'd love to try."

"You'll consider the job offer?" Frank asked Tim.

"I'll make sure he does, Mr. Sawyer... Frank."

Frank checked to see if Tim had issues with Lucy answering for him. He didn't seem to mind. If a girl was going to have her hooks into his son, Lucy wasn't a bad option. Her obvious drive might be good for the boy.

Chapter 12

Washington, DC, George Washington Memorial Parkway

Frank needed this meeting with the president to be successful. His investment of billions in research over the last five years was in jeopardy. If the Chinese beat him in the race to commercialize fusion, there would be no participation trophy.

Ben interrupted his musings. "I'm sorry to hear about Tim's latest escapades. I know it wears on you and Lisa. Anything I can do?"

Frank stared into the distance before answering. "It's not the first time I've been in the press because of Tim's recklessness, but it does get old. By the way, I recommended he join us and that he work for you."

"That's great news. It would be great to have him around again."

"Let's change the subject. It puts me in a sour mood."

"You're right. We're on in a few minutes. You sure it's a good idea to push Gladwell out of this meeting? He can't hurt us now, but he will likely be in the Oval Office in a couple of years."

"I know you believe it's expedient to have him attend, but I won't have that man be a party to these conversations. I've never trusted him."

"You seem able to work with the president despite your political differences. Why not Gladwell?"

"President Brown was raised by a single mother in Houston, Texas. She parlayed valedictorian in her high school and money from beauty contests winnings into a Harvard Education. Gladwell was given everything by wealthy parents."

"Still, their politics are the same."

They passed an electronic speed-limit sign that adjusted based on the amount of traffic and time of day. A fifteen-person crew was repairing it. Frank pointed at them. "Look at them working on a speed-limit sign for a road populated entirely by automated cars. Ten of them are standing around. The Ellen Browns of the world create those useless jobs, because they want those people to have a paycheck to feed their families. President Brown's views are irrational, but they at least come from a place of compassion."

Frank jabbed at the air with his index finger. "Gladwell is a different beast entirely. He wants those same people to have the same make-work jobs so that he can have their votes."

"You know, he proposed a role in his administration for you at the proving ground."

"That's laughable."

"He offered me a job at the same time."

Frank whipped around to face his friend. "And you didn't tell me? You aren't seriously considering it?"

"Relax, buddy. You know I never would. I didn't want you to be distracted by it."

"What did he want in return?"

"More of the same... political support... financial support."

"And what do we get?"

"He indicated that we wouldn't need to bid on government contracts going forward."

Frank wrinkled his nose as if the mere mention was noxious to him. "I'm OK without that kind of support. We can win contracts on the merits."

"Though he wasn't explicit, he's likely behind the holdup of our current military bid."

Frank slapped the armrest. "Don't you find Gladwell's job offer mildly insulting?"

"How so?"

"It's rich that a loser like Gladwell would offer you a lapdog role in his administration. You should run against him."

"Come on. I like big government as much as you do. I'm a business guy. Have been for most of my life."

Frank glanced at the scars spidering across Ben's head. "Prior to that, you were a war hero. And prior to that, you were a college football star. You have the perfect resume. I would vote for you."

"Who would manage the business side of Automated Technologies? If your meeting with President Brown goes well, things are going to get busy."

"Having the political side of things solved may be even more important than the business aspects. I agree that Gladwell will be a problem if he gets upgraded from the Naval Observatory to the White House."

Frank's mobile rang and his assistant's picture appeared on the screen. Frank accepted the call. "You are on speaker. Ben's with me."

"I'm sorry to interrupt, but I thought you would want to know."

"Know what?"

"The president's office called and said there would be a last-minute attendee at the meeting."

"Don't keep us in suspense."

"It's Vice President Gladwell."

Frank looked at Ben as he spoke to his assistant. "I made it clear that I didn't want him there."

"They insisted," his assistant said.

"We'll deal with it." Frank shook his head and hung up.

Before Frank could launch into another tirade about Gladwell, the car's soothing electronic voice chimed in, "Nearing White House."

Chapter 13

Washington, DC, The White House

The bodyguard switched to manual control as they neared the gates of the White House. The security guard approached the car. He checked everyone's credentials. "Good to see you again, gentlemen. Please proceed."

Inside, they passed through another round of security. A cheerful young aid escorted them to the Oval Office. As they approached, they heard Gladwell's voice. When the vice president saw Frank and Benjamin, he smiled a politician's smile. "Welcome to the White House, gentlemen. I heard you were meeting with the president. I was able to clear my busy schedule last minute in order to join you. By the way, sorry to hear about your son."

Frank frowned and opened his mouth to speak as they entered the oval office.

Before he could respond, President Brown interrupted. "I know you wanted to keep this meeting small, but I wanted Thomas to attend primarily as an observer. I'm trying to keep him more involved in issues that may span our administrations."

Frank forced a smile and held out his hand. "Mr. Vice President, it's good to see you again."

"I know this is your meeting, but I have good news. You won the contract for your Dogs of War. An initial thousand units. By the way, I love that name," Gladwell said slapping Frank on the shoulder.

"The contract was for three thousand initial units." Frank looked at his shoulder as if a bird had just dropped something unsavory on it.

"The U.S. government is going to split the contract between you and Defense Mechanics."

"Our technology is infinitely better."

"But Frank, everyone has to win. It can't only be about what's best. People will think we're playing favorites with Automated Technology."

"We'll have to see if it makes sense to spin up our production lines for an order of that size."

President Brown interrupted again. "Perhaps we can start. Frank, you asked for this meeting."

Frank turned to face her as she came around her desk. At sixty, she was still an attractive woman. She cut an elegant figure in her dark, understated Armani pants suit. "Madam President, I'm sure you've seen China's news regarding their plans for fusion energy production?" Frank asked.

"I have. Our own scientists, and those of our allies, insist it's fifty years away at best. It's more Chinese propaganda."

"Your advisors are wrong. We've duplicated most of their work in our labs. We're a few months behind them, worst case. They also have everything they need to scale up mining operations on the moon."

Frank continued, "Their last mission to the moon brought back over five hundred pounds of helium-3. Over the last five years, they've used it to perfect commercial fusion. We know because we have the plans for the machinery. Incidentally, their team is also working on fusion weapons, despite the international ban."

"That sounds like corporate espionage, which is a federal crime even if it involves another nation. I assume they didn't share the technology with you willingly?"

Frank was in dicey international legal waters, but he gambled. "When China stole our AutoDrive technology for their highway system, the gloves came off. I despise their business ethics. Their theft of my intellectual property has cost me billions."

"You risk causing a major international incident."

"If they aren't America's enemy, they are our most fearsome competitor. I would dread the day that the Chinese had a monopoly on fusion. Over time, that will amount to a monopoly on all energy production," Frank said.

President Brown shook her head in disagreement. "There are too many competing technologies: oil, coal, wind, solar."

"Solar and wind will never generate enough power to serve the needs of modern industrial nations. And what will the European countries do given a clean alternative to fossil fuels to power their cities? For that matter, what will the far left in your own party want?" Frank asked.

"Even if you have their technology, what good does it do you? They still control access to helium-3. Our space program is decades behind theirs."

Benjamin said, "We believe we have an answer. You've heard of space elevators?"

"I have. It's another technology that is fifty years out. Building a tower into space is a ridiculous idea."

"Not so ridiculous. Frank has one, and it is ready to deploy within a year. All he needs is minor help from the American government," Benjamin said.

"I agree that it's ridiculous to build a tower into space. But this works more like a rope extending from the earth. It stays up due to centrifugal force," Frank said. He spun his index finger in a circle. "It's like spinning a lasso."

"I don't believe you. Even if I did, the Chinese space program is too far ahead for us to close the gap."

"We can build the elevator fast enough to catch up. The economics are staggering. It takes over ten thousand dollars to move a single pound from earth into orbit using rockets. We feel we can drop this to one hundred dollars per pound, perhaps less as the technology matures. Even China won't be able to compete against that cost difference."

She was thoughtful for a moment. "Assuming NASA could vet your plans, what would you want from me?"

"An aircraft carrier."

"You want me to give you an aircraft carrier?"

"Of course not. I would be willing to pay for it. Perhaps one that is ready to be mothballed? You can strip out the military technology." He smiled. "Of course, I would want a discount."

"Why would you need an aircraft carrier?"

"I need to tether the space elevator to it. It's better to attach it to a floating object near the equator than a fixed position on land. That way, you can move it out of the way of storms. The physics also work better if it is closer to the equator. I can use a regular ship, but it will slow me down. I need something that can receive tons of cargo quickly."

"Assuming an aircraft carrier can be repurposed for civilian use, what else?"

"We propose to build two elevators. The U.S. government maintains ownership of the first. We own the second. We supervise the construction of the elevators as well as the related technology. The company gets tax-free status, freedom from lawsuits, freedom from OSHA, freedom from union laws, and freedom from bureaucratic interference. This will be like building the first transcontinental railroad. It will be physically and financially dangerous. In a word, I need control to take on this kind of risk."

She held up her hands to stop Frank. "Slow down. That would be political suicide with my constituency."

"Not to be impolitic, but your run in politics is coming to an end in the not-too-distant future regardless. Ellen, we've known each other a long time. What will be your legacy? Are you going to be the president that lost control of space and international energy production to the Chinese? I assume it's not lost on you that military dominance will follow?"

He paused for effect, knowing the political heroes President Brown idolized. "Will you get a sentence in the history books like Carter, or will you get a chapter like Kennedy?"

"Why do this? You're already rich. The business community worships you. If this fails, you will be a laughing stock. The space elevator could be your Spruce Goose."

Frank looked thoughtful for a moment. "We both come from Texas. I assume you've been to Johnson Space Center?"

"Of course."

"I went there when I was a child with my father and my grandfather. Just the guys. I of course knew about the space program, trips to the moon, etc. What young boy doesn't?"

"Knowing about it and seeing it isn't the same thing. I was amazed at what these men accomplished. The courage of the first astronauts. The sheer will it took the country to come from behind and beat the Russians.

"My grandfather has since passed, but he was alive during that first space race. A tear came to his eye when he talked about what we accomplished as a country. That's not an everyday thing for an old Texas rancher. He said something that might sound trite today. 'Frankie, this is what America can do when we put our back into it.' It's always stuck with me."

The president nodded thoughtfully. "That doesn't sound trite to me at all. I'll get you what you need, assuming our scientists can validate your fusion claims and your elevator designs."

Frank stood and extended his hand to President Brown. "Thank you, Madam President."

President Brown didn't move. "Sit for a moment longer, Frank. Do you know how my father died?"

Frank sat back down on the couch. "I read that it was an accident on an oil rig, but I don't know more than that."

"He was a blue-collar worker on an offshore rig in the Gulf of Mexico. A chain cut loose from the drill and killed him instantly. The funeral was closed casket."

"It must've been tough to lose your father at such a young age and with such violence."

"The oil company refused to pay his death benefits. They accused him of drinking on the job."

She paused and looked Frank in the eye. "The problem is my father didn't drink. We didn't have enough money to fight it in court. It made for a hard life for my mother and me, but we got by."

Frank leaned his chin on his hand and leaned forward in concern.

"I wanted you to understand that my distrust of business is based on the harsh reality of my childhood. I like you. I always have. However, I don't trust the motivations of any big corporation," she said.

"I'm sorry to hear that, Madam President," Frank said.

"I want you to work with Gladwell on this. I know that won't sit well with you, but I insist."

Frank leaned back as his empathy drained away. "I told you I need control. I'll do this without you."

Benjamin grabbed Frank's arm. "We need government support if we are going to catch up with the Chinese. You know we do."

President Brown defused the situation. "You will have your control, but I need to know what you are doing. My party will insist on his involvement. He's the heir apparent for the presidency, so you might as well get used to it. Take it or leave it."

"We'll take it, Madam President," Benjamin answered for Frank.

Frank grudgingly nodded his head. "We'll take it."

Frank frowned and turned to Gladwell. "I'll try to make it work."

Gladwell smirked in return.

Chapter 14

Shanghai, Nuclear Engineering Research and Design Institute

Dr. Yang was at the office early again. The rest of the lab tended to work late, and so the early morning hours were less crowded. He could pull information off the servers with less chance of detection. He used different computers each time to avoid creating a pattern.

He checked his watch. The terabytes of data slowly copied over to the high-capacity storage device. He glanced at the clock on the wall.

"You are here early."

Dr. Yang jumped. Director Lu stood behind him. "You surprised me, sir."

"Engrossed in your work as usual? You know, you would get more recognition if you worked hours similar to your colleagues. You are always running out the door in the evening while the rest of us are working."

"I do always come in early."

"I don't dispute that you work hard. I am saying you would get more recognition. But perhaps you don't need it. You seem to have friends in high places."

"I do not understand."

"I heard that your wife is pregnant with your second child."

He froze, unsure of how to respond.

"Relax, your secret is out. I assume the government knows as well, which means you must have handled it somehow. I hear that it can be quite expensive to get the government to look the other way. How did you ever afford it?" He laughed. "I know how much money you make. I approve your paychecks."

He gave a rehearsed response. "Not money, sir. My uncle is high up in the party. He used his influence to help me."

"What is his name? Perhaps he can assist me and my wife with a similar situation?"

Dr. Yang's mouth hung open.

"Ha-ha. It's a joke. Do you think I've been eating tiger penis for lunch? You give me too much credit. We're almost sixty years old. Our parenting years are done." The director laughed so loud he shook.

Dr. Yang laughed along, but his laugh sounded hollow. His hands were clammy, and the room spun.

"What are you working on so early? You are well ahead of where you need to be."

"I am finalizing the round-seven tests." A bead of perspiration rolled down his forehead. He dabbed at it with his hand.

"But you sent those to me last week. Are you feeling ill? You look like you might be coming down with something."

"I mean to say, I am going over them one more time. I was worried I had made an error."

"Have more faith in yourself. Your work is impeccable. By the way, why are you not at your desk?"

Dr. Yang paused again. He was doing that a lot in this conversation. "I think more clearly when I walk around. I had an idea that I wanted to check, and this workstation was close at hand."

"Well, carry on. I will see you at our morning meeting. If you are feeling ill, please go home so that you don't make the rest of us sick."

"Thank you, sir. Perhaps I will go home early if I don't feel better."

The director closed the hallway door and walked off.

Dr. Yang put the storage device back in his pocket, and wiped the sweat from his forehead.

Chapter 15

Dongfeng, Jiuquan Satellite Launch Center

The Chinese built the Jiuquan Satellite Launch Center in 1958 as their first fledgling space hub. It was located deep in the Gobi Desert away from prying Western eyes. Miles of flat, dry land spread out in all directions punctuated only by periodic launch towers. Over the last decade, the number of towers had grown from one to eight. The original administrative buildings constructed in the 1960s were all gone. Gleaming icons of modern architecture replaced them. Interspersed with the civilian buildings were China's nuclear weapon research facilities.

Today's opening ceremonies would start at exactly eight minutes past eight. Eight rockets out of an eventual eighty-eight would carry the Chinese taikonauts back to the moon. Eighty-eight thousand Chinese civilians had been brought in by bus or railroad to ensure a large crowd.

Secretary Feng was a rational man, but he hoped that the recurring use of the number eight in today's events would be auspicious. As the March of the Volunteers anthem concluded, Secretary Feng went to the podium.

"Fellow citizens, today is a great day for China and a great day for mankind. Eighty-eight brave men and women will revolutionize energy production for the entire world. They will bring back enough helium-3 from the moon to power mankind's energy needs for thousands of years to come.

"But they will not be leaving China. Rather, China will go with them. We will be the first country in history to build a permanent colony in space. The moon will be an Autonomous Region like Tibet and Inner Mongolia. Like these Autonomous Regions on earth, the moon will thrive under the firm, benevolent hand of China.

"I leave it to Colonel Feng, my son, to introduce these heroes of China and the world to you."

Colonel Feng marched to the podium and saluted his father. With solemnity, eight teams of eleven taikonauts came on stage. Colonel Feng introduced them all by name as the civilian crowd cheered them on. As he called the eleventh name, each team walked off stage to a small bus waiting to take them to their respective launch pads.

In a coordinated show of force, the eight rockets launched one after another in the largest space mission ever conducted by mankind. Secretary Feng knew billions watched the spectacle on television around the world today.

He also guessed American spy satellites monitored today's events. While there were clear security disadvantages to holding this launch at a location that also did nuclear weapons research, there were hidden benefits as well. In violation of international law, the eighth rocket contained three tactical nuclear weapons.

Most atomic weapons required a conventional explosion to make them go nuclear. This required oxygen. However, these new bombs were designed to detonate in the vacuum of space. China's lead in the race to dominate the moon was now insurmountable. However, should anyone challenge this lead, China would be able to back up its position with force.

Chapter 16

Malibu, Executive Drug Treatment Center

Tim strode to the podium at the front of the room. The small group of staffers and other clients had been his only human contact for the last thirty days. In addition to his fellow patients, everyone had a person or two in the audience attending today's graduation ceremony.

"I'm not one to give big speeches," Tim said. "But I wanted to say thanks to all of you. I came here with a chip on my shoulder. I wasn't a loser junkie who needed to be sequestered away from polite society."

An actress, two Hollywood producers, and three business executives nodded their heads in agreement.

"I know now that I'm not a loser, but I am an addict. Now, however, I'm an addict with the tools I need to keep my life in order. Thanks to all of you."

There was a polite round of applause from everyone in the audience.

"In closing, I want to thank my girlfriend for convincing me to come here. Lucy, thanks for your insistence. I wouldn't be here graduating without your prompting."

Lucy dabbed her moist eyes as the rest of the audience turned to look at her and smile. Tim rejoined her in the audience.

The program leader took the podium to close the meeting, and then Tim was free at last. He shook hands, hugged his fellow patients, and rejoined Lucy.

"I meant it," he said. "I couldn't have done this without you."

"You did the work, not me," Lucy said. "I'm proud of you. Let's celebrate. Where do you want to go?"

Should I pick a high-end place with all the temptations that I supposedly now have the tools to overcome? Should I play it safe and pick a place without a bar?

"Let's go somewhere small that doesn't serve alcohol. I've never been to Hollywood Boulevard before. How about that?"

Lucy cocked her head at him. "You know Hollywood Boulevard is kind of a dump, right?"

"So I've heard, but I still want to see it."

The clinic arranged a Town Car service for them. They stepped out into the warm night and climbed into the back of the car. Traffic was light for a change, and the car dropped them off at one end of Hollywood Boulevard fifty minutes later.

Tim looked down the street and smiled to himself.

"What's on your mind?" Lucy asked.

"You're right. This place is a bit of dump."

"Told you," Lucy said as she elbowed him gently in the ribs.

They strolled down the dark street, looking at the offbeat shops and denizens of the Hollywood underbelly. The weekday foot traffic was light. A handful of out-of-towners craned their necks to look at the sites like tourists everywhere. The occasional pink mohawk or silver-spray-painted mime provided some variety.

They reached the end of the retail and dining section, and Lucy said, "Let's turn around. They've cleaned up the touristy parts, but we shouldn't stray too far off in any one direction."

As if in response to Lucy's comment, they heard a bottle shatter nearby and a slurred shout of pain. Lucy grabbed Tim's shoulder and said, "Leave it. Let's go."

Tim looked into her eyes for a moment then shook off her arm and ran around the corner. He could hear Lucy chasing after him.

An old drunk leaned against a dumpster, blood running down his face. Broken glass surrounded him. Tim smelled the alcohol and urine wafting off him from twenty feet away.

Two men in their early twenties stood over the old guy. One of them cocked a second bottle back in the air.

"Drop it," Tim said.

The men spun around to look at Tim.

"Who the hell are you?" the first one asked.

"Leave it," Lucy whispered into Tim's ear. "You don't need to risk getting hurt over some old homeless guy. We'll call the police. He'll be fine."

Tim didn't acknowledge her comment. "I said drop it. Now."

"Or what? What are you and your girlfriend going to do about it?"

"Leave her out of it," Tim said.

"A bit late for that, brother," said the second, grabbing his crotch. "I'll tell you what. We'll trade you. You can have the old guy, and we'll have your girlfriend."

"Let's get out of here," Lucy said, no longer whispering.

"Not so fast, honey," the second one chimed in. He smashed the bottle against the side of a dumpster and slashed the jagged remainder back and forth. Tim recognized the telltale gleam in the man's eyes. He was high on something, which meant this wasn't going to be an easy fight. On top of that, two against one didn't seem like good odds.

I'm over-thinking it. Tim took two rapid steps toward the man with the bottle. The man slashed at Tim's face. Tim caught the incoming arm and kicked him in the crotch with all his strength. The man doubled over, and the arm with the bottle went limp. Tim grabbed the limp arm and drove the jagged bottle hard into the man's face. The man shrieked in pain and fell to the ground, clutching at his torn cheek.

Tim stepped toward the other man, but he glanced over Tim's shoulder and fled down the street. Tim's fists shook from the excess adrenaline. *I did it,* he thought. *Two against one. They never had a chance.* He turned to check on Lucy and pulled up short. She had a small automatic pistol in her hand.

"What the hell is that?" Tim asked. He replayed the conversation over dinner a few months ago. "I thought you never shot a gun before."

Lucy looked at the gun in her hand, then back at Tim. "I wasn't lying. I bought it for protection, but I've never actually fired it."

"Never fired it? What are you doing carrying a gun when you don't know how to use it? That's crazy."

"You're probably right. And it's going to be more trouble than it's worth if the police come. Can we please get out of here?"

Tim turned to look at the man on the ground. He was already hobbling up. His face was a mess of blood. The bottle had pierced his cheek in several places, but missed his eye. The man stumbled after his friend.

Tim walked over to the homeless man. "You OK, buddy?"

"I'm OK, thanks to you. Give me a hand."

Tim winced. The man wreaked and was dripping blood. He considered saying no, then reached out his hand.

"Thanks, son," the old man said.

Tim took a hundred-dollar bill out of his wallet and slipped it to the man. "Do me a favor, and don't drink this. Get yourself to a clinic and get your face patched up."

The old man's eyes lit up. "Can't promise you that son, but thanks for your concern."

Lucy grabbed Tim's arm. "Enough. Let's catch a cab and get off this street." She turned and marched back toward the retail part of the boulevard, looking for a cab.

Tim nodded good-bye to the man and jogged after Lucy.

"What the hell was that?" she asked.

"Come on, Lucy. They would've maimed or killed him for sport. I couldn't let them beat the crap out of some old guy like that."

"You've done it before," she spit.

Tim grabbed her shoulders and spun her gently to face him. He looked at her for a second before answering. "I know I did. The first day I met you. I let a crowd of people beat an old man, and I chose to run to safety."

"So what's different now? Why risk your life over a derelict?"

"I did it for us," Tim answered.

"Not for us. I said I wanted to get out of there." She folded her arms and glared at him.

"All right. Then I did it for me. You know how everyone always asks a couple how they met?"

"Yes, so what?"

"I don't want you to view me as gutless every time you remember the day we met. That's not the real me." Tim paused for a moment and considered his statement. "That was the real me, but it's not who I want to be."

Lucy waited an uncomfortably long time before responding. "You saved that old guy because you didn't want me to think you're a wimp?"

"It comes from a better place than that, but, yeah, that's part of it."

Lucy unfolded her arms and her dark expression softened. "You're not a wimp." She hugged him. "That was very brave. Very stupid, but very brave. How about if we make an agreement that you don't do anything like that again to prove yourself to me?"

Tim pushed her gently back so he could look into her eyes. "I'll tell you what. No more foolish chivalry on my part. In return, you get rid of the gun. You shouldn't be carrying that thing around if you don't know how to use it. Someone's going to shoot you with it."

She raised an eyebrow at this, but then smiled back at him. "Deal."

Chapter 17

Austin, Automated Technology Labs

Sam Sawyer reviewed the results of her last several attempts at fusion. She considered going home to shower but rejected the idea. That nicety could wait. The research she received from China was helping, but she was still too far behind.

Her father's recent conversation with the president added to the time pressure. He would need to sell the president's advisors on his plans soon. If Sam couldn't show better results in the lab, there was no point in going to the moon. The recent Chinese launch further stressed how far behind she was. On top of it all, Benjamin was struggling to find enough helium-3 to support her research.

Sam spoke to her lead engineer. "Have you recalibrated everything based on the latest updates I gave you?"

"I have. We're ready."

"Let's review it one more time."

The engineer sighed and walked through the changes for the tenth time. Ninety-five percent of the approach was lifted from the Chinese efforts. The remaining five percent was guesswork on Sam's part. She hoped she was right.

"Let's get started," she said.

The engineer typed a couple of quick keystrokes, and the fusion reactor spun up. At this low-energy output, everything looked normal. Then again, it had in every other test run in the last several months. Commercially viable fusion would require much more energy output. The current process consumed too much helium-3. Without improvements, the business would lose money.

She waited for everything to stabilize then said, "Increase the output to twice its current level."

The engineer held his breath and entered the commands. The reaction was the most efficient to date. "It's working," her engineer said with a sharp exhalation.

"It's a personal record, but it's still not enough. Increase the output by twice again."

The engineer typed a few more keys, and they watched the results. The reaction was still stable.

"It's working. That's a commercially viable level of energy extraction."

They had reached the minimum level of energy production her father needed for the economics to make sense. It was Sam's turn to hold her breath. "Boost the energy output by five times," she said.

"Shouldn't we pause and take a victory lap? We run the risk of breaking the reactor if we do it."

"Do it. It's a prototype. We need to know how far we can take this."

The engineer increased the output and waited for inevitable systems failure, but it didn't come. The reaction kept going.

"Give me a second." She jabbed at her tablet. She mumbled equations and numbers under her breath. She erased her calculations and ran them again.

She slapped him on the back. "At this level of efficiency, we'll be able to meet the earth's energy needs for over five thousand years."

She sent her father a message that he would remember for the rest of his life. "Daddy, we did it!"

Chapter 18

Austin, Sawyer Family Ranch

"Pull," Sam yelled.

One clay pigeon sailed left and one right. She fired twice in rapid succession, and both exploded into shards. She grinned at her father. "You're up, Dad."

"Pull," Frank yelled.

Two clay pigeons sailed over his left shoulder. He took aim and pulled the trigger in rapid succession. One of the pigeons exploded, and the other landed in a puff of dust in the distance.

"Ouch," Stephen Clark said.

Benjamin was less diplomatic. "All that military training and you still can't take down two inanimate objects with a twelve-gauge. I would venture a guess that there is no one else on earth with their own shooting range who is worse with a shotgun."

"Don't you worry about him, Frank. You're doing great," Lucy chimed in.

Sam couldn't handle it anymore. *Stop kissing ass.* "New girl, no words of encouragement. This is a grudge match. Boys versus girls. Which team are you playing for?"

The smile stayed on Lucy's face, but disappeared from her eyes. Sam felt her competitive nature getting the best of her. She was trying and failing to like Tim's new girlfriend. "Sorry, Lucy. No offering of aid or comfort to the enemy. Let's run up the numbers on the boys. It's your turn again."

As usual, the men were woefully behind at the Sawyer's traditional Thanksgiving shoot-out. Benjamin and Tim pulled their weight. Stephen Clark also did his part. As always, Frank struggled. Sam loved her father, but it made her happy that there was one thing in life that he wasn't great at—skeet shooting.

It briefly appeared that the men might have a fighting chance this year with the addition of Lucy Lee to the women's team. However, Lucy proved to be an exceptional student under the expert guidance of Lisa Sawyer. Having grown up on a Texas ranch herself, Lisa always had the highest scores for the day.

Lucy was last up. "Pull."

The Benelli semi-automatic boomed twice in rapid succession, and both clay pigeons exploded.

"Victory," Lisa Sawyer whooped in her strong Texas twang. She let Lucy put the gun back in its rack, hugged her, and said, "You'll fit in just fine." She turned to the group and said, "Everyone, let's head up to the house and get cleaned up. We'll eat at three p.m."

They headed up to the sprawling Sawyer residence and showered to get the gunpowder smell out of their hair. Everyone changed into something comfortable.

As Sam sat down, she noted that her mom somehow maneuvered her into sitting next to Stephen. Her mother deftly guided him into his seat without him realizing he was being manhandled. It was one of her mother's many talents.

Frank said grace. "Thank you, Lord, for this wonderful meal and the hard work that has gone into preparing it. We thank you for allowing us to gather as family with our old friends as well as our new friends, Stephen and Lucy. We thank you for all the blessings you have given us this last year. We pray these things in Jesus's name. Amen."

"Amen," everyone echoed.

"Thanks for including me in the prayer," Lucy said.

Sam glanced at Lucy again. Sam had never had any real issues with any of Tim's other girlfriends in the past. In retrospect, Sam had not invested any emotional energy in them, as they were all flakes. If Tim's attitude over the week was any indication, Lucy was the real deal. She knew she should be happy for him.

"Let's eat," Lisa said. They had two turkeys. Lisa always ordered one from Greenberg's Smoked Turkey in Tyler, Texas. Sam wasn't much good in the kitchen, but she had killed a wild turkey on their ranch to add to the meal.

Frank raised his glass and said, "I have a toast and an announcement to make."

Everyone put down their silverware and looked expectantly at Frank.

"I want to congratulate Tim on his hard work getting clean over these last several weeks. You've worked hard, and we are all proud of you." Frank beamed at his son who held up a glass of water with a smile on his face.

Everyone raised their glass and toasted Tim's progress.

Frank added, "I would also like to thank Lucy for her part in that recovery. Thanks for supporting him through the process. It's been wonderful getting to know you, and we hope to see you at a lot more of these family events." Sam bristled at the heartfelt affection on her father's face.

Lucy blushed at this and smiled at Tim. Everyone nodded toward her and said a second "Cheers." Sam hoped hers sounded genuine.

"Last, I have an announcement to make," Frank said. "Tim and I spoke earlier today, and he's agreed to take a leadership role in media relations for our new green initiative."

Lucy clapped her hands and put her arm around Tim's shoulders. "That's wonderful news, honey. What's this new green initiative?"

Frank held up his hand. "I'm not at liberty to say yet, but at least it won't be the weapons division. Suffice it to say, it's going to be much bigger and more important than anything we've ever done."

Lisa Sawyer said, "Samantha, honey. You should take Stephen to the lab to show him what you are working on. I understand that you've been collaborating on the same project."

Before Sam could answer, Lucy interrupted. "Stephen, I didn't realize you were a researcher. Weren't you in the military?"

Stephen paused momentarily and said, "I met Frank back in my army days. I handle his affairs in China now." He turned to face Sam. "I'm definitely not a researcher, but I would love to see your lab."

Lucy turned to Tim and asked, "Perhaps we can join them and make a double date of it."

Sam immediately blushed and cleared her throat. She glanced at Stephen and noted that his ears were turning red.

Sam was thankful when Frank stepped in to say, "Lucy, how about if we give you a rain check. Much of the work we are doing at the lab needs to remain secret for competitive reasons."

"Come on, Dad. Lucy would be fascinated by what we're doing," Tim said.

Lucy looked expectantly at Frank. She did everything but bat her eyes. Sam was already on a roll with Lucy today, so she added, "I agree with Dad. This project in particular isn't quite ready to see the light of day."

Lucy's smile evaporated as she turned from Frank to Sam and said, "I guess I'll take that rain check then."

"Sounds like that's the plan," Sam said and popped another piece of turkey into her mouth.

Sam's mom, always the good hostess, changed the subject to something innocuous. The meal continued with an abundance of joking and wine drinking. As dinner ended, Lisa Sawyer stood up and cleared the dishes. In the spirit of the holiday, she had sent her staff home to enjoy Thanksgiving with their families.

"Mom, I'll help you dry the dishes," Samantha offered.

As the men wandered off to watch football, Lucy stood up as well.

"Lucy, please join us in the kitchen, but pull up a stool and relax," Lisa said.

"Absolutely not, let me help. But first, can you point me to the restroom?"

"It's the second door on the right down the hallway. If you reach Frank's office, you've gone too far," Lisa answered.

Sam watched Lucy walk down the hall. She dried another dish but noticed that she hadn't heard the bathroom door shut. She set her dishtowel on the counter and went to check.

The bathroom door was open, and the light was on. She walked farther down the hall to her father's office. Lucy was flipping through the documents on her dad's desk with one hand. She held her mobile phone in the other.

"Wrong turn?" Sam asked.

Lucy jumped, and one of the papers fell on the floor. She glanced at her mobile phone. She tried to attach it to a charger on Frank's desk, but the plug didn't fit. "I must've missed the bathroom. Then I saw the charger on the desk, and I noticed my battery was low."

"Not a fit?" Sam asked. "Let me see your phone. I'll find a charger for you."

Lucy looked at her phone and slid it into her back pocket. "I don't want to trouble you."

Sam walked farther into the office and picked up the paper from the floor. She scanned it, then grabbed the other papers on the desk and set them to the side. "My dad can be a little old school. He's the only person I know that still prints things out to read them. He usually puts them away inside his desk. Sloppy of him." She looked at Lucy with deadpan eyes.

"I lied," Lucy said.

"Excuse me?"

"I saw your father's open office, and I wanted to peek inside. It's not often that you get to see the inner sanctum of one of the world's most prominent business leaders."

"This isn't his inner sanctum."

"I just meant—"

"Dad's inner sanctum is the lab. He's happiest when he's working on a challenging new technical problem that no one else can solve."

"I've heard that about him. Well, I should have respected his privacy." Samantha waved this off with her hand, but her face remained expressionless.

"Let me take you to the rest room."

Samantha escorted Lucy to the bathroom and watched as Lucy shut and locked the door. Samantha walked back to the office and rifled through the papers. Most of them were harmless enough. A CERN paper on helium-3 fusion was in the mix. Not surprising with all the recent press regarding helium-3.

She found the paper that Lucy had dropped on the floor. The paper had Chinese writing on it. She frowned at this and stepped back to the doorway. She clicked the inside lock on her father's door and shut it behind her.

Chapter 19

Austin, Automated Technology Headquarters

Sam and Stephen exited the elevator to the executive floor of Automated Technologies and walked toward Frank's office. Since she was a little girl, Sam had the run of the place. She never knocked on her father's door. As she burst into his stark office, she wished she had.

"It's b.s. that you wouldn't let Lucy tour the labs today," Tim shouted.

"It's premature. There are no more than twenty people in the world that know what your sister is working on," Frank said.

"But you're going to tell the world in three weeks anyway."

"Today isn't three weeks from today. You're handling the press orchestration. You should know this."

Tim turned to Sam. "And you. Could you have been more unwelcoming over dinner? Lucy asked me after dinner why you hate her."

Sam met her brother's stare but then looked at the floor. "I tried to stop myself. I felt like she was trying too hard. I could've been a better sister."

"Trying too hard? She's been there for me this entire time. My life is in order for the first time in years, and it's all because of her."

"Doesn't that seem the tiniest bit odd to you?" Sam blurted. She bit her tongue immediately, disgusted with herself for not filtering her thoughts.

"I don't even know what that means," Tim exploded. "It's odd that a girl cares enough about me to help me get my head clear? Rather than just going along for the ride. You yourself have told me a million times--"

"That you need to find a girl that likes you for you, not for the family name," Sam completed the sentence for him.

"Then why did you treat her that way?"

Sam clamped her mouth shut briefly, but then forged ahead. "Dad, I found her going through your papers."

Frank leaned back and pursed his lips. "I had the fusion papers on my desk from CERN as well as some documents from China. That was irresponsible of me."

"What of it?" Tim asked. "I'm sure there is a perfectly rational explanation for it. I'll ask her."

"Don't bother," Sam said. "She told me she couldn't resist peeking into the inner sanctum of one of the world's wealthiest men."

Frank thumped his hands together and laughed. "Now that is a rational explanation. Who could resist seeing my inner sanctum?"

Sam frowned at her father. "I'm not joking. She was up to something."

"I can run a background check on her," Stephen offered.

Tim aimed his wrath at Stephen. "Who the hell are you to be checking up on my girlfriend?"

"Enough, everyone," Frank said. "Stephen, there will be no background checks. Tim, your sister apologized. Sam, I don't want to hear anything more about concerns over Lucy. Drop it."

Sam nodded and squeezed Tim's shoulder. She turned to Stephen. "Let me give you that tour of the fusion lab."

As they rode the elevator down, Sam said, "I'm sorry about that. I should've saved that for later so that you didn't have to see it."

"Frank speaks highly of your ability to judge people. He says it's better than his, and I know how good your dad is."

Sam found herself blushing for the second time in two days.

"Perhaps it's worth digging into her background," Stephen continued.

"I'm not above going behind my dad's back on the rare occasions that I know he's wrong. In this case, I have no evidence, and I can't be the person that messes up Tim's relationship. We should let it lie."

"Consider it done."

Sam ushered Stephen through the door into her lab. Since it was the day after Thanksgiving, they had the place to themselves. "Check this out. This machine fits in a lab and can produce enough megawatts to run a medium-sized city for a year."

"Is it safe this close to the reactor?"

"I thought you army guys were tough. Afraid of a little radiation?"

"Radiation? Should we be wearing exposure badges?"

"I wouldn't worry about a badge. Besides, with fusion reactors you don't have to worry about radiation when they fail. It's the blast."

"What blast?"

"Well, in the case of a noncommercial reactor like this one, the blast radius could be as large as seven miles. Our big commercial reactors will have to be fifty miles away from any major city. All those pesky government regulations. I told my Dad we should move this one a bit farther away from Austin, but he told me not to worry so much."

"A blast of that size in this part of Austin would kill half a million people. Even for Frank, that's a big risk." He ran his fingers through his hair and looked like he would like nothing more than to conclude the tour.

Sam raised her eyebrows and stared at him.

"And I'm guessing I just got played?" Sam noticed that his ears were turning red again as they had at Thanksgiving dinner.

Sam laughed and slapped him on the shoulder. "I'm sorry. I get to show so few people my work. I've been saving that story for months. You're my first victim."

"I see you inherited Frank's sense of humor."

She smiled and nodded. "But what do you think of my reactor? This has been my life for the last five years."

"It's amazing. You've accomplished what a two-thousand-person team took years to do by yourself."

"Not by myself. That's why I wanted you to see it firsthand." She waved her hand at the rooms of equipment and computer monitors.

"I'm not sure I follow."

"I would've never been able to catch up with the Chinese without the work you did for my father. I'm smart, but I'm not that smart. I wanted to let you know how important your role was in making this a reality."

"That means a lot to me."

She pointed out a few of the more interesting technical details and then wrapped up the tour. As much as she loved the technology, she knew from experience when she was sharing too much information.

"Why don't we grab lunch?" Sam asked.

"That sounds great."

While they walked in silence, Sam glanced at him. His ears were red again. "Is something wrong?" she asked.

"You know I travel to China a lot. I'm heading back there tomorrow morning."

"That doesn't surprise me. I would imagine much of the work you do for my dad is pretty hands-on."

"I don't have a place that I call home when I'm back in the States. I crash in a hotel in whatever city I happen to be in."

"That must get old."

"It does. I was thinking of getting a place here in Austin. I'm here enough to meet with your Dad and Benjamin... and others."

"You would love it here."

"Problem is, I don't know Austin well." Sam glanced at his ears and saw they were even redder.

"I would be happy to show you around."

"Really? I would appreciate getting the tour from a native. I could buy you dinner to say thanks."

"Are you trying to ask me out on a date?"

"Well, I don't know that I would say that. I wouldn't want to get sidewise of Frank. He might not appreciate me dating his daughter."

"Because if you were, I would say yes."

Stephen stopped. "You would?"

"I hoped you would ask. I would've asked you, but I didn't want you to feel like you had to say yes to the boss' daughter. Awkward."

"I guess I should say something to Frank and your mom?"

"You can hold off unless you plan to propose over dinner. My mom and dad knew what they were doing when they invited you."

Stephen laughed, and Sam saw that his ears were no longer bright red.

Chapter 20

Austin, Automated Technology Labs

"If you can please follow me," Frank said to the group of government scientists. Representatives from the JPL, NASA, Lawrence Livermore, the Department of Energy, and various other government organizations lined up to follow. As the group followed Frank into the labs, an assistant passed out the requisite hardhats and eye protection required by government regulations.

"We'll see a number of things today. First, I want you to see our fusion reactor. Next, I'll show you the building blocks of our space elevator. Finally, you'll see some of the ancillary technologies that will make this a commercial success."

Frank guided the team into the cramped lab where Sam waited to give them an overview of the fusion reactor. "This is my daughter, Samantha Sawyer. More than anyone, she has been responsible for our fusion program," Frank said.

"Thanks, Dad," Sam said. "Let me give you the high-level statistics on what we've accomplished in the lab so far."

"This reactor can produce a peak of five hundred megawatts. To put that in perspective, a city like New York might use ten gigawatts of power on average. That number varies based on time of year, weather, et cetera."

"That's a pretty big gap," one of the scientists said. Frank could tell by the sarcasm in the man's voice that he was not impressed. He would be soon. Frank winked at his daughter.

Sam continued, "We're not done yet. We scaled the reactor down for a laboratory environment to conserve our limited helium-3. In the real world, we would have a much larger reactor and much more helium-3 at our disposal. We will also make efficiency improvements to the process over time."

"Yes, yes. We understand all that. But what's the final result?" the scientist pressed.

"A single reactor will easily handle the New York City metropolitan area on a day of peak energy usage. Say the hottest day in summer or the coldest day in winter," Sam said.

Heads nodded.

The representative from the Lawrence Livermore National Laboratory raised his hand. "How can you possibly have done what CERN, the U.S. government, and a host of well-funded universities haven't accomplished? Only the Chinese claim these kinds of results, and they won't let anyone see their research."

Frank responded, "We've been doing research in parallel with the Chinese. It's unfortunate that they're ahead of us, but we're making good progress. In terms of how, it's good engineering and hard work. I would like to spend less time today on how we got here and more time convincing you that it works."

Another scientist raised her hand and asked, "How much helium-3 did you consume, and where did you get it?"

Sam answered this question. "We consumed well over one hundred million dollars of helium-3 to run these tests. We were behind the Chinese, so the investment was worth it. There is a large first-mover advantage with this technology."

Most of the audience nodded appreciatively at the large figure, but the scientist pressed the issue. "You only answered the first half of my question."

"We used shell companies to ensure that no one knew that we were using helium-3 in these amounts. The Chinese would've known immediately that they had a competitor."

Frank decided to move the tour along. "If I can ask the nuclear engineers to stay here with Sam, she can share the technical details with you. I'll remind you that everyone is under a strict NDA for everything you see today."

For the next part of the demonstration, Frank opted for a bit of showmanship. "I'm going to ask each of you to come in individually and stand exactly in the red shoeprints you see on the floor. We're going to play a game."

Frank brought the first scientist through the double doors and pointed to the painted footprints. "Stand there and look at the truck." A huge Ford F-350 pickup painted in the Automated Technologies red and white corporate colors floated ten feet above the ground. "Tell me how it stays up."

The rest of the scientists cycled through, and Frank asked the same question. The answers ranged from optical illusion to antigravity field generator. Frank didn't know what this last thing might be, but it was encouraging they thought he was smart enough to build one.

Only one person had a decent answer. "Hundreds of transparent, micrometer-thick carbon-fiber threads are supporting the truck."

"Close enough. You win the Ford F-350."

"What on earth am I going to do with a huge pickup truck?"

Frank laughed. "I'll get you something more appropriate to your needs. Give my assistant your supervisor's name, and I'll make sure we appropriately navigate whatever rules you have on receiving gifts. Now, let me show you how we're doing it."

This time, Frank allowed the group to view the truck from different angles. They saw that the truck hung from a four-meter-wide carbon-fiber ribbon. It was so thin in one direction that you couldn't see it.

The group nodded their heads in appreciation. A whip-thin scientist with a sunken chest pursed his lips.

"You, in back," Frank said. "You look like you have a question."

"Carbon fiber strong enough to hold up a truck has been around for decades. This is showy, but it doesn't convince me that you can build a sixty-two-thousand-mile-high space elevator. It convinces me that you can hold a truck a few feet off the ground."

"Smart man. Look at that roll behind you." Frank pointed to a twelve-foot-wide roll that towered above them.

"What is it?" the introvert asked.

"That is a sixty-two-thousand-mile-long roll of carbon fiber. It will take several of those rolls to complete the elevator. We'll deploy the first roll from space, then a climber will scale the ribbon adding additional layers to it. When it is done, it will be able to support several tons of cargo per trip."

"I'll direct you to my lead operations engineer who can answer your detailed technical questions," Frank said. He did the introductions, and a small group of scientists stayed behind to continue the conversation. "Everyone else come with me."

Frank saved his favorite part of the tour for last. He turned to the remaining scientists. "I need a volunteer."

A woman in the back raised her hand and walked up to Frank. Frank's assistant handed out ear protection.

Frank walked the volunteer to the end of a twenty-five-yard-long track to a large red button. "When you are ready, push it." She obliged Frank.

The machine hummed, and Frank felt his chest vibrate. A loud crack followed a blinding electrical flash. The woman jumped back, tumbling into Frank.

He caught her and gave her an encouraging wink. "Nice shot. Let's take a look at your handiwork."

They walked to the target and saw a gaping hole in the massive steel plate at the end of the track. The metal was molten around the edges.

"What is the point of this? Is it a weapon? Weaponization of space is murky legal territory."

Frank shook his head. "This is our helium-3 return system. Rather than using conventional rockets, we'll shoot it back to earth."

"Are there other applications? Could you transport humans or other cargo with it?"

"A human wouldn't survive the acceleration to over five thousand miles per hour. Most cargo can't survive that kind of acceleration either. But it will work for helium-3.

Frank reconvened the entire team back in one of the conference rooms. He surveyed the audience. He counted more smiles than frowns. He saw more nodding heads than folded arms. "Comments?" he asked, confident the day was a success.

"We didn't see any spaceships today," a man from NASA said.

"I can show them to you before you leave. We have two. They're not particularly complicated since they don't have to climb out of earth's atmosphere. They can be completely controlled by remote operators using our proprietary technology. I didn't think they would be the highlight of today's tour."

The man looked crestfallen at the response. *He probably thinks his job is in jeopardy*, Frank thought. *I'll have to mend some fences with the NASA folks.*

The second question came from a woman in the front row with a severe expression. Her question matched her demeanor. "I noticed that there are a number of men and women working for you that have physical handicaps. There are a disquieting number of people with prosthetic limbs. Does your operation have safety issues?"

Frank's anger built as he raised his finger to retort then reminded himself that he needed to win these people over. "Thanks for your question. We have never had a serious safety issue in any of my facilities. These people are like my family. Many of the people you see are veterans, some of whom I served with in my army days. Their prosthetic limbs were built here in the lab to see if we could push the limits of the technology."

The woman blushed and shocked Frank by having the good taste to apologize for the tone of her question. "I should not have assumed that you wouldn't treat your team well. I apologize. It's noble of you to have a program focused on the disabled."

"No need to apologize," Frank responded. "You're kind to call it noble, but these men and women go through the same rigorous interview process as everyone else. They are here because they are the best people for the job. Any other questions?"

After the shaky opening, the tone of the questions changed dramatically. A number of the scientists gushed about the technology. No one had any negative comments.

As he scanned the room, he noticed that the man with the sunken chest from earlier in the day continued to purse his lips. "You look like you might have another question," Frank said.

"Not a question, a comment," the man said. "The technology I've seen today is amazing. It's ahead of anything I've seen in the public or private sector."

"Thank you," Frank said. "I want you to believe that Automated Technologies is ready to start immediately."

"I do, but I have an issue."

"I don't understand."

"The technology is too good. One company led by one man shouldn't control it."

"You would rather the Chinese control fusion energy production?"

"My recommendation to the president will be that this technology be nationalized. Private industry shouldn't be allowed to have this much power. This needs to be handled by those of us in the public sector to ensure a more egalitarian outcome."

Frank looked around at the audience and saw several heads nodding. *This is unexpected.*

Chapter 21

Beijing, Great Hall of the People

The first Chinese lander touched down on the surface of the moon to great fanfare. Over the last twenty years, the Chinese had transformed their oafish internal propaganda machine. It was now a well-oiled marketing engine with the sophistication of a Madison Avenue ad agency. From the moment they landed, the Chinese team was broadcasting to the world.

One of the requirements for the first taikonauts was a strong, unaccented command of a second language. Children in classrooms across the world heard about a day in the life of the Chinese team in English, Hindustani, Russian, Spanish, and French. Taikonauts answered all the typical questions regarding food, breathing, and the inevitable bathroom queries. They lifted four-hundred-pound objects in one hand to demonstrate the effect of low gravity. One of the taikonauts with acrobatic skills did double back flips for the children. To the outside world, the return of mankind to the moon was going perfectly.

Colonel Fei Feng wished the reality matched the hype. When they left the temporary moon base several years ago, they did their best to mothball it for future use. However, the harsh environment had taken its toll. The extremes of hot and cold had damaged equipment. Solar arrays had micro cracks in them and needed replacement. The ever-present dust degraded anything mechanical.

On top of repairing and restarting the existing equipment, the team needed to tend to their own basic human needs. Biologists restarted hydroponics labs to create a self-sufficient food supply for the colony. Maintenance engineers fixed micro breaches in door seals to ensure an uninterrupted air supply. Safety engineers tested fire-suppression systems to preempt catastrophic fires in the highly oxygenated environment.

Against this backdrop, Colonel Feng gave his first report to the twenty-five person Politburo. "In closing, I expect that we will begin mining operations in three months. The first helium-3 shipments will arrive on Earth six months from now."

The party chief of Shanghai spoke. "When we agreed to this investment, we were told that the Chinese industrial base would be well on its way to switching to fusion within a year. Where does this stand?"

"Those projections were too aggressive. However, it will be possible to power Shanghai with fusion within twelve months."

The Shanghai party chief nodded his head in satisfaction, but the Beijing chief bristled. "What of Beijing? Our air quality problems are even worse, and we are the capital city. When will Beijing migrate to fusion?"

General Secretary Feng interrupted. "It is also critical that we provide power to Taiwan and North Korea to cement our control over them. Our customers in the West are an equally high priority. We need paying customers. We need to create demand on a worldwide basis, even if that means slower deployment at home. Beijing will be dealt with in the appropriate order."

The Beijing chief frowned but remained quiet. Colonel Feng hoped that his father's presence would intimidate the others as well. He braced as his father turned his attention back to him. "What do you need to accelerate this schedule?"

"More resources will not expedite things at this point. The team is engaged in basic tasks such as establishing a sustainable source of food and stabilizing life support. These systems need the highest priority. Sending more engineers will exacerbate the problem as more people will consume more resources."

"Send more unmanned rockets with food. Do not focus on creating sustainable food stocks for the time being. Safety of our personnel is important to the success of the mission. However, be judicious. Where else are you wasting time?"

"The team is crowded into a single living facility at this point. One of their first tasks is fixing the second living facility, which has fallen into disrepair. A third, larger facility is also planned to accommodate the significantly larger team."

The general secretary slapped the table in front of him and fired back. "Postpone both activities. Taikonauts know how to live in tight environments. Have them share bunks like our submariners do."

"It can be done, but it will come at a human cost. The team can handle it for a few months. Beyond that, productivity and safety will suffer. Mistakes that might cost time or money on the earth will cost lives in space."

The Beijing chief waved his response off. "Bah. I hear the same complaints from many districts in my city. People live on top of each other ten people to an apartment. Your team should feel honored to represent their country in this endeavor. Their privations are nothing compared to those of us who experienced the revolution."

Colonel Feng sighed. For the old guard, it always came back to the revolution. They had admittedly suffered through decades of famine, but their own foolhardiness caused that. To voice this thought was tantamount to treason.

"It will be done, ladies and gentleman of the Politburo."

Chapter 22

New York, United Nations

The Chinese ambassador climbed out of his Town Car in front of the United Nations building. He rehearsed his speech for the day. He and the rest of the Chinese diplomatic core had lobbied governments around the world tirelessly to gain their support. He fully expected that the United States and their closest allies would block China's proposed treaty today. However, this was an important first step to formalize China's legal status on the moon. High-minded westerners may feel that access to space should be democratized. However, the ambassador was confident that the commercial reality of having nearly free energy for the foreseeable future would chip away at this resolve. This would be the speech of his life.

***

Frank reviewed the final copy of Tim's first meaningful press release on behalf of Automated Technologies. It was exceptional.

He picked up his phone and dialed his son.

"Dad?"

"Nice work on the press release. It strikes the perfect tone."

"The hard work was getting all the news agencies coordinated to release at the same time without telling them the actual news."

"How did you manage that?"

"They're used to covering high tech news stories. Everyone wants to be first, and everyone wants to get it right. If you mislead them directly, you burn bridges. Instead, I indirectly leaked a plausible false story to throw people off. At the last moment, I'll rally our team to release the real story to all major outlets at once. I hope you don't mind."

"It's perfect." It was good to have the old Tim back. He hoped the warmth showed in his voice. "Wonderful job. Time the release five minutes into the ambassador's speech."

***

The Chinese ambassador stepped up to the podium. "Honored delegates, China thanks you for the opportunity to speak here today regarding our plans for the commercialization of the moon." He bowed slightly to the audience.

"Many of us in this room are signatories to the 1967 Outer Space Treaty. Among the treaty's provisions is the idea that space should be free and open in order to benefit the world community. It also bans nuclear weapons from earth orbit or the moon.

"This focus on nuclear proliferation is appropriate. The treaty was drafted at the height of the cold war when nuclear annihilation was a real threat. While all responsible nations agree we should not weaponize space, many of the provisions in the treaty are an anachronism. As an example, no nation is allowed to claim territory on the moon."

He gauged the audience's reaction and knew that he had them in the palm of his hand. He pulled the microphone from the podium and wandered across the stage waving expansively. "This provision made sense in an era when the moon was a curiosity for researchers. All that has changed with the establishment of China's moon base and our discovery of commercial levels of helium-3.

Our base and the land it occupies are the property of China. To claim otherwise would be preposterous.

"China is decades ahead of the nearest country in terms of being able to colonize the moon to successfully harvest helium-3. Even if a country could bring back helium-3 from the moon, they would not be able to do anything meaningful with it."

Several of the diplomats in the crowd murmured to each other. The ambassador masked his annoyance at this breach of etiquette. "We propose the following. China will meet the energy needs of the world at no more than twenty-five percent of the current cost of fossil fuels. On top of the massive financial savings of parties to this agreement, greenhouse gases and pollution will be effectively eliminated.

"In addition, we will open our moon base to member nations to conduct research. We will allow non-Chinese astronauts to travel to the moon on our ships. It is our responsibility to support ongoing scientific inquiry."

Twenty diplomats headed for the exit with mobile phones in hand. He noted that the United States, the United Kingdom, and several other key allies remained in their seats with rapt attention.

"In return, we wish to have formal recognition of our base as Chinese territory. In addition, we wish to have sole rights to harvest helium-3 from the moon's surface. With our current technological lead, this is effectively already a reality…" His comments trailed off as one of his junior aids handed him a note. He sucked air through his teeth, making a whooshing sound, and said, "Ayaa." He regained his composure and abruptly concluded his comments. "Ladies and gentleman, China wishes to continue this dialog at a future date." As he exited the stage, he noticed the smirk on the face of the U.S. ambassador. China would punish this affront to her national pride severely.

Chapter 23

Austin, Automated Technology Headquarters

The Chinese ambassador was ushered into the executive conference room. He sat erect with his hands on his knees.

"You asked for this meeting. What do you want?" Frank asked.

"I will forego the usual diplomatic patter as you have a reputation for putting little value on these niceties. You have not perfected fusion. You misrepresent the current state of your research to complicate our negotiations with the international community. A single company with limited history in fusion research cannot have matched our results. The time and financial investment is simply too large."

This was not Frank's first rodeo. He knew better than to respond. Better to leave the accusation hanging. The ambassador would rush to fill the uncomfortable void.

The ambassador rewarded his patience. "Do you have nothing to say in your defense? It is the height of irresponsibility for you to create difficulties for the world community on a topic of such global importance. And why? Some imagined slight that we stole your technology. We tried your cases, and we found them meritless."

Frank opted not to comment on the kangaroo courts that dispensed justice in China. The ambassador rewarded his silence with even more vitriol.

"You haven't even vetted your results with the international community. No one has independently validated your achievements. Why should anyone believe you?"

This did warrant a response. "Neither has China. You've asked the international community to have faith that you've discovered a commercially viable approach to helium-3 fusion. Why should I be held to a higher standard than China?"

"We are a nation, not a commercial interest. We back up our claims with massive investments in space, which go back decades. You have nothing more than artist's renderings of a so-called space elevator and a press release saying that you have mastered fusion. This elevator is science fiction nonsense."

Frank raised an eyebrow. "You assume I'm bluffing?"

"We know you are bluffing. If we had time, we would take you to international court for willful interference in our commercial interests."

"China is guilty of intellectual property theft, bribery, and misrepresentation of financial results. Your human rights record is abysmal. Good luck getting someone to hear your case. I'm guessing your results will be similar to mine in the Chinese court system."

"Enough. You have nothing. You will withdraw your claims. In return, we propose the following. We will reopen all your court cases and deal with them expeditiously. You can expect rulings in your favor."

"And my lost profits? Billions by my count."

The ambassador waved this off. "We will pay your paltry billions. In return, you will admit to your lies. We will also take your cartoonish drawings of your space elevator and the associated intellectual property. This is a most generous offer."

Frank smiled at this. "Your plan is to pay me what I am owed and steal more of my technology? What else do you have for me?" Frank knew an opening offer when he heard one.

The ambassador frowned. "In addition, we will give you fusion power distribution rights in the United States. We will license our technology to you. You will effectively own power generation in the Americas. You will be wealthy beyond your wildest dreams."

"I'm already wealthy beyond my wildest dreams."

The ambassador straightened and grabbed the arms of his chair so hard his knuckles turned white. "What else could you possibly want?"

"What do I want? I want to dominate fusion energy production. I want to beat China in the space race. I want to operate at such a fraction of your cost that I can undercut you by half. I want to bankrupt your programs and force you to buy your helium-3 from me. "

"Then you must have stolen our technology. It is the only explanation."

"Prove it. By the way, I'll let you buy helium-3 at market price despite your theft of billions of dollars of my intellectual property. I am, after all, a capitalist."

"You dare to challenge the People's Republic of China!" The ambassador slammed the conference room table with his fist. "I will show myself out."

Frank motioned to one of his security personnel. "Escort the ambassador to the edge of the property and make sure that nothing is missing after he leaves."

Chapter 24

Beijing, Office of the Chinese General Secretary

The minister of state security was shown into the general secretary's office. His role in the state security apparatus of China was much broader than his western counterparts. Many western governments went through great pains to ensure separation of internal and external intelligence efforts to protect the rights of their citizenry. China viewed this as a wasteful duplication of effort.

General Secretary Feng had supported the man's elevation to his current post. In his younger years, the minister had been brutalized during one of the early Communist Party purges. Rather than succumbing to the punishment, the man channeled his rage into his job. His ruthless pursuit of party goals made him one of the most feared men in China. He continued to receive the secretary's support because the only thing he feared was Secretary Feng himself.

The security minister took in the rich furnishings and the walls adorned with decades of awards and achievements. Secretary Feng saw with pleasure that the man's eyes lingered on the gold plated AK-47 hung on the wall. Prior to its gilded coating, party insiders whispered to each other that Feng had personally used the rifle to execute a number of his more intractable enemies. In reality, the rumors were false, but Feng did nothing to squelch them. He felt it set the right tone for meetings like this one.

"The American liar Frank Sawyer will pay for his deceit. I have plans that will severely punish him and any of his associates for these lies," the minister said.

"He has stolen our technology. You have failed the Chinese people," Feng responded.

"But sir, my people assure me that our fusion program is secure. The American government is using Sawyer to block our progress in the United Nations."

"Our ambassador to America met with Sawyer personally. He doesn't seem to agree with you."

The minister leaned forward and pounded Feng's desk with a fist. "Then the man is a fool. We developed fusion over two decades with a two-thousand-person team. Only an idiot would believe that a single man accomplished the same thing in a quarter of the time."

Feng raised an eyebrow and looked at the hand touching his desk. "Am I also a fool?"

"I speak only of the Chinese ambassador. He has been feeding you lies."

"Do you think you are the only one with intelligence assets in America?"

The minister snapped his hand back from the table. Feng watched the man wither. He enjoyed having this rabid dog in his kennel, but it was sometimes necessary to muzzle him.

"Sir, I had no idea. Perhaps if you were to share your sources with me, I could more quickly get to the bottom of the leak."

"You've done much worse than give up our lead in fusion energy production. You failed to get any intelligence on Sawyer's space elevator. The Americans have gone from being two decades behind us to six months behind us overnight."

"I will fix it."

"You will do three things. You will find and fix the internal security leak. You will neutralize this space elevator. When those two things are done, you will resign and retire to the countryside. If you fail, you will face a different kind of retirement."

"I will not fail you." The minister leaned backward in his chair as if trying to escape.

"Convince me." The general secretary leaned forward to prevent the man's retreat.

"We have an extensive human intelligence capability in the United States. We will redouble our efforts to gather information on Sawyer's progress. With regard to the space elevator and potential actions in the United States, I would suggest using one of our allies."

"I agree. China must have plausible deniability if anything is to be done in America."

"We have many allies that stand to lose a lot from the discovery of fusion. Many Middle Eastern countries depend on oil exports. We can make promises to them regarding their role in a new world order led by China. United States aggression in space is a threat to them. Their actions would stand alone and could not be easily tied to us."

"And the leak?"

"I will personally lead the effort to interview all personnel at the Shanghai Nuclear Engineering Research Center. It will be like the purges of old."

General Secretary Feng pointed at the minister's chest. "If it is, you will be among the purged."

"Sir?"

"The researchers there are national treasures. Their technical leadership will allow us to dominate this planet for the next two hundred years."

"I... understand."

"If I get a sense that you are randomly punishing scientists to appease me, you and your family will pay dearly for it. Get out."

Chapter 25

Washington, DC, The White House

Frank sat down for the second time in as many months with President Ellen Brown. He noted that she had opted to be diplomatic this time—Gladwell was not at this meeting.

"I've had a chance to meet with all my top science advisors," she said.

"And?"

"Positive feedback across the board with regard to the feasibility of your plans. They believe your timelines are overly aggressive, but they feel it will work. They stressed the technical elegance of your solution compared to the Chinese approach."

"I'm glad everyone is on the same page."

She broke eye contact before responding. "There was another common theme."

"Let me guess, the Livermore guy wants you to nationalize my technology, pay me a fair price, and turn this into a governmental affair. Ellen, that's not going to happen."

She met his eyes again. "It will if you want my help. I'm inclined to agree with the scientists."

"As a patriot, I'm happy to let America play a central role in this endeavor, but this is my technology. You can't have it, and there is no legal way for you to get it."

"Automated Technologies has a very convoluted corporate structure. I don't know how many international laws we'd be breaking if we nationalized your technology," the president said.

"Coupled with the fact that you would be ostracized by the world. Half the world doesn't trust the Chinese to dominate world energy production. The other half would never trust the United States."

"That's why we need you to voluntarily give us your technology. In return, you get the navy support you want, and you get to play a pivotal role in how this unfolds."

"I would rather go it alone."

"It's a dangerous world out there, Frank. Your plans to float the elevator in the middle of the Pacific will leave you exposed. You could be attacked by pirates."

Frank rolled his eyes. "I may not have my own navy, but I can fend off guys in motorboats with rocket launchers and AKs."

"And what about nations with a standing navy?" the president asked.

Frank shook his head in disbelief. "You're right on the second point. But it says something about America that the one thing you Feds should be doing, protecting your citizens, has to be purchased."

"You are making a mistake. You'll be back."

"I'll take my chances."

***

Frank left the White House and headed for a nearby restaurant to meet Tim. Frank had tried unsuccessfully to get his son to move back to Austin when he accepted his new job, but his life was here. Tim had his circle of DC friends, but Frank still missed having him around.

Their relationship over the last decade had been strained at best. However, as Tim matured personally and professionally, Frank treasured the time they spent together more every day. He was proud of the boy.

Frank walked into the restaurant and saw Tim at a corner table waving him over. *He's even on time for dinner*, Frank thought. Frank extended his hand, but Tim stood and gave him a warm hug.

"It's good to see you, Dad."

"Where's Lucy? I figured she would be joining you. You guys have been inseparable the last several months."

"I asked her not to join us tonight."

Frank sighed and rested his jaw on his fist. "Please tell me everything is OK with you guys."

"Everything is fine between us. I just wanted to catch up alone for a change."

Frank nodded and smiled. "It's been a while since we've had a chance to talk without others around. By the way, great job on that press release. I wish you could have been a fly on the wall in my meeting with a very pissed-off Chinese ambassador. Angry competitors make mistakes."

Tim grinned at the compliment. "Thanks. It's strange being on the other side of the press. I don't remember being quite so pushy. On top of that, I annoyed a few of them by hinting that the story was related to a simple acquisition."

"Probably so. Figure out how to mend fences. You want them on your side. We rarely get a fair shake in the press, but even the liberal media should get behind cheap, green energy."

"I have more news. I'm going to ask Lucy to marry me."

Frank sat bolt upright, but then leaned forward and squeezed Tim's shoulder. "You guys are great together. She's been good for you. I notice you're drinking club soda. Quite the change."

Tim made a sheepish expression at his glass, but then grinned back at his dad. "Yeah, well. She sets high standards. For a change, I feel like living up to them."

"Behind every good man and all that, I suppose? Congratulations, son. When are you going to tell your mother and Sam?"

"Soon. I wanted to tell you first since you were going to be in town. Hold off on telling them so that I can surprise them. By the way, how did your meeting with the president go?"

Frank frowned. "Every time I work with the federal government, I am reminded why I am in private industry."

"What happened?"

"No naval protection or support of any kind unless I let the government nationalize all my technology. Voluntarily."

"I take it you refused?"

"Of course. Bad enough to have the Chinese government take my highway automation technology. I won't let my own country steal this. It's too valuable."

"Are you're sure that's the best decision?"

Frank waved the question away. "I don't want to wreck tonight by talking about the government." His enthusiasm returned as he changed the subject. "Things will accelerate now, son. There will be lots of news to share with the media."

"I have to change the messaging based on your meeting with the president, but I'll be ready."

"I hope you know how good it is to be working with you on this. And let me know when you pop the question."

Chapter 26
Tijuana, Restaurant Terraza Vallarta

Colonel Amir Mokri had lived in Mexico long enough that everyone assumed he was a native. VEVAK, Iran's Intelligence Agency, had recruited him immediately upon graduation from college. He was now a wealthy western businessman. His import/export business provided transportation services to the agriculture industry between the United States and Mexico. His business thrived, but not so much that it drew unnecessary attention.

He pondered his unlikely life as he sipped his beer on the patio of one of his favorite Mexican cantinas. He preferred the Baja seafood cuisine at this restaurant over the more traditional fare found in the interior of the large country. He spoke the language fluently and understood the culture. He even drank the occasional beer. He couldn't bring himself to attend Catholic mass, but neither could fifty percent of the Mexican population.

In general, his job as an Iranian agent was easy. Once a month, he would send an encrypted update on his mundane activities over the Internet. Occasionally, his superiors would contact him to sneak a fellow agent across the border into America. However, he always used a Mexican coyote for this work. The coyote's extensive people-smuggling operation worked equally well for domestic labor and foreign spies. He could have moved them across the border in one of his trucks easily enough, but this risked blowing his cover. His job was to keep his head down, move the occasional agent across the border, and wait.

He signaled for his bill and paid with cash. The day was hot, so he hailed a cab to take him back to his spacious apartment in the Aqua Caliente district.

At home, he logged into one of the millions of anonymous websites on the Internet for his monthly check-in. He downloaded a document on handcrafting beer. He always chuckled at this. The leadership in VEVAK may be ruthless, but they did have a sense of humor. There was a certain logic to hiding encrypted information for an Islamic state on a beer site. He even brewed the occasional batch of beer as a hobby to build his cover story.

He decrypted the file using a series of ciphers. He reread the document three times. It directed him to contact his handler in Iran on an encrypted phone. This type of risk had only happened a handful of times in the last twenty years. He was being activated.

Chapter 27

The Moon, Zhulong Base

The taikonaut popped another Dexedrine pill. She knew she was exceeding the dosage directed by the team's medical officer, but she also felt she was still within safe limits. Children with ADHD used the prescribed amphetamines, and the effects were well understood. Militaries around the world used Dexedrine to heighten the awareness of troops during long patrols and periods of reduced sleep.

This was her third straight eighteen-hour day. Her team was repurposed to mine helium-3, and she had to pick up the slack. She knew morale on the team was low. She hoped some homegrown food would improve everyone's attitude.

Overcrowding in the living module required a rotating sleep schedule, which further compounded the long hours. The constant noise and movement around her always made the eight hours of bunk time seem more like four. The long hours, the lack of sleep, and the harsh lunar environment took their toll on everyone.

The pill started to have its effect, and the room brightened. She hated the way the Dexedrine made her chest hurt when it first hit her system. It always felt like indigestion. She shook her head and focused.

She led a team of three PhD botanists on this mission. All of them had done extensive research growing plants in low-gravity environments. Her four decades of professional and academic experience made her one of the oldest members of the entire mission. She was fortunate to be one of the Lucky 88 selected for this mission.

She made her rounds inspecting each of the hydroponic grow stations. Her rice was doing quite well. On earth, using normal crops, it typically took three months for rice to grow. Using genetically enhanced rice, advanced fertilizers, and a little tender loving care, she expected to have edible rice within two months. There was a practical need to grow food on the moon to preserve the precious cargo space on rockets from earth. As important, she knew fresh food would improve the morale of a mission team that was surviving on freeze-dried rations.

She checked her cabbages. They were not growing quite as aggressively, but they looked healthy enough. Her final stop was a small kiwi bush. The kiwis were a luxury. Kiwis were the national fruit of China. She knew that they in particular would improve everyone's demeanor. It would take longer for them to bear fruit, but it would be worth it.

She recorded the relevant plant data in the computer, then climbed back into her suit. The modules weren't connected yet. The tubes that would eventually connect the living and working areas were deemed non-essential until mining operations stabilized. She understood the need to prioritize, but the minor inconveniences annoyed her.

She attached her helmet to her suit. She paused to rub her chest. Damn the Dexedrine. The indigestion was worse than usual. She would avoid the spicier of the freeze-dried food this evening. It must be aggravating the situation. As she reached to close the inner airlock door behind her, she doubled over in pain. She clutched her chest through the thick suit.

She hit her transmitter. "Help. Something is wrong. It's my heart. Can someone hear me?" Her transmitter was set to the wrong channel. She fumbled with the radio, unable to remember the right one. She reached for the outer airlock and spun the handle.

She realized her error and reached to shut the door, but she was too late. In her rush to get help, she forgot to close the inner airlock door. She heard escaping air whistling by her helmet, as she watched her plants and equipment fly out the door. Something struck her in the chest, and she fell back onto the lunar soil. All her work was ruined. She pushed to her knees to shut the airlock, but she was too weak. She made one more sharp cry for help and fell silent.

She had the ignominious honor of being the first human being to die on the moon.

Chapter 28

Houston, Johnson Space Center

Frank had invited his entire family, Benjamin and his wife Beth, as well as Lucy to watch the launch of the space elevator components. The rocket would deploy the space elevator that Frank would eventually attach to the floating platform in the Pacific Ocean.

The countdown timer reached zero. The massive boosters ignited, and the rocket climbed into the sky, accelerating with every second. Frank had never seen a launch in person.

He turned to his wife and said, "Ironic, isn't it?"

"How so?"

"If this works, we're witnessing the end of an era. The elevator will eliminate the need for most of these launches in the future."

"In other words, I'm working myself out of a job?" a nearby mission specialist asked.

Frank grinned at the man. "No, but the job will change, like all jobs do. It will become more about controlling flights between the earth and the moon rather than flights between the earth and orbit."

"It seems like that's going to require a lot less manpower than our current approach."

"Don't think of it that way. The elevator will move multiple shipments per week. That means multiple flights to the moon per week. If you get seriously worried about your job prospects, call me before you hit the unemployment line."

The man looked skeptical until Frank handed him a business card and said, "I'm not joking. Call me if you're interested."

"How much longer before we're ready to deploy the ribbon?" Benjamin asked the mission controller.

The man glanced at the computer. "Another couple of hours before it reaches geostationary orbit at twenty-two thousand miles. From there, you guys take over."

"We have some time to kill," Frank said. "Anyone hungry?" The group wandered over to the StarPort café to dine on overpriced, overcooked hamburgers.

As Frank talked shop with Benjamin at one end of the table, he noticed Tim whispering to Lucy. She smiled, blushed, and nodded her head. Frank put his hand on Benjamin's forearm to interrupt him and whispered, "Hold on. Tim has something to say."

Tim stood up and cleared his throat. "Everyone, Lucy and I wanted to share something with you." Lucy stood up as well, and Tim put his arm around her shoulder. They stared into each other's eyes for a moment.

"Lucy's been an important part of my life these last several months. Before meeting her, most of my many relationships fizzled after a couple of months." Lucy raised an eyebrow at this, but then smiled up at him.

"She supported me with my addiction challenges. She encouraged me to come work for Dad. I'm a better man because of her. Thank you for that honey."

Everyone nodded at Lucy and smiled. Frank noted that even Sam's smile appeared heartfelt.

"We love each other, and I've asked Lucy to marry me."

Everyone congratulated them at once. Lisa Sawyer jumped up and put her arms around both of them, hugging them tight. "I am so happy for both of you. It is so wonderful that you are going to be part of our family. You have to let me plan the wedding with you."

The group continued discussing the wedding. Frank noted that Lisa was already helping the newly announced couple pick dates, venues, and colors. He could already tell it was going to be an expensive wedding. He checked his watch and nodded to Benjamin. "We should get back to the launch center to supervise the next steps of the deployment."

Frank glanced at Sam as he stood to leave.

She took the cue and tapped Lucy's shoulder. Lucy stood up, and Sam hugged her. "I wanted to welcome you to our family," Sam said. "I also wanted to apologize for my behavior over Thanksgiving. I wasn't myself. I'm happy to be gaining a sister."

Lucy returned the hug, and Frank noted that her eyes were moist. Frank smiled at them both. *That's one family disaster averted.*

Chapter 29

Houston, Johnson Space Center

Frank gave an abbreviated wave to Sam as they dangled ten feet above the pool in their spacesuits. She gave what looked like a half-hearted thumbs-up. Between the bulk of the suits and the high pressure, even basic movement was difficult.

NASA agreed to let Frank train using their suits. He wasn't sure when or if he would need it. His goal was to operate all his equipment on the moon remotely. Actually going there in the next year would imply something had gone badly wrong with his plans. Even so, it seemed like a worthwhile skill to develop.

The cranes lowered Sam and Frank into the massive forty-foot-deep pool. A team of scuba divers descended on them like a helpful school of pilot fish. The divers guided them to the bottom where they would learn the basics of spacesuit operation.

"How are you guys holding up?" the instructor asked.

"Claustrophobic," Sam gasped. She flapped her arms inside the suit in a feeble attempt at swimming.

"Just relax. Don't fight the suit. It will win," the instructor said. "It takes getting used to, so let us know if you need extraction."

"I'm fine," Sam said. Sam shared Frank's fear of tight spaces. Frank heard a tremor in her voice, but he let it go. Sam's pride would be hurt if he inserted himself into the conversation.

"How are you doing?" the instructor asked Frank.

"I'm doing OK. The ball-bearing joints are hard to use," Frank said. He tried moving his arms and legs in different directions. It was slow going, but he was getting the hang of it.

The cranes placed them on the bottom of the pool where they would do their work. The training facility simulated the gravity of the moon by carefully balancing the air pressure of the suit with its weight. It wasn't a perfect simulation, but it would at least give them a sense of the challenges of low gravity.

"For your first exercise, you are going to use a cordless electric wrench to loosen a bolt," the instructor said.

Frank looked at the wrench attached to his suit and turned it on briefly.

"Hold on," the instructor said. "Don't play with the tools until the exercise commences. We don't want any accidents."

"Sorry," Frank mumbled. He wasn't used to being reprimanded for playing with mechanical tools. He had to remember that this was their lab, not his.

"You each have a bolt in front of you. I want you to loosen it with your wrench. Once you have removed the bolt from the structure, it will stick to the wrench magnetically. Remove it from the end of the wrench and place it in your EVA trash bag," the instructor said.

"EVA?" Sam asked.

"Extravehicular. If you were in zero gravity, you would secure the bolt in the bag so that it doesn't float away."

Frank and Sam turned on the wrenches and carefully extracted the bolts. Frank pulled his wrench back, and the bolt stuck to the magnetic end as expected. This wasn't much different from working in one of his labs. He manipulated his arm until his fingers were on the end of the bolt. He pulled it loose from the wrench and dropped it.

He grabbed at it reflexively, but he was too slow in the bulky suit. He clenched his jaw as it dropped to the bottom of the pool.

He looked over at Sam. She was laughing at him as she dropped her bolt into her EVA trash bag and closed the top. "Oops," she said.

Frank smirked back at her. He leaned forward in his suit to check where the bolt landed and smacked his head into the space helmet.

"Slow down," the instructor said. "Remember that you can't lean forward the way you would if you were wearing street clothes. The suits don't bend that far. Use the mirror on your right arm to locate the bolt."

Frank twisted his arm until he saw the bolt. It was next to his right foot.

"Now," the instructor said. "Back up and fall forward so that your hand lands near the bolt."

Frank backed up until he could see it. He eyeballed the distance from his hand and let himself slowly topple forward. He grabbed the bolt and held himself up with his other arm. Frank placed the bolt into his EVA bag and sealed the top.

Now, how to stand up? He pushed off with both his hands and lifted two inches off the floor of the pool. He floated straight back to the bottom still on his hands and knees. *This suit sucks.* Frank started to redesign the suit in his head. This suit must weigh around two hundred pounds. While the weight would matter less in space or on the moon, the sheer bulk was ridiculous. *What if I used my next gen carbon fiber and combined it with Kevlar? Are there any fabrics that would provide enough elasticity to make movement easier? What about one size fits all?*

"Frank, are you there?" The operator's voice snapped him back to the moment. He would redesign a better suit when time permitted.

"I'm stuck," Frank admitted.

"This would be easier on the moon. You wouldn't have the drag from the water slowing you down. Do you need assistance?"

"Not yet. Let me see if I can figure it out." He inched forward on his hands and knees until he came to the structure from which they had extracted the bolts. He grasped the edge of it with his right hand and pushed hard. He came to a satisfying rest on both feet.

"Excellent job," the instructor said. "Why don't you guys get out, and we'll go over some other things."

The divers reattached the crane cables to Sam and Frank and pulled them out of the pool. As they exited their suits, the harsh smell of chlorine assaulted them. The instructor joined them.

"What other tools do you guys have?" Frank asked.

"We have drills, wrenches, and cutting tools. Everything fits into this modular device. I wanted to give you the basics today. We can schedule time for you to come back and familiarize yourself with the rest of the tools."

"What happens if the suit springs a leak?" Sam asked. "For example, what if you cut your suit using one of the tools? Are they self-sealing?"

"No, they aren't. You want to avoid puncturing your suit. We've been playing with some new designs, but they are still just prototypes. But for now, don't cut your suit."

Frank made a popping motion above his head with his hands. "You explode?" Frank asked.

The man chuckled at Frank's pantomime. "Not quite. We have kits that will seal minor tears for a short period. They aren't great, and it would be hard to apply to yourself. However, it's a workable alternative if you use a buddy system. You would need to get back to a pressurized environment as soon possible."

"How much time in the pool to learn the basics?" Frank asked.

"You're a fast learner," the instructor replied. "We could teach you the basics in three months."

"Sign me up," Frank said.

Chapter 30

Pacific Ocean, Oil Rig

Frank paced the rusted deck of the floating oil rig, glancing at the sky. He knew there was nothing to see yet, but he couldn't help himself. He forced himself to inspect the rig instead. It certainly wasn't an aircraft carrier. It had two helicopter pads, but you couldn't land a cargo plane on it. That would limit its effectiveness. It was cluttered with drilling equipment that he would also have to remove at some point. It would have to do for now.

He looked again at the sky. The carbon fiber ribbon would stretch from a tether on the oil rig to a point sixty-two thousand miles above the earth's surface. The ribbon deployment had three distinct stages.

The first stage was complete. From geostationary orbit twenty-two thousand miles above the earth, the ribbon had launched toward the Pacific Ocean at one hundred twenty miles per hour. The other side of the ribbon deployed at a slightly faster rate out to an eventual distance of sixty-two thousand miles above the earth. At first, rocket propulsion pulled the earth-bound side of the ribbon down to the edge of earth's atmosphere. As the ribbon approached earth, gravity took over. The space side of the ribbon spooled out due to centrifugal force.

The more difficult second stage was just completing. Earth's atmosphere extended up to around three hundred miles. The ribbon and its deployment vehicle experienced minor buffeting at this height, but the atmosphere was still very thin. Eighty percent of earth's atmosphere existed below ten miles. Below that point, high winds buffeted the deployment vehicle all the way to the ground. He prayed that the ribbon was strong enough to withstand the punishment of the upper atmosphere.

The third and final stage was the hardest. The high atmospheric winds meant they couldn't predict exactly where the ribbon would touch down. With enough fuel, the deployment vehicle could fly itself all the way down to the earth's surface where the team could capture it. However, that much fuel weighed too much. All sixty-two thousand miles of the ribbon would crash into the ocean from the extra weight of the fuel.

Frank thought he had a workable solution. The deployment vehicle would crash into the water within a five-mile radius from their current location. At touchdown, buoyant devices would deploy to keep the ribbon from sinking. This would give his ocean-going tugboat time to retrieve it and return it to the oil rig.

One of Frank's engineers alerted him. "The end of the ribbon is approaching the ocean's surface." The man pointed to the northwest and handed Frank a pair of high-powered binoculars. "It should be a mile away from us."

Frank looked out over the water. A series of floating balloons inflated explosively on the ocean's surface to the cheers of the engineering team. Frank kept his eyes on the balloons, trying to catch a glimpse of the actual elevator ribbon. *Nothing.* His stomach knotted.

"What is the telemetry data telling us?" Frank asked.

"Everything looks good."

Frank pulled the binoculars away from his eyes. He glanced outside at the helicopter pad and saw the windsock change directions. He looked through the binoculars again. As the wind shifted, the buoyant devices spun and he saw the ribbon.

"I see it," he shouted. It was his design, but it was still amazing to think that the ribbon extended tens of thousands of miles into space. "Send the tug over."

The tugboat headed to the touchdown site. As it pulled alongside, an operator extended a crane over the floating deployment vehicle. A Zodiac raft launched off the back of the tug with five sailors in it. The sailors clambered up the sides of the inflatable rafts and attached the crane's hook to the ribbon. The crane operator hoisted the ribbon onto the rear deck of the ship where deckhands secured it with chains. The ship's locomotive-sized diesel engines roared to life as it lumbered back to the oil rig.

Once at the rig, another operator used another crane to move the ribbon onto the huge floating platform. He gently lowered it onto the rig where five mechanics bolted it permanently to the deck.

When a mechanic tightened the last bolt, a cheer went up from the crew. One of the engineers uncorked a bottle of expensive champagne and poured glasses all around. Another engineer cracked open a bottle of Shiner Bock, which Frank accepted with a smile and a nod of his head.

"Ladies and gentleman, we've done it," Frank said. "This is the single greatest engineering achievement of this century, perhaps for the last one thousand years."

The team gave rousing cheers, gulped their champagne, and got back to work. The riskiest part of the project was done.

Chapter 31

The Moon, Zhulong Base

Colonel Feng sat in the comfort of his office at Dongfeng mission control communicating with his commander on the moon. "Why are you so far behind schedule? And more importantly, explain to me how—"

"We have had some initial successes. We have successfully harvested two hundred pounds of helium-3," Commander Chow interrupted.

Colonel Feng shut his eyes and gripped his head. The three-second delay in round-trip communication to the moon made conversation difficult.

"If you would let me fin—"

"Sorry. I did not mean to cut you off."

"Be quiet. Let me finish my questions. When I am done, you will answer. Tell me why you are behind schedule and how you are going to fix it. Your turn, Commander Chow."

"The base was in complete disrepair when we arrived. Morale and productivity are suffering. The loss of our chief horticulturist was a blow. It was like losing a beloved grandmother."

"I understand the morale issues, but you must show results. There is pressure from the party and my father to get back on schedule. The Americans are still well behind us, but Frank Sawyer is a tough competitor."

Commander Chow shrugged his shoulders defensively on the small screen. "The initial goals are impossible. People are on top of each other in the living quarters. I was planning a celebration with the team to coincide with our first batch of homegrown food. Instead, we had a funeral."

"You should be driving the team to produce helium-3 rather than planning parties. You can hold a celebration when you are back on schedule. I do not want to discuss your problems. I want to hear how you will fix things."

The commander's eyes narrowed as he considered the alternatives. "I... I do have an idea," he said. "It will compound the risk to our team, but the danger is tolerable."

"Please continue," he said gesturing impatiently.

"As you know, our mining vehicles serve dual purposes. Not only do they harvest helium-3, but they also generate hydrogen and oxygen. We are producing more oxygen than hydrogen right now."

"We agreed to use the rocket capacity from earth for equipment rather than oxygen. Your point?" Feng asked.

"This overproduction of oxygen will ensure that we have more than enough for the team. But this comes at the expense of reduced hydrogen. We could instead produce more hydrogen," the commander said.

"I see. Your plan would be to switch the mining vehicles over to hydrogen power sooner than planned?"

The Chinese mining vehicles had dual power sources. Initially, they used solar energy. However, as hydrogen stores grew more plentiful, they would switch to their hydrogen fuel cells. The goliath machines operated at a much slower speed using solar power.

"Yes. Faster trucks means more helium-3 sooner. However, we will have much less backup oxygen available. I would ask that you have a ship standing ready with oxygen supplies should we need them."

"This is a creative idea. You have temporarily restored my confidence in you. Store no more than a week's reserve oxygen."

"Can you give me assurances that a standby ship will be available?"

Colonel Feng clenched his fist at the sudden forcefulness of his subordinate. "I am as concerned about the welfare of the team as you are. Do not question my dedication to them again."

Commander Chow stammered, "Yes, sir. We will push to get back on schedule immediately."

Colonel Feng dropped the connection. A rocket could fly to the moon with spare oxygen in three to five days. The risk was necessary to stay on schedule. If he was wrong, the entire team would die.

Chapter 32
Kiribati, Kanton Island

Even seated in the cramped helicopter, Benjamin dwarfed the smallish president of Kiribati. Benjamin banged his elbow against the metal door for the fifth time in the tight space. The steady thumping of the blades and the whine of the turbine engine, combined with the man's accent, made for difficult conversation. "I'm sorry, Mr. President. Can you please repeat that?"

"This is Kanton Island. Many decades ago, it used to be the primary commercial runway into Kiribati." He pointed at the weed-choked asphalt strip below.

Benjamin could barely make out the runway under the jungle foliage. The pilot landed in the only visible clearing. As Benjamin exited the helicopter, the combined scent of jungle foliage and salt water assaulted him. The island smelled... primitive. The asphalt was a patchwork of cracks. He frowned at the dilapidated buildings as he wiped his face with a handkerchief. Even in lightweight pants and a tropical shirt, the sun was hot on his black skin.

"How much did you say you want for the island?"

"One hundred million U.S.," the president responded. "As you can see the runway is still in good condition. If you spray defoliant on it, it is almost ready to use."

If Benjamin were negotiating with an American, he would immediately point out in the inanity of the statement. He didn't know this culture well, so he kept his comments to himself for now. "And how many people live here?"

"That is the beauty of it. No one lives here anymore. There will be no need to relocate anyone. It will make the process of approving the sale through our parliament that much easier. Fewer backs to scratch."

Benjamin strode toward one of the airport buildings with the president trotting behind him to keep up. Benjamin turned the door handle, and it came off in his hand, falling to the ground. He put his thick fingers into the hole left by the doorknob and pulled. Like the knob, the door came off its hinges and fell to the asphalt.

"I wouldn't go in those buildings. They may not be safe," the president said.

Benjamin looked at him and smiled at what sounded like sarcasm, but the president seemed sincere. "You said the buildings would be part of the deal."

"Indeed, indeed. Like the runway, they need minor work. What do you think?"

"My definition of minor work is different than yours." It mattered little. Trailers and other temporary accommodations would be sufficient at first. A large cargo plane could transport them with ease.

From his military days, he knew C-130 cargo planes could land on uneven dirt runways. Defoliant might be enough to make the runway usable for these rugged military aircraft. It wouldn't work for a commercial airliner, but at least it would be a start.

"Your island is beautiful, but one hundred million is too much. The infrastructure is in worse condition than I was told."

"But you are asking for much more than a mere land purchase. You are asking us to permanently cede one of our islands to an undisclosed foreign country."

Benjamin stared at the president through his mirrored sunglasses and didn't respond.

"Perhaps we could negotiate the price down in return for other items?" the president asked.

"Such as?"

"We have limited industry and tourism. A new employer would be most welcome."

Automated Technologies would need more people if this venture was successful. But they were more likely to hire people from major U.S. and international universities with advanced degrees. However, they would also need support roles like material handling and food preparation. There might even be an opportunity to provide more advanced training to the local residents. Presented correctly, it would be a great public relations victory for Automated Technologies that would also help the people of Kiribati.

"We'll need people. We can come to an agreement in that regard. Let's check out your beach."

They struggled through the weeds and undergrowth until they reached the ocean. Benjamin gazed out over the pale blue lagoon as schools of tropical fish darted about in the clear water.

"I thought you guys were supposed to be underwater by now," Benjamin said. "Two of your previous presidents have publicly stated that you would be the first casualty of global warming."

The president shrugged and grinned broadly. "We did receive international aid based on those concerns. What did you think of our government offices back on South Tarawa Island?"

"They were beautiful. I don't mean to be rude, but I was surprised to see how modern they were."

"You are not being rude at all. We used the international aid to build the offices. At the time, we expanded the buildings dramatically to allow global warming researchers to have a place to office. When they left, we filled the offices with other personnel."

Benjamin smiled at the minor deception. "That was savvy negotiating. Now I know you are overcharging me. I'll give you forty million U.S., and we can work out a guarantee to employ a reasonable number of your people. I will also throw in free training."

"Fifty million and I will put people to work clearing this airfield immediately."

"Deal," Benjamin said. "But let's discuss the parameters and the timing. This can't be public knowledge yet. This can't come to a vote in your parliament for at least three months, perhaps longer."

"I understand. I am to rally support with a handful of people to ensure the deal goes through. You will let me know when it is time to put it to a broader vote."

"We understand each other perfectly."

"And you cannot tell me what you are doing and why?"

Benjamin shook his head. "It's premature. But when we're done, Kiribati will be a household name."

Chapter 33
Pacific Ocean, Oil Rig

The *Al Gore* was one of many ships making up the flotilla of onlookers watching the elevator deployment. The ship was named for the politician and activist from the early 2000s who had championed the cause of global warming. He remained one of the patron saints of the green movement to this day.

Onlookers on more than fifty other ships came together to witness this historic event. The Automated Technologies security team grudgingly agreed to allow the Mother Earth Militia's ship to be part of the flotilla. While the militia's roots were in tree spiking and arson, their protests had been nonviolent for the last ten years.

Today, they would be going back to their roots. An activist scratched his chin through his long beard and set his binoculars on the deck. He could see the climber accelerating up the elevator dragging another layer of ribbon behind it. It was time.

The climber was already a mile above the deck of the oil rig. It should be in range based on the specs for the Chinese weapon. One of his fellow activists brought a missile from underdeck and handed it to him. He took careful aim at the climber and launched the rocket. The missile streaked off the bow of the ship toward the elevator. The crew calmly dropped their sails and chained themselves together on the deck. There was no point in running in a sailboat.

***

The huge spool of carbon fiber ribbon unrolled as the first of many automated climbers accelerated up the elevator. The machine would ascend slowly at first, but it would reach a speed of fifty kilometers per hour as it added a second layer of carbon fiber to the existing ribbon. More climbers would follow until the ribbon was thick enough to support twenty tons of cargo.

Frank removed his oil-stained work gloves and tucked them into his back pocket. He shielded his eyes with his hat. A growing smile crept across his face as he watched the climber ascend. "I still can't believe it's all coming together," he said to no one in particular. He turned to go into the control room to check the computers monitoring the process.

Frank heard a barely audible pop in the sky. The ribbon went slack, then proceeded to fall back onto the deck. Frank moved fast.

"Everyone, get under something now." One of Frank's engineers stared unmoving into the sky trying to make sense of the commotion. Frank grabbed him by the collar and dragged him into one of the enclosures. Carbon fiber collapsed onto the rig, wrapping around equipment and trailing into the ocean. The wafer-thin ribbon wasn't a problem, but the one-ton climber wouldn't be far behind.

Frank looked left and right praying that the equipment wouldn't land on the rig and kill one of his people. *What could I possibly have done wrong?*

The climber crashed into the water with a loud splash inches from the edge of the platform and began to sink.

He still held his engineer by the scruff of his neck. "Sorry," Frank said as he slapped him on the back and stood up. The man stared back at him slack-jawed.

"What the hell happened?" Frank asked into his headset. "What was the telemetry data telling us before the ribbon failed?"

"Everything was fine up until the explosion," someone on the bridge said.

"What explosion? There wasn't anything flammable on the climber," Frank said.

A breathless engineer ran up to Frank, eyes still wide from the narrow miss. "I saw something shoot up from the *Al Gore*." "What do you mean?" "I think they shot down the elevator with a rocket." "That makes no sense. Why would the Mother Earth Militia sabotage the largest green energy initiative the world has ever known?" "I'm sure of it. I saw a rocket. You said yourself it couldn't have exploded."

Frank couldn't fathom why anyone would launch a rocket at the elevator, but that didn't matter right now. He called up to the bridge. "Put me on the loudspeaker." After three seconds, Frank was about to ask what the holdup was when the bridge told him they were ready.

"Everyone, we can salvage this effort. I need the tug to grab that climber before the entire thing sinks to the bottom of the ocean. I need another team to cut the excess ribbon off my rig. We can't work with it covering our equipment. I need an armed security team with me on a Zodiac now. Bring me a rifle."

Everyone moved. Frank met the security team, and they climbed into the Zodiac raft. "Get me to the *Al Gore* now," Frank ordered.

The boat raced across the water at fifty knots. As they approached the sailing vessel, Frank said, "Weapons ready. We don't know what to expect."

As they edged up to the boat, the militia members held their hands above their heads. They were attached to the main mast with heavy gauge chain.

"What the hell is going on here?" Frank shouted.

A tall man with a long beard stepped forward and spoke. "The Mother Earth Militia won't allow you to decimate Daughter Moon with the same reckless abandon mankind has unleashed on Mother Earth."

"Daughter Moon?" Frank asked, confused.

"Mankind has been a plague on the earth. We've destroyed her natural beauty in our race to dominate her rather than live in harmony."

"Fine, whatever. What does that have to do with the moon?"

"We will never let you wreak the same havoc on the moon. We will never allow you to rape her the way you've raped her mother."

Frank could see this was going nowhere. *These people are, quite literally, insane.* He turned to his chief of security and said, "Unchain these idiots. Get them back to the rig and detain them. Search this ship from stem to stern. Take everything. I want to know what happened here."

The chief of security checked the chains on the anklets and wristlets and the locks around the main mast. He turned to the man with the beard. "Tell me where the keys are."

The bearded man stared back vacantly. "I threw them overboard."

"Son of a bitch," Frank shouted. "We're miles out at sea. What is wrong with you?"

Frank rubbed his temples and turned back to his security team. "Take their ship back to the rig. Cut the mast off this boat so you can detach them from it and sink it. What's the weather tonight?"

"Balmy," one of the security team answered.

"Move these guys from the boat to the rig using one of the cranes. Leave them chained up overnight five feet above the ocean and throw chum in the water. I hear sharks can jump ten feet into the air. I want to see if it's true. It will give these idiots an opportunity to bond with nature. Get me back to the rig."

The Mother Earthers railed about murder, theft of their vessel, and Daughter Moon. Frank ignored them. The security team stayed behind on the *Al Gore*. Frank and his chief of security jumped into the Zodiac to return to the rig.

"Sir?" the chief of security asked.

"Yes, I know," Frank said. "Leave them chained up for an hour on the crane. Let them sweat for a while, then lock them up. Let's not add murder to this already rotten day."

"Thank you. I wasn't sure if you meant it."

"Just make sure you don't distract the team with niceties like cutting their chains off. They can stay that way until we hand them over to the authorities. Make sure they have food and water."

Frank's eyes narrowed. "Make sure they have plenty of steak and chicken to eat. No fruit. No vegetables. Let's see if these nut jobs have the courage of their convictions. Once you soften them up a bit, I need to know who put them up to this. When they tell you, they can have all the vegetables they want."

They arrived at the rig, and Frank jogged up to the bridge. "Get Ben on the line for me."

A bridge hand passed him a phone. "Ben, get me another meeting with the president. I'm going to have to go beg for naval protection. We're sitting ducks out here."

"You know it's going to come at a price?" he asked.

"That goes without saying," Frank replied.

Chapter 34

Washington, DC, The White House

"I guess you can't defend yourself from thugs with rocket launchers after all," Gladwell laughed.

Frank gripped the edge of his chair and tried to remember that punching the vice president in the face was a felony. "Would the situation be as humorous to you if some of my people had died?"

Gladwell flipped his wrist in a backhand motion. "But they didn't. Don't be so melodramatic."

President Brown broke up the argument. "Gentlemen, let's move forward. Thomas, don't gloat."

A sneer passed across Gladwell's face at the reprimand from his boss. *Good,* Frank thought.

"When we last spoke, you were determined to refuse assistance from your country," the president said.

Unbelievable. "I was unwilling to give up the most valuable technology of the last two hundred years to buy off the U.S. government."

"What is the purpose of this meeting if we are going to rehash the last one? Should we adjourn?"

"Benjamin has a proposal that may give us a resolution."

Benjamin cleared his throat to summarize everyone's positions. "Frank doesn't want to lose control of his technology to the U.S. government. You feel an effort of this magnitude doesn't belong in the hands of private industry. Neither of us wants to see the Chinese win. Is that an accurate enough summary?"

"It is," the president answered.

"We realize now that we need U.S. Navy protection. We're too exposed."

"Even the most casual observer of the situation would agree with you."

"We propose to build a second elevator in the Pacific Ocean to be operated by the U.S. government. You must pay for the construction at reasonable rates, but you will control it. We will control the first elevator."

The president leaned forward to listen. "I'm intrigued. Go on."

"It balances private industry control with governmental control. We push the Chinese out of the picture."

"Who controls helium-3 production and by extension the entire energy industry?" the president asked.

"We do."

"Then the conversation is done."

"But the United States government has a strong influence in the decision-making process. For example, if there is a nation that is on the U.S. terrorist list, we won't sell to them."

"That goes without saying. Existing laws already forbid it. I'm not clear what America is getting in this deal."

"That was a simple scenario. A more complex one might be the Russian or Chinese government playing hardball with a U.S. ally. As an example, Russia might see their access to helium-3 drying up if they threatened Poland."

Gladwell raised his hand to force his way back into the conversation. "And you would be willing to put that in a contract?"

All eyes turned to look at Gladwell and his raised hand. It was as if he had stepped in something and tracked it into the Oval Office.

"Thomas, we don't want that kind of agreement in writing for someone to share with a hungry news media," President Brown said. "This will be a quiet agreement between a patriot and his government."

Frank hoped that was enough to cow Gladwell into silence, but the man wouldn't stop talking.

"I have another issue with these plans. The second space elevator should be in southern California."

Frank held his head between his hands and screwed his eyes shut. "Why?"

"There are clear technical advantages to having the elevator on land rather than the ocean," Gladwell answered.

"Did your political science degree help you come to that conclusion? Name one."

"It's easier to move freight back and forth."

"There is no place in the southern continental United States that doesn't suffer from massive dust storms, tornadoes, hurricanes, or earthquakes. We did an exhaustive check."

"You can get hit by a hurricane in the Pacific Ocean."

"We can also move the elevator out of harm's way. It floats. That's the point."

"It's also vulnerable to attack."

"Not with the U.S. Navy supporting it. You are fifty times more vulnerable on land. Any idiot with a truck bomb can destroy a land-based elevator. Ellen, this man isn't qualified to make these kinds of decisions."

The president did not meet Frank's eyes when she responded. "California is a dark blue state. Thomas has a campaign coming up, and he needs funding."

"So we are going to make a bad decision for political reasons?"

Benjamin interjected, "Frank, it's their elevator. Let them put it where they want."

Frank knew Benjamin was right. He was boxed in. He slowly nodded his head. "You have a deal. We'll put the elevator wherever you want it. When can I expect my fleet?"

Chapter 35

Washington, DC, Eisenhower Executive Office Building

Benjamin was not looking forward to today's meeting with the vice president, particularly after the last round of unpleasantness between Frank and Gladwell. There were real risks in burning relationships with the next administration. He hoped to walk out of this meeting with those relationships intact.

Gladwell invited Benjamin to take a seat in his office and got right to the point. "My campaign is getting ready to kick into high gear. In light of your request for help to President Brown, I wanted to see if you and Frank had discussed my offer. Getting the support of both of you would set the right tone with the business community in my upcoming campaign."

"We've discussed it. Frank's not amenable to the idea. He's not willing to throw the support of his name or his company behind you," Benjamin said.

"That's extremely shortsighted. I can offer a lot in return."

"Like I said, I've discussed your offer with Frank. He doesn't want a governmental role. His passion is in the business world."

"I get that. He's a busy man. But what about the governmental contracts? I can guarantee that you will win any contracts you want. You will have to go through the bidding process with everyone else, but you and I know how deals are really done."

"Frank thinks we can win on the merits of our products."

Gladwell's voice went up an octave. "That's naïve. He's crazy if he thinks a sitting president can't effectively shut him out of military and civilian contracts. Or guarantee him the ones he wants. I'm going to remember my friends."

"It's a risk."

"Forget Frank for a minute. What about you?"

"Me?"

"I would like you to be my vice president. It would be a real reach across the aisle. There is no better person to have on the ticket with me to show I care about the business community."

"Wasn't it Daniel Webster who said, 'I do not propose to be buried until I am really dead' when he turned down the vice presidency?"

The vice president wrinkled his nose at the reference. "I've had to pay my dues. But you are thinking too small. The vice presidency is a stepping stone to the most powerful job in the world."

"I don't agree. I wouldn't be an obvious choice to run for president after a stint as your VP. Democrats would see me as too conservative. Republicans would view me as a traitor."

"I'm going to win this election regardless." The vice president lowered his voice and leaned toward Benjamin. "Let's be honest. President Brown hasn't done a stellar job. The economy is struggling. We've lost ground against China—"

"Agreed," Benjamin said.

"But name a realistic option from the conservative side of the aisle. Even without your support, I can still claim to be the political force behind the space elevator. The man who beat the Chinese."

Benjamin raised his eyebrows at the shameless land grab. "It's more realistic to say it's Frank's idea."

"No one cares about reality. I'll be in the media twenty-four seven as the politician that made it all possible."

"All that assumes you don't have Frank pushing back equally hard in the media saying you had nothing to do with it."

"I'll have the bully pulpit. Frank won't. He'll be a voice crying in the wilderness."

"Frank can be pretty loud when he wants to be."

Gladwell scoffed. "He'll seem shrill and petty if he doesn't allow the U.S. government to share the spotlight. And the U.S. government and I will be synonymous." Gladwell paused for a moment, put his head back, and looked at the ceiling. "You're Frank's friend. You know him better than anyone. What's your read on him?"

"I'm biased. He's my best friend."

"Humor me. What makes the man tick?"

"Love of country, love of freedom. Bold ideas that seem unachievable to other men."

"Like controlling the world's energy supply."

"He doesn't view it that way."

Gladwell rolled his eyes. "Everyone views it that way."

"Not Frank. He believes human civilization changes if there is unlimited nonpolluting energy. He doesn't want to control people by doing this project; he wants to set them free."

"Me too. I want to help him make that vision a reality."

"He won't buy that."

"Maybe he should. Maybe the alternative is that it gets taken away from him. If he doesn't back the right team, maybe there isn't a spot for him long-term."

So this was the end game? He and Frank could get behind the Gladwell ticket and effectively give away their control of their own technology. Alternatively, Gladwell would take it through legislative gamesmanship. The vice president did have decades-old relationships in the congress. Gladwell might even be bold enough to use an executive order and bypass congress all together. He would say that the space elevator must be nationalized as part of America's strategic defense or some such nonsense.

"He could always throw his financial support and name recognition behind another candidate."

"Again, there is no realistic option on the other side of the aisle. They're all clowns. You know it, and I know it."

"You've convinced me, Thomas."

Gladwell raised his eyebrows and smiled. "That was easier than I expected."

"You've convinced me that Frank is right. I need to run myself."

"What are you talking about?"

"I'm forming an exploratory committee," Benjamin said. The clichéd political vocabulary made him wince.

"I don't understand. An exploratory committee to do what?"

"To beat you, Thomas. I'll be running against you in the upcoming election. You won't be the guy that beat the Chinese. I will be. I'll be the guy in front of the cameras every time there is a success with the space elevator. I'll be the politician that brings cheap green energy to the planet."

"You son of a bitch. You can't win. You don't have an ounce of political experience."

"You consider that a disadvantage? You guys have run this country into the ground. The people will welcome an alternative from outside the Beltway."

"We will bury you. Get out of my office."

"Gladly. I'll see you on the campaign trail. You need to let me know if the last eight years were worth it after your concession speech."

Chapter 36

Pacific Ocean, Oil Rig

Frank tapped the expended Chinese QW-1 missile launcher on the table in front of him. They had recovered three more from the *Al Gore*.

"Have you been able to establish any link between our Mother Earth Militia guests and the Chinese?" Frank asked his chief of security.

"Nothing yet. They are being tight-lipped. They could've also purchased it on the open market from any arms dealer."

"How are they faring after not having access to vegetarian fare for a week and a half?"

"So far, everyone has refused to eat with one exception."

Frank raised his eyebrows. "Do tell."

"We've been interviewing them individually, and she pleaded for a vegetarian meal during the interrogation. She wouldn't eat in front of the group, but she sure wolfed it down when she was away from prying eyes."

Frank picked up the missile launcher and examined it. "You have a couple of women on your team, correct?"

"I do."

"Bring the girl down so I can speak with her. Have one of your female security guards here to avoid any signs of impropriety."

As the chief of security stepped out, Frank's radio buzzed. "Yes?" he said.

"The U.S. Navy fleet is within helicopter range. They are asking to send over one of their officers to pick up the Mother Earth Militia folks.

"Tell them it will have to wait."

"They were quite insistent."

"Tell them there is nowhere to land. Tell them our own helicopter is on the pad or something."

"They can see that we have a second helicopter pad."

"How long do I have before they get here?"

"No more than twenty minutes, best case."

"Then pile crates on the second pad and stall them. Also, send down a vegetarian meal in ten minutes."

Frank knew the U.S. Navy was anxious to get their hands on the Mother Earth Militia folks. The navy officers themselves were certainly no fans of eco-terrorists or pirates. However, they reported to politicians who would find Frank's vigilante justice unseemly. This was Frank's last chance to get any information. After that, he would be dependent on the government.

Frank heard a rap at the door. "Come in," Frank said.

An athletic woman dressed in a black security outfit ushered in a waify, haggard-looking young lady. Frank could tell by her matted hair that she hadn't bathed in over a week. The security team had made sure that the terrorists had no more than two hours of uninterrupted sleep. The dark circles under the girl's eyes told him the tactics were working.

"Sit down," Frank said.

The girl collapsed into the chair and stared at the metal tabletop.

"How old are you?" Frank asked.

"Twenty-five," she mumbled without looking up.

"Do you know piracy carried the death penalty for many years in the United States? You're lucky that times have changed. You'll be out of jail by the time you are forty-five."

A sarcastic smirk crept across her face, despite her physical state. "We're not pirates."

"I've had several of my lawyers research it for me. Any act of robbery or criminal violence on the open seas qualifies. They are still checking on whether there are additional arms-trafficking charges."

Her smile faded and her eyes grew wet. Frank sighed. *This misguided kid is the same age as Sam.*

"I need to know who put you up to this," Frank said in a softer voice.

"I'm new to the militia. They invited me to join the crew because I know how to sail. No one shared any of the details with me."

There was another knock at the door. "Come in," Frank said.

One of the cooks brought in a steaming dish of pineapple and potato curry. She set it in front of Frank with silverware, a cloth napkin, and bottled water.

"Hungry?" Frank asked.

"Is this where you entice me with food until I tell you something useful?"

"No, I'm asking if you are hungry."

"What do you think?"

Frank slid the dish to her along with the silverware and the water.

She gave him a suspicious stare. "What's in the food? What's in the water? Is this some type of truth serum thing?"

Frank laughed at this. "I'm not in the habit of drugging people. Eat. You know, my daughter is about the same age as you."

She picked up the fork and poked at the food but didn't reply. She sniffed cautiously at the rice.

"I would hate to see her lose twenty years of her life for a stupid mistake. For hanging out with the wrong crowd."

Her eyes watered again as she ate a small forkful of rice.

"Everyone else in your crew is pretty tight-lipped. If you give me useful information, my lawyers will get your sentence reduced. I might even have enough pull to keep you out of jail entirely."

She ate some potatoes and opened the bottle of water. She responded with a full mouth of food. "I told you I don't know anything."

"I get it. You didn't buy the missiles. But you must've heard something about the deal."

"You can keep me out of jail? What about my friends?" She wolfed down several large bites of potatoes and pineapple.

"Your friends are going to jail. They could have easily killed some of my people. This is your opportunity for a deal. It ends when you finish that meal."

At this, she put down her fork and cried in earnest. "I really don't know anything. I don't want to go to jail."

"You must have overheard something. The beer is flowing one night. People are passing around a few joints. People say things they shouldn't."

Frank could see the gears turning in the girl's concentrated expression.

"One night six months ago we had a big party. Everyone was pretty high."

"And?"

"One of the guys talked about this totally hot Asian chick that helped him procure the weapons. Typical guy stuff about how he would have liked to do this or that."

"A Chinese national?"

"I never met her, but I gathered not. As American as you or I."

Frank rocked back on his chair at this news. *Could Sam be right? Could the Asian girl possibly be Lucy?* The rhythmic thumping of a large helicopter approached. "Finish the rest of your meal. My lawyers will be in touch with you."

Frank left the room. He dialed Stephen on a satellite phone. "I need you to dig into Lucy's background."

"That's quite a change in direction. Any particular reason?" Stephen asked.

"Just being cautious. And Stephen, no one can know you are checking. Not Sam, not Tim, not Ben."

Chapter 37

Tijuana, U.S. Border Crossing

Colonel Mokri rode in the passenger seat of one of his trucks as it crossed the border into California. One of his Iranian agents was at the wheel. The colonel could drive his own trucks, but it would look strange to have the company's prosperous owner driving the vehicle. If they were stopped, he would claim that he was training a new driver.

His fellow agent said in Farsi, "That was easy." He ground the gears as he upshifted.

Colonel Mokri cringed. "Watch the gears. It's bad for the truck, and it will call attention to you. Spanish or English only. Señor Jose Martinez, not colonel anything. I know we're alone, but you need to get into character."

"Yes, sir. My apologies. Where do we go now?"

"I need you to drop me off so that I can rent an off road vehicle. I need to meet our true believers in the desert. I paid a coyote to shuttle them across."

"True believers? Are we not all true believers?"

The colonel looked out his window and smiled at the youthful enthusiasm. "Of course. I mean only that every asset has its purpose. College educated VEVAK agents with exceptional language skills tend to view the world differently than illiterate goat herders."

"Those goat herders are martyrs. Surely, you must respect them for their willingness to die for Allah and the cause? Do you have the faith it takes to martyr yourself? I can only hope that mine is that strong. Perhaps you have spent too long in the land of the infidel."

The young man's insolence shocked Mokri. The colonel had indeed been away from Iran for many years. Apparently, respect for one's superiors had declined during that time. Despite his irritation, the colonel held up his hands to placate the young agent. "I hold them in the highest regard. They have a purpose, and we will use them to advance Allah's needs. However, we advance Iran's agenda more by staying alive and doing our job."

"But the glory of martyrdom—"

"Your job is to scout the target and determine an effective way to infiltrate it. Do you think Iranian peasants with no English skills are going to devise a workable plan to destroy the space elevator? The Americans are not stupid. The work you will do gathering intelligence while delivering food to the base is invaluable. "

The young agent visibly relaxed at the compliment. The colonel signaled for him to pull over near a car rental storefront. "Drop me off at the corner. We'll part ways here. Take the truck north and continue your run. I'll be in touch soon."

"Allahu Akbar, Colonel," the agent said.

Colonel Mokri shook his head at the agent's brazen lack of professionalism. "Vaya con Dios, señor."

Chapter 38

Simi Valley, Reagan Library

Benjamin Whitman had a far-away look in his eyes as he mentally rehearsed his responses to potential questions. He looked around at the other Republican Party candidates. Their political careers spanned decades, and many of them had run for president in the past. They had participated in scores of political debates at all levels of government. Benjamin had done a year of debate in high school, and he hadn't enjoyed it.

He felt a hand on his shoulder. "I wanted to say good luck. You nervous?" Frank asked.

"I look nervous?"

"To everyone here, you look like a calm and collected captain of industry. But I know you better than most."

"I'm used to the business world. I'm used to saying what I'm thinking in the clearest terms possible. These debates are all nuance and nonsense. The moderator doesn't want to know what I think. He wants to have a gotcha moment that he can replay on television for the next twelve months."

"Just be yourself. The other candidates will meander and refuse to take a stand. If you are the one guy speaking your mind, you are the candidate the audience is going to remember. Crush these guys."

Frank walked back to his seat to give Benjamin more time to prepare.

The national anthem played, and the candidates walked onto the stage. Benjamin looked at his competitors: three governors, two senators, and one congressman. Between the six of them, they had a combined century and a half of political experience. However, they had a combined total of five years in business including childhood lemonade stands. Frank was right. The only way to stand out from this crowd was to be himself. He wasn't going to out-politic the politicians.

The moderator explained the rules to the participants and the audience. He directed his first question to one of the governors. "The Republican Party is generally associated with business and industry. Your entire adult life has been spent in politics. Can you tell me what you would do to improve the competiveness of American businesses compared to other economic powerhouses like China?"

"Let me first say thank you for being here. What a wonderful venue here at the Reagan Library. I can't think of a better place for the first Republican primary debate. As a young staffer, I worked for Ronald Reagan on one of his campaigns. He was like a father to me. God bless America."

The audience clapped respectfully. The moderator nodded at the governor, but checked his watch.

"Let me tell you what I did in my state. By partnering closely with the business community, we've grown our state economy at two percent a year while I've been in office. That's well above the national average for the last decade. We've established innovation hubs and funded college universities to ensure the best research is getting into the hands of our business leaders."

The moderator thanked him and moved on to the next question. "Mr. Whitman. This is for you. I would like to ask the opposite question of you. You have spent most of your career in the private sector. Why should voters believe you are adequately prepared for a life of public service?"

Benjamin cocked his head at the moderator. "You will have to explain your question. What do you mean by public service?"

"Sir, the question is straightforward. The other participants in today's debate have extensive experience governing where as you don't."

"I'm sorry. I thought you said public service, not governing."

"I did. Most people understand public service and governing to be one and the same. It's a generally understood term." The moderator's sarcastic smirk risked cracking his pancake makeup.

"You and the people on this stage may see the two as synonymous. But I don't, and many Americans don't." Benjamin turned to the governor who had answered the first question. "Governor, are you paid a salary?"

"Of course. What kind of question is that?"

"And do you live in the governor's mansion? I assume for free?"

The governor's jaw muscles tightened as he responded. "Yes, of course I live in the governor's mansion. And of course I don't pay for it. I have to maintain a separate residence. I need to be protected from the public so that my family and I can have a modicum of privacy."

"Governor, I wouldn't call a job that pays a handsome salary and provides a complimentary mansion public service. That sounds like something else entirely. I've spent decades working with inner city youth trying to teach them the fundamentals of the business world. I don't get paid for that work. I don't get a free house for that work. Perhaps that is what we should mean when we say public service?"

The audience and the moderator laughed at this. Benjamin couldn't tell if the moderator agreed with his sentiments, but the man knew how to play to the camera. His network's ratings would be good.

The debates continued with the usual questions around religious faith, perspective on abortion, and women's rights. The pat answers were non-differentiating. Other candidates in other elections had given these same answers for the last four decades.

The moderator came back to Benjamin with another question. "Mr. Whitman, I'm sure our viewing audience is familiar with the work Automated Technologies is doing with the space elevator and fusion technology. You are pro-business, while seeming to have little respect for government—"

Benjamin interrupted. "I have little respect for government overreach."

The moderator plowed forward without adjusting his characterization of Benjamin's views. "However, President Brown has tasked Vice President Gladwell to give the effort his full attention. Is it not hypocritical of you to accept all that government support?"

"Your implication is that Automated Technologies couldn't build the space elevators without government support?

"Of course. Vice President Gladwell talks daily about all that the administration does to support your business initiative."

"My business initiative? I am not currently in private service at Automated Technology. I am apparently interviewing for a job in what you call public service."

This received loud applause and laughter again from the audience. The moderator interjected to move things along. "That is fair. I mistakenly called this your business initiative, and you are technically on a leave of absence. But the spirit of my question remains."

"I do get the thrust of your question, but I must again disagree with your premise. Automated Technologies owns all the technology for the project. The government is getting a free ride, because the owner of Automated Technologies is a patriot."

"But sir, the vice president regularly highlights the fact that federal lands in California have been reserved for the space elevator. Automated Technologies has co-opted part of the American naval fleet. Some viewers might view your position as disingenuous."

"Automated Technologies is building a second space elevator for the American government as part of that deal. We are allowing the U.S. government to license our technology for free. The scales are balanced."

The moderator scoffed at Ben's response. "I can't let that go. You aren't charging for the licensing of the technology, but you are being paid for the cost of the construction. All while you are using U.S. Navy resources to protect a private-sector investment."

"It would be hypocritical to dispute that. However, the primary purpose of government should be to protect its citizens from foreign and domestic lawlessness. And the U.S. Navy is doing an admirable job in that regard. This is government doing what government should be doing."

This drew hearty applause from the audience. The moderator wrinkled his papers as yet another one of the night's zingers missed its mark. Benjamin looked down at the podium and noticed he was gripping the edges. He released his death grip. He had survived his first debate.

***

Later that evening, Frank joined Benjamin in the bank of hotel rooms that the campaign used as a temporary headquarters. They turned on one of the cable news channels to see the results of the debate.

One of the national commentators that they both respected summarized the evening. "Overall, the debates were mundane. The candidates had stock answers to stock questions. The one highlight of the evening was Benjamin Whitman. His willingness to go aggressively after both the other candidates and the moderator made for great entertainment."

His fellow journalist asked, "It was comical, but did Mr. Whitman's feisty responses have more than entertainment value?"

"Rather than giving my opinion, let's look at one of our informal polls from the evening. We asked, 'Who won tonight's Republican primary debates?' Eighty-five percent of respondents chose Benjamin Whitman."

Applause erupted in the hotel room. Frank slapped Benjamin on the shoulder in congratulations. "You have a lock on this nomination if you keep this up. Time to focus on Gladwell."

Chapter 39

Austin, Sawyer Family Ranch

Frank answered the incoming video request from Stephen Clark. "How's China?"

"I'm looking forward to getting back to the states. But I'm calling you to discuss Lucy." Stephen answered.

"Give me one moment." Frank stood up and discretely closed the door to his office. He didn't want Lisa to walk in and hear the conversation. His wife would have no patience for this type of clandestine activity if directed at her future daughter-in-law.

"I've researched Lucy's background as you asked. I've been careful. I haven't left a trail," Stephen said.

"That's important. If this gets back to Tim or Lucy, it would create a huge divide between Tim and me. What's the summary?"

"I've been able to trace her back through early high school using a combination of social media, school records, employment data, credit-checking services and the like. She's a model citizen with left-wing leanings."

"That's good, right? Her public persona matches what we know about her. She certainly doesn't hide the fact that she's pro-environment. She restrains herself when she's talking with me about her left-wing political views, but they aren't secret."

Stephen paused for a moment, prompting Frank to ask, "Are you there? Do you agree?"

"My gut is telling me something is off."

"Not based on what you just told me. Is there something else?"

"There's not, and that's the problem. It's too perfect."

"I don't understand."

"Her academic and professional lives are impeccable. I can find no record of any arrests at demonstrations, no minor drug charges, not even a speeding ticket."

Frank laughed out loud at this. "Come on, Stephen. You can't seriously penalize her for being a model citizen. Honestly, that's why she's so good for Tim. She shares his political beliefs, but she has avoided the chaos that seems to swirl around the left."

"And that isn't the least bit strange to you? Getting arrested at a protest would be a badge of honor for many in her peer group. It's as if her environmental credentials were designed from the ground up."

"Designed? Strange choice of words."

"It was intentional. It's like she's a cardboard cutout of a hippie chick. But a very special cardboard cutout. One that would remain palatable to a prominent business man."

At this, Frank's humor evaporated. "That sounds paranoid. Nothing you've said supports that kind of logical leap."

"That's not the extent of it. She literally falls off the face of the earth prior to high school. I can't find anything about her in public schools, private schools, or a newspaper. She goes from total obscurity to getting into a prestigious East Coast prep school. There should be the obligatory spelling bees, musical competitions, art contests, athletic teams. Something…"

"What about her family?"

"Single child, parents deceased. Again, almost as if she was designed from the ground up. There is no way to check farther into her background without doing human interviews."

Frank replied immediately. "No. Absolutely not. The second you interview people from her past, she will know."

"I can be discreet."

"You can't be discreet enough. Think about it. If someone asked your friends questions about your background, wouldn't they tell you? What happened when we background checked you during our hiring process?"

"You have a point. All my friends told me that they had been contacted and asked whether it was legit."

"There you have it," Frank said.

"You seem to place a lot of faith in Samantha's opinion."

"So?"

"She's suspicious."

"I told you not to tell anyone you were doing the investigation," Frank said in measured tones.

"Relax boss, I didn't. I'm telling you she was still very suspicious the day we saw you and Tim in your office. She told me to let it go for Tim's sake, but I could tell it was against her better judgment."

Frank considered whether he was too close to the situation. Sam loved her older brother dearly, but she also tended to be more suspicious. She was a strong judge of character, but she also didn't trust others easily. Sam's opinion meant a great deal, but was he willing to risk Tim's relationship with Lucy? By extension, was he willing to risk his own relationship with his son, particularly now that things were going so well?

"Frank?" Stephen said, pressing him for a response.

"Sorry. I know you need an answer. Let's put a brake on things. I have what I need."

"I can do this without alerting Lucy or Tim."

"I know you believe that, but I have to play the boss card on this one. Perhaps I should say I need to play the dad card. There isn't enough in what you've shown me to risk alienating Tim."

"It's a risk," Stephen noted. "And I think it's a material one."

"I understand, and I appreciate your candor. It's on me if I'm wrong. Let's drop it."

Chapter 40

Shanghai, Nuclear Engineering Research and Design Institute

The minister of state security sat across the table from Director Lu of the Shanghai Nuclear Engineering Research and Design Institute. After the threats from the general secretary, the minister had decided to fix the leak personally.

"You have broad overall responsibility for the fusion program?" the minister asked.

"Yes, of course. My team is over two thousand, but I am the man most responsible for the success of the program. I am bringing fusion to China and the world."

"The world?"

"This is a Chinese accomplishment, but the entire world will benefit."

"Perhaps you should focus more on China and less on the world. Within your team of two thousand, do you also handle security?"

"Everyone reports to me. You could say that I am the father of China's fusion program. One of my primary tasks has been to mislead the world and the Americans in particular regarding our efforts. I surprised the world with our progress to ensure there would be no competition."

"But there is competition. Surely you have heard Frank Sawyer's claims."

Director Lu laughed out loud. "Yes, but he is lying. He has nothing. His animosity for the Chinese people is well known. He's trying to confuse the market with his trickery. I have no doubt it is from some misguided notion that China has stolen his intellectual property in the past."

"You have a leak. Frank Sawyer has fusion, because you failed to keep the program secure. You have single-handedly given away our lead in fusion to the Americans."

Director Lu's smile evaporated. "That's not possible."

"As the 'father of fusion,' I am holding you personally accountable for this leak. You will help me find out who did this. I have a list of your senior team leaders and chief scientists. We will start with them and work our way down through the organization."

"It cannot be one of my senior people. Their futures here are too secure. They have a strong sense of national pride. It must be someone lower level."

"We will see."

***

Dr. Yang sat alone in a small conference room. He wasn't sure why he'd been called away from his work. He had much to do. A police captain in a blue uniform opened the door and sat across from him. She brushed her short bobbed hair out of her eyes and pulled out a small red notebook.

"Dr. Yang?"

"Yes. How can I help you? Has there been an accident?"

"Nothing like that. My name is Captain Sun. I have some questions for you."

Dr. Yang glanced nervously at his watch. "I am quite busy with my research. Perhaps at a future time."

"You don't have time to assist with a state security issue here at your lab?" Captain Sun said raising an eyebrow.

"I... didn't know it was so serious. Yes, of course I have time."

"We are interviewing everyone at the Institute. Someone leaked sensitive information to the Americans. You are to tell no one on your team about our discussion. They will all be contacted shortly, and they must not have time to prepare their answers."

Dr. Yang played dumb. "Leaked? Everyone knows about it. We announced fusion to the world at the United Nations. I saw it on television."

The captain frowned. "I am talking about detailed technical information."

Dr. Yang prayed his expression conveyed legitimate shock. "That is a different matter. We all knew it was essential that we maintain our competitive edge through secrecy. Everyone on the team was carefully vetted to ensure they were not a security risk."

"I would like to discuss that."

"Have you identified someone on my team that might be a risk?"

"I would like to discuss you, Dr. Yang."

"Anything to help the investigation."

"Have you ever had any clandestine meetings with any foreigners to discuss your research?"

"Of course not. I would have let Director Lu know if I had been approached by someone."

"Yes, you have clear protocols should this happen."

Dr. Yang nodded, as Captain Sun perused his file.

"I see that you are a Christian. You attend a local house church. That is uncommon within the institute's senior staff."

"Our church is registered with the state. We follow all the laws."

The captain nodded. "You are correct that it is registered. There are millions of Christians in China, and they do not generally interfere with the state. Still, it is uncommon at your level."

"I assure you my religion in no way diminishes my feelings for China," Dr. Yang said.

"I also understand you never joined the Communist Party. Again, uncommon. Do you harbor ill will toward the party? Are there any conflicts that you face between your religion and party affiliation?"

"No, no. Nothing like that. I am a researcher. Party affiliation is for political and business types."

"Party affiliation is not only for political and business types; it is for everyone with a love of China."

Dr. Yang bowed his head and looked at his lap. "Director Lu chastens me for not prioritizing my membership. Perhaps he is right."

She smiled and brushed it off. "Even though you're not a party member, I am guessing you must have strong family ties within the party?"

"Why do you say that?"

"Your wife is pregnant with your second child. I understand it is a girl. Congratulations."

Dr. Yang's mouth hung open briefly. He tasted bile in the back of his throat. The captain again raised an eyebrow.

He forced to share his rehearsed story. "Yes, thank you. It is indeed our second. My uncle is in a leadership position in one of the rural districts. He helped me get an exception with the authorities. He went to school with one of the magistrates here."

"I would assume that someone who was granted such an exception is likely not someone who would steal state secrets." She smiled. "I would like you to create a list of everyone on your team. Evaluate whether any of them are a security risk. We will meet tomorrow afternoon to review it. You are free to go."

"Thank you, captain."

Before he could walk out the door, the captain said, "One more thing. Just to tie up loose ends. Can you give me the name of your uncle?"

"Yes, his name is Wei Yang. I don't have his contact information handy, but I can get it."

"Bring it to tomorrow's meeting."

Chapter 41

Shanghai, Mandarin Oriental Pudong Hotel

"We have a problem, Frank," Stephen said. "I heard from Dr. Yang. The Chinese State Police are investigating a leak. He passed the first interview, but he lied to them to explain the exception for his second child. He doesn't think the lie will stand up to scrutiny beyond tomorrow."

"Damn it. When the Chinese trade delegation visited my offices, I should have assumed they would interrogate everyone at his lab."

"What do you want me to do?"

"What do you recommend?" Frank asked.

"We put Dr. Yang in this situation. We have to get him out of here." Stephen shuddered to think that he had put the entire man's family at risk.

"Relax. Let's talk through it. Do you have any ideas?" Frank reiterated.

"We can use one of your corporate jets. It would be less conspicuous than trying to get him through a commercial airport. They may have everyone at the lab on a no-fly list."

"If they believe we stole fusion research from them, they'll be watching our jets. They'll be watching all our people, including you."

"You're probably right. What about contacts at the port?"

"Good idea. I know people there. It's the busiest in the world, and you can probably get lost in all the activity. Let me make some calls. I have something else that will help. What's the name of the director at the research institute again?"

"It's Director Lu, why?"

"Sam developed a backup plan in case we were caught. She created some computer files that we can use to incriminate him."

"It's a good idea, but what will they do to the poor guy? They'll kill him." Stephen tensed. Killing in battle was one thing. Putting civilians in harm's way felt entirely different.

"The files only need to serve as a temporary diversion. As soon as Dr. Yang leaves Shanghai unexpectedly, all the blame will go back on him. They certainly won't execute his boss for espionage."

Stephen relaxed at Frank's assurances. "I like it. It gives Dr. Yang some extra time."

"There's one problem. The Chinese are pretty good with computer security and hacking. Sam can't break through their computer defenses from the outside. Dr. Yang will need to do it himself. If he uploads them in the morning, the police may discover them first thing. He can step out for lunch like he would on any other day and not return."

"He's already scared to death."

"It's the only solution. I need time to make things come together at the port."

"I'll do what I can to keep him from breaking," Stephen said.

"One more thing, Stephen."

"Yes?"

"Watch yourself. Chinese-American relations are going to unravel."

Chapter 42

Beijing, Office of the General Secretary

General Secretary Feng reviewed the most recent helium-3 production data with a scowl on his face.

Colonel Feng waited for the inevitable tirade.

"We fall farther behind every day," Secretary Feng said. "The moon is a harsh environment that continues to cause problems for our equipment and people. Much of our effort continues to be on the basics of life."

"But we have done this before. Much of the infrastructure was there from the last mission."

"It was a smaller team with smaller aspirations. The current mission includes a larger team with a goal to establish a permanent colony on the moon."

"Irrelevant. This is the first uniquely Chinese accomplishment in centuries. If you fail, we remain cheap labor for the big ideas of western civilization."

Colonel Feng knew this to be true. Despite being the largest economy in the world, Western nations withheld the respect that China was due. To them, China was cheap labor. China was not viewed as a place of ideas. China received third-world respect despite its first-world economy.

"I like your idea of refocusing gas production on hydrogen over oxygen to increase available power to your harvesters. This is a bold idea."

"Thank you father. It comes with risks. I promised my mission commander that I would send oxygen in one of the upcoming supply rockets."

"Have you done that?"

"I have not. The flights have to carry essential replacement parts for the equipment. My mission commander hounds me on a daily basis."

The general secretary scowled even harder. "Perhaps he is not the best choice as the leader. We who lived through the revolution knew real risk and real sacrifice."

Always the revolution. Anything but rapt attention would only antagonize his father.

The general secretary continued, "When we struggled to reform China, the leaders were in the trenches with the workers. We fought side by side during the war. When the war ended, we worked side by side in the rice fields with them. Everyone did his part. We all dressed the same, and everyone worked equally hard."

Colonel Feng imagined that his father had harvested enough rice in his life to fill a small bowl. Yes, everyone wore the same Mao suit, but a brutal hierarchy had ensured everyone knew their place.

"You will personally return to the moon. You will replace Chow and lead the team yourself."

Colonel Feng tempered his response. "Father, I treasure the time I spent in space, but the time for that has passed. I have as much or more that I must supervise on earth as on the moon. There are eighty-eight people there, but there is a team of one thousand supporting them on earth."

Secretary Feng continued as if his son was no longer in the room. "This is the right answer. It will send a good message. I am glad we are in agreement."

"This is more show than substance. I understand the message it sends, but it is not the fastest way to increase helium-3 production."

"The message matters more. Go. Now."

Chapter 43

Arizona, Near the U.S.-Mexico Border

When Colonel Mokri opened the door to Billy Ray's Rental Emporium, he couldn't help but notice the pinup calendar behind the desk. The woman in the picture wore a red, white, and blue bikini and cutoff jean shorts. She held an AK-47. Her expression somehow managed to be dangerous and pouty at the same time. The calendar was two months behind. He was about to mention it when he noticed that it was also set to the wrong year. He had picked the right establishment to rent his SUV.

"Can I help you, brother?" the man behind the counter asked.

"Mr. Ray?"

The man looked confused for a second, then said, "My last name's Jensen, but you can call me Billy Ray."

Yes, indeed. This establishment is perfect.

"I wish to rent an SUV for the week. I need something with four-wheel drive. What do you have?"

"Well, sir. I have a couple of Fords, a Chevy, and a luxury Jeep. Jeep costs a bit more cuz of the luxury aspect." Billy Ray's eyes danced over Mokri's tailored suit and his Rolex.

Mokri raised an eyebrow. "I'll take one of your Fords."

"I rented both Fords out yesterday to other customers. They ain't available."

"Then, I'll take the Chevy."

"Chevy's broke."

Mokri's dark eyebrows lowered and drew together. "Then, I'll take the Jeep. I assume it is available for rent?"

"Why would I mention it if it wasn't?" Billy Ray asked.

Mokri nodded and smiled as if this was of course self-evident. He pulled out one of his American drivers licenses. He chose Thomas Gonzalez.

"Well, Tomas, let's get this paper work filled out."

"It's Thomas. Thomas Gonzalez."

"My bad. Where are you going to be taking my truck?"

"I want to tour the national parks in the area. The Grand Canyon, the Petrified Forest, perhaps others."

"Don't need four-wheel drive for that."

"Well, I don't want to go to the visitor centers. I want to use the back roads to get away from the tourist traps."

Billy Ray folded his arms and squinted his eyes. "You better not be going down to the border. My trucks aren't for that. Better not be picking up any illegals."

"Mr. Ray… excuse me… Mr. Jensen, just because my surname is Gonzalez doesn't mean I'm planning on spiriting any Mexican nationals across the border. I'm as American as you."

"So you say."

Mokri shook his head in mock frustration, but this conversation was going quite well from his perspective. "Is your truck capable of jacking into the AutoDrive system?"

"No, it isn't. A real man should drive himself. Besides, I don't trust the feds. Don't need them monitoring me or my customers."

Mokri smiled and agreed. "I plan on driving myself. It's more fun that way."

"I also don't have any of those GPS trackers in my trucks, but trust me. I'll know if you go somewhere you shouldn't. Like the border."

And that, Billy Ray, is why I am here. "Mr. Jensen, I told you I will be visiting our National Parks." He pushed the completed paperwork back to Billy Ray. "Do you take cash?"

Billy Ray's eyes lit up. "Mr. Gonzalez, I can indeed accept cash."

Mokri paid the man, and Billy Ray escorted him to the Jeep. The twenty-year-old Jeep Cherokee had indeed been a luxury vehicle at one point. The map console in the dashboard was cracked, and the leather seats were split from overexposure to the harsh desert sun. Mokri noted the car didn't reek as he thought it might. The pine tree air freshener hanging from the rear view mirror did its job.

He disregarded his conversation with Billy Ray and drove deep into the Arizona desert. To protect his cover as an upstanding Mexican businessman, he rarely ventured out into the desert himself to deal with border crossings. However, this situation required his personal attention. He hoped this mission didn't blow his cover, but his superiors insisted.

He wore infrared goggles to avoid using his headlights. He was close enough to the arranged pickup to use his encrypted radio. "Luis, can you read me? Over."

Luis responded immediately. "Copy, señor. I have your two friends here. Over."

The colonel knew he could rely on Luis's professionalism. He was a rough man who had no doubt left many to die in the desert over the years. However, he was coin-operated. He handled sensitive border crossings personally and could be relied upon to keep his mouth shut.

Luis greeted him. "Welcome, señor. Here are the two gentleman you wanted to cross the border."

"You are reliable as ever, Luis. I appreciate you handling this situation yourself."

"De nada, señor. I noticed they don't speak Spanish. For that matter, not much English." He motioned to the two men.

"I would imagine you didn't have a very lively conversation. They aren't here for their language skills."

"It is expensive and time-consuming for me to use this crossing. It is one of the least trafficked, but I risk exposing the route every time I use it."

"That is why I pay you so much more money for these delicate situations."

"But perhaps a bit more money would be warranted in this case for the extra care."

The colonel laughed quietly at this. "I'll tell you what, Luis. I've always appreciated your professionalism, and I value our ongoing business relationship. I will make it up to you with the next transaction, rest assured."

Luis appeared quite proud of himself for reading the situation correctly. "Excellent, señor. We should go. It isn't good to spend any more time here than necessary."

"Of course," the colonel responded. He moved forward as if to shake Luis's hand and shot him twice in the chest and once in the face.

The Iranian terrorists jumped at this, taken aback by the suddenness of the attack. It was interesting that violence could so unnerve two men willing to drive a truck bomb into a building filled with civilians.

Perhaps it wasn't too surprising. After all, their training consisted of swinging across monkey bars and crawling under barbed wire with unloaded AK-47s. No serious military man would risk giving men of this caliber live rounds. Still, they had their uses. He opened the back of the Jeep and threw them each a shovel.

"Dig," he said in Farsi.

Chapter 44

Shanghai, Nuclear Engineering Research and Design Institute

Dr. Yang arrived early at work. Director Lu was already meeting with the police. The director motioned him into his office and shut the door.

"I'm sure you've heard?" Director Lu said.

"Yes, sir. I came in early this morning to review my team to see if anyone is a potential security risk."

"It is critical that we find who did this. By the way, are you feeling all right? You still look ill."

Dr. Yang, already thin, had lost twenty pounds in the last several months. The director inspected him more closely.

"It's the long hours and the revelation that all our hard work is now in someone else's hands. I did not sleep well last night."

"Nor I. Well, don't let me keep you from your efforts."

Dr. Yang walked down the corridor to his office. He pulled the memory chip out of his pocket and inserted it into his workstation. He uploaded the files to the appropriate servers, wishing the process would go faster. According to Stephen Clark, the files couldn't be traced back to him. As he completed the task, the captain from yesterday's interview knocked on his door.

"Do you have the personnel files we discussed? I know we were going to meet this afternoon, but I am anxious to review them," she said.

"Not quite yet. I came in early to go over it again to ensure I didn't miss anything. I can give you a more thoughtful list if we keep our original meeting time."

"As soon as possible, please. Also, since you are at your desk, can you give me your uncle's contact information? I will call him now."

He paused and his mouth hung open.

"Dr. Yang?"

"Yes?"

"Your uncle's contact information?" She put her hands on her hips and frowned, which snapped Dr. Yang out of his stupor.

"Yes, of course. Sorry. I was up all night thinking through the list of personnel."

"But now you are at your desk," she said.

"I am not myself. One second."

She couldn't see his screen. He opened up an Internet browser and found the number for the railway station in the province where his fictitious uncle lived. He wrote the number down on a scrap of paper. At least the prefixes would match. If she didn't call immediately, he would be all right. He handed her the scrap of paper.

"I'll make the call right now so that we can clear this up. That way it won't be hanging out there when we meet this afternoon." She walked back to the conference room that served as her temporary office and shut the door.

It was over. The state police would execute him. They would imprison his wife and abort his unborn daughter.

Run. Now. If he could get outside, he could call Stephen Clark. *Yes, this will work. They will capture me, but Stephen will save my family.*

He broke out of his trance at the sound of a commotion. A group of police officers ran down the hall with guns drawn.

The door to the conference room opened and the captain looked at him quizzically. "This number—"

One of her superior officers grabbed her by the elbow and said, "Captain, come with me. We've found our traitor."

"But, sir, I... Dr. Yang and I—"

"Now, Captain. We've found our spy, and we are under strict orders to stay out of the researchers' way. They have work to do."

A hulking uniformed officer pushed a handcuffed Director Lu down the hall. The director sobbed and shouted at the officers.

Dr. Yang waited until they were gone and then ran out the back exit.

***

Stephen scanned the hotel lobby for tails. A young man in a light grey business suit looked in the opposite direction as soon as their eyes locked. Stephen assumed the man was keeping tabs on him. Thankfully, the fact that he was so easy to spot meant that he was probably not very good.

The police had no reason to suspect him more than any other Automated Technology employee currently in China. The Chinese police couldn't spare enough personnel to cover everyone.

Stephen's eyes burned as he exited the hotel into the polluted city streets. He climbed into a waiting taxi and watched the tail in the taxi's rear view mirror. The man jabbed his finger in Stephen's direction several times. He could almost hear the man shout, "Follow that car."

The taxi crawled through the crowded Shanghai streets. Stephen checked his watch. *I know I should have walked.* Then, they hit a gap in traffic and made good progress.

His phone rang, and he recognized Dr. Yang's number. He answered, "I'm on my way."

"I left early. They arrested Director Lu as soon as I put the files on the server. They must have been right in the middle of checking the computer records. What will they do to him?"

"He will be all right once you leave the country. For now, all suspicion will be on him, but that will change when you and your family disappear."

"That is good. He is not a bad man. He doesn't deserve this."

"Put it out of your mind. Focus on your family. How long before you are home?"

"Thirty minutes."

"The police are following me. I need to shake them. It will take me some time. When I arrive, you need to be ready to go. Don't bring any luggage. You don't want to look like you are going on a trip. You can get new things once you're in the U.S."

Stephen hung up. He was getting closer to the Yang's apartment, so he motioned the car to pull over. He climbed out and entered a large department store. This would be a good place to lose the tail. If he could shake him, Stephen guessed that the man would return to the hotel to reacquire Stephen's trail later in the day. It would be easier for the man than explaining his mistake to his superiors.

He weaved through the men's section looking at dress shirts and ties. Nearby, a crowd gathered around some new digital consumer item. Stephen mixed with the throng. He kept one eye on the agent. The officer was close now, trying hard to remain inconspicuous by hiding behind clothing displays.

Stephen looked right at him. He hoped that the officer would get nervous and create some distance. It worked. The agent turned and pretended to be browsing in the women's underwear section of all places.

Stephen jutted into a nearby men's restroom and entered one of the stalls. Hopefully, the agent wouldn't check the bathroom before scurrying off to a different part of the store to pick up the trail. Just in case, he sat on the toilet and lifted his legs off the ground. He remained in the stall for ten minutes then left.

The officer was gone. He strode toward the revolving-door exit. As he reached it, he met the frantic officer trying to push his way in. The man looked into Stephen's eyes and froze. *Damn it. The dumb luck of this guy.* Stephen stopped pushing on the door forcing the man to enter the store. "Sorry sir. After you," Stephen said.

The frantic officer mumbled something and entered the store. Stephen exited and walked down the street assuming the man would follow. He came to a quiet alley and turned left. He sprinted to the end. He slowed enough to allow the officer to see him round the corner, then froze out of sight.

Stephen heard the officer switch to a slow jog. Stephen's antics were having the desired effect. The man was getting sloppy.

As the officer turned the corner, Stephen punched him hard in the throat. The man's mouth opened in a scream, but no sound came out. Stephen punched him hard in the solar plexus several times, and the man fell to his knees. He pulled a syringe out of his jacket pocket and injected the officer in the neck. The man flopped about for a moment, then passed out. He checked the officer's pulse. He wasn't dead. He buried the unconscious man under a pile of trash.

He checked for witnesses. The alley was empty. He headed toward the Yang's apartment knowing that he was now running late.

***

After brief introductions to Dr. Yang's family, Stephen outlined their escape plan. "We are going to leave through the Port of Shanghai. We bought time with Director Lu's detention. However, I had to incapacitate an officer who was following me."

Li Yang put her hand over her mouth. "Incapacitate?"

"He's unconscious, but alive. I don't know how long before he's missed. We could have several hours, or they could be searching for me now."

"Should we be seen with you?"

"No. We need to minimize contact, so we will take separate taxis to get there. However, you will need me once we get to the port. "

They hailed different cabs. Stephen took the opportunity to call Frank on an encrypted satellite phone. "We're headed to the port. Anything I should know?"

"Our contacts with the Shanghai police haven't heard about an all-points bulletin on you, but we may not know immediately. To be safe, we purchased a first class ticket for you from the Shanghai Airport to Kennedy in New York. That should throw them off track for a while."

"Thanks. I have to go. I'm at the port."

Their taxis pulled up near one of the employee entrances just as a police officer walked up to the security guard at the gate. He pulled out a photograph, showed it to the guard, and asked some questions. Stephen told the driver to wait. Through the window, he motioned to Dr. Yang to stay in his car. He called Frank again. Stephen asked, "Any updates?" He glanced at the rearview mirror to see if the driver was listening to his conversation.

"Give me a second." The guard and the police officer were deep in conversation. The security guard shook his head slowly. Frank returned. "Nothing, Stephen. Again, I wouldn't know immediately if they were searching for you. As far as we can tell, you should be fine."

The police officer handed a copy of the photograph to the security guard and walked off in the opposite direction. When the policeman left, the guard glanced up at Stephen and motioned him over.

Stephen climbed out of the taxi, paid, and motioned the Yangs to follow him.

"We are here for the port tour," he said.

"Yes, of course you are." He held up the picture to the window. Stephen froze. It was a picture of him from this morning in the department store. Someone must have discovered the man he left in the alley.

The guard said, "Relax. I only want you to know that you must be careful." He turned and looked at Li Yang. She was still trying to hide her pregnancy, but it was increasingly conspicuous. Congratulations, madam," he said.

Li opened her mouth to speak, but nothing came out.

The guard continued, "We recently had our second and third children. Like you, we already had a young son. My wife discovered she was pregnant with twin girls. We had no idea."

Li nodded slowly in understanding. The guard smiled and turned to Stephen. He pointed to the security camera behind him.

"Cameras," he said. "You must be careful. This one is apparently malfunctioning. When I get time later today, I will need to put in a request to maintenance to fix it. You should assume that the other port cameras are not having similar problems."

"I will stay alert."

"You should go."

"Thank you for your assistance."

"There is no need to thank me, but I must ask for a favor."

"Of course."

"Tell Mr. Sawyer that my wife and I are forever grateful. Let him know that he is in our prayers every night. We will never forget what he did for us."

Chapter 45

California Desert, Space Elevator Complex

Vice President Gladwell walked into the backstage area with his entourage of aids and security personnel. This inaugural use of the U.S. government's space elevator was the political opportunity of a lifetime. It was his chance to permanently attach his name to the greatest endeavor of the twenty-first century.

As he looked out over the crowds attending the ceremony, he saw Frank Sawyer's son. He turned to his team and said, "Give me a minute."

They stepped back a respectful distance, and Gladwell held out his hand. "Tim Sawyer, I presume?"

"Yes, sir, Mr. Vice President." The boy's formality pleased Gladwell. "I voted for you and President Brown in the last two elections."

Gladwell raised his eyebrows. "I hope I can count on your vote again this time?"

"I…"

"Relax. I'm giving you a hard time. I know that's an unfair question."

"Yes, sir. Ben has been like an uncle to me my entire life. My politics are more in line with yours, but he's like family. To be honest, I'm not sure what I'm going to do this year."

"I'd like to make your decision a bit harder. Your work as your father's press secretary has impressed me. I particularly liked your timing of the release to coincide with the Chinese ambassador's speech at the United Nations. I like a man who can use communications as a weapon."

"Thank you, sir. It had the desired effect."

Gladwell put a paternalistic hand on Tim's shoulder. "I'd like to offer you a job in my administration if I win the presidency. I could use some younger blood in the press secretary role. What do you think?"

"Wow, I have to admit I'm stunned. I've learned a lot in the last several months, but that's a big step up. On top of that, wouldn't it cause you some political challenges to have to deal with my tabloid baggage?"

He released Tim's shoulder and patted it. "Son, that's water under the bridge. As I understand it, no charges were filed. It's just the tabloids spreading their libel. I'm surprised you didn't sue."

"Well, I'm honored, sir. I'd like time to consider it."

"Of course. I wouldn't expect an immediate answer. Consider it, and my team will be in touch with you. Excuse me, I have to get ready."

In reality, Gladwell would never offer the dumb kid a job. However, the offer would surely get out to his father as would the fact that Tim was seriously weighing it. Anything that caused strife in the Sawyer family household was a good thing.

He checked his hair and smiled at himself in a nearby mirror. They cued him to go on. His face formed an expression that he hoped combined warmth with steely American determination.

"My fellow Americans, today is the dawn of a new era. For the first time humans will use this elevator to leave the earth. America will once again be the dominant power in space. And it's possible only because of the tight collaboration between the U.S. government and private industry.

"We're Americans, and we're never selfish." He stopped and waited for the expected applause to abate. "We'll use this power to benefit all mankind."

"On top of this, we're generating thousands of new jobs right here in California. Between the federal government employees and California state employees alone, we'll create five thousand new jobs. From that public sector investment, thousands more jobs will trickle down to private industry. Ladies and gentlemen, these are your tax dollars at work."

He turned to the team of six travelers seated on the stage behind him, including Tim Sawyer. "These brave souls will be the first to make the climb. You'll note there isn't an astronaut among them. This technology democratizes space for all men and women. With the exception of a representative from Automated Technologies...," Gladwell turned and winked at Tim, "...these civilians were chosen by lottery to be guests on this inaugural trip."

"I put my name in the hat, but the idea was vetoed by my Secret Service detail." In reality, Gladwell would never risk his life on such unproven technology. He was quite comfortable taking credit for its success here on the ground. Reading the teleprompter, he quickly introduced each of the passengers as they waved and entered the climber. Their seats were not luxurious, but they had ample room for the twenty-two-thousand mile multi-day journey.

"Let us wish them Godspeed on their trip to the stars. The hearts and prayers of America and the world go with you."

Gladwell basked in the applause. With a little more work and a few more speeches, he would be the face of America's push into space. He walked backstage and nodded to the Secret Service detail. "Get me back to DC."

***

Frank shielded his eyes as he looked at the point where the space elevator disappeared into the clear blue sky. Hundreds of friends, family, and employees of Automated Technology surrounded him. Lisa prodded him with her elbow. "Are you OK? You're not going to get all sentimental on me, are you?"

Frank gave her a lopsided grin and cleared his throat. Benjamin said, "This is going to change everything. I'm proud of you, buddy."

"I'm proud of us. This is the culmination of a lifetime of work for you and me. I can't believe we did it."

"I never doubted you guys," Lisa said.

"Me neither, brother," Benjamin added. "But you need to get going. I know how much you like giving speeches, but you have to say a few words before you ride this thing."

"You sure you're ready for me to share your news?"

"I can't think of a better time and place to announce. The Automated Technologies family should hear it first."

Frank grabbed a microphone from one of his assistants. "Friends, you've all been part of this journey over the last several years. This is your accomplishment. You're part of a team that will revolutionize energy production the world over. In a matter of years, energy will be a tenth of what it costs now. We'll eliminate man-made pollution in a decade.

"But it's much more than that. Many of you have been with Benjamin and me since the days that we revolutionized terrestrial travel. Today you're part of the team that will revolutionize extra-terrestrial travel. This is the first step toward colonization of our solar system and beyond."

He paused while he let his words sink in. The applause and cheering was deafening, but he also saw a lot of teary eyes in the audience. He let their emotions ride over him, soaking it all in.

"I also have an announcement that I wish to share today that both saddens me and excites me. Benjamin Whitman, your CEO and my closest friend, has officially won the nomination of the Republican Party for president. His temporary leave of absence will now be a permanent leave of absence. He will be leaving Automated Technologies to focus all his time on his campaign. I will be filling his role on a temporary basis."

People in the crowd put their hands over their mouths and looked around in disbelief. No one in the audience had worked at the company without both Frank and Benjamin at the helm. They were inseparable.

"I share this news with mixed feelings. Like you, I can't imagine this place without Ben."

Benjamin grabbed the microphone for a second. "I guess this means Frank's actually going to have to look at our financial statements now."

"I don't know about that, Ben. I always have a backup plan." Frank winked at Sam. He put his left arm on Benjamin's shoulder and looked at the crowd.

"Ladies and gentleman, we've all seen the polls. It isn't premature to say that you're looking at the next president of the United States." He grabbed Benjamin's wrist and raised it in the air as if Benjamin had won a prizefight. The crowd went wild with applause.

Frank handed the microphone back to Benjamin and joined in the ovation. "Thanks everyone for your friendship and support," he said. "It means the world to me. But we're here today to celebrate our success with this space elevator. Frank, you have a ride to catch."

Frank and the other volunteers stepped into the climber and took their seats. Engineers closed the hatch, and the climber started its weeklong journey up the elevator.

Chapter 46

California Desert, Villa Real Motel

"The north entrance is the best route for an attack. You are familiar with it, and it is a shorter distance to the space elevator," Colonel Mokri said.

"I disagree strongly, sir," the young agent replied. "There are swarms of guards, people, living quarters, and other buildings that would impede the attack."

"But the south entrance is four miles from the space elevator. Even at top speeds it would take five minutes for a truck to reach its target." Mokri paused to step on a cockroach that had skittered under the door to the hotel room and felt his stomach turn. Perhaps his last two decades masquerading as a prosperous business owner had softened him. The motel offered an anonymous location off the beaten path, but it came at a price.

The young agent spun his laptop to face Mokri and pounded his finger on the screen. "It is four miles from the gate to the elevator, but there is nothing in the way."

"That's four miles for military guards in Humvees with fifty-caliber machine guns to rally and catch the vehicle. The guns have an effective range of well over a mile. They won't even need to get close."

"We could always use one of your trucks. I could drive it. I am ready to give my life for Allah and my country."

Mokri put his hand over his face and sighed. "I have told you before that you are not a suicide bomber. We have two uneducated peasants with no language skills and no knowledge of spy craft. Besides, if you blow up my truck, you blow my cover."

"Perhaps you are too comfortable with the life you have built for yourself. Perhaps you are merely afraid. Perhaps you lack the required dedication."

"Enough. My orders are to maintain my cover. You need to grow up and think long-term. Perhaps you are not clever enough to devise an intelligent plan."

The young man folded his arms and drew back in his chair. His face grew red. *Good*, Mokri thought. *He will channel his anger into coming up with something better. He will own the plan, because it will be his.*

"Give me an idea that makes sense, assuming you have one," Mokri said, further goading the young man.

The young agent glared at Colonel Mokri but looked away after ten seconds. Gradually, his face returned to its normal color.

"I have an idea. It blends both approaches."

"Tell me."

"We use two trucks."

"But we have two men. The plan is to have them both in the same truck. If one is shot, the other can take over."

"Hear me out. We use two trucks. One at each gate."

"What does that accomplish?"

"We can create an effective distraction if we time the attacks appropriately. The first attack will be at the north gate."

"As I've always said."

"Listen to me. The first truck bomb will go off at the gate, not near the space elevator. All security and emergency personnel will race to the blast. They will focus all their attention on rescuing the survivors."

"And the second truck?"

"The second truck will come in through the south gate. It will still be guarded, but most of the guards will be dealing with the explosion at the north gate."

Colonel Mokri leaned back in his chair and studied the young man's face. "This is an exceptional plan. It is thoughtful and daring. It preserves our cover. I can rent a second truck. We can divide our explosives in such a way that both blasts will still be large enough."

The young man grinned and smacked the table. "When do we execute my plan?"

"Two weeks from today. In the meantime, you will continue your deliveries. We will conduct the attack on one of the days when you don't have a scheduled stop."

"But I would like to be there to see it."

"Everyone will be a suspect. We can't risk having you interrogated."

"But—"

"You cannot be on-site, but I will make sure you have a good seat for the fireworks."

***

Two days later, the colonel watched his young agent pull his delivery truck into the receiving bay through a pair of high-powered binoculars on a small tripod. After five minutes, he pulled a disposable mobile phone from his pocket. "Go now," he said in Farsi.

From his vantage point, he could barely make out both entrances. He looked down at his GPS tracker to check on the progress of the first suicide bomber then switched back to his binoculars.

The first delivery truck pulled to a stop at the south gate as the guard walked up to the driver's window. Mokri watched the truck, waiting for the man to push the button that would detonate the bomb. The man shouted something that Mokri couldn't possibly hear at this distance and held up his hand.

The button triggered a small detonator in the back of the truck. The detonator set off a chain reaction. The ammonium nitrate in the fertilizer vaporized, creating an excess of flammable oxygen gas. The gasoline mixed into the fertilizer then ignited, releasing even more gas. The resulting pressure wave destroyed an area the size of three city blocks.

Mokri turned his attention back to the north gate. Security personnel were already locking it. Military and emergency vehicles raced to the south gate to check for survivors. There was no point. They were all dead. The entire area was leveled. Only rubble and small fires remained.

Mokri knew his agent would hear the blast at the south gate even miles away. He would likely be confused. Perhaps he would think Mokri, the foolish old man, had somehow botched the plan. The attack was a week and a half early and at the wrong gate.

Mokri watched the first responders arrive as a coordinated unit. Their professionalism impressed him. They had drilled for this eventuality. He chuckled as he watched the little ants focus on the pointless task of looking for survivors.

He checked his GPS readout for the second truck. He switched back to his binoculars. None of the guards noticed it barreling down the highway toward the destroyed gate until it was two hundred yards away. He saw an American soldier aim his rifle at the truck. Mokri was impressed that the man had the presence of mind to shoot without giving any warning. He also knew it wouldn't matter.

The truck weaved erratically one hundred yards from the gate, but it kept going. The truck rolled to a stop no more than fifty feet from the remains of the south gate. Mokri adjusted the binoculars to see if the driver was dead. Then a satisfying second explosion erupted. Seconds later the sound wave reached him. The second explosion killed all the first responders instantly.

Excellent, he thought. *And now, my young friend, you get your wish to be martyred.*

He packed up his binoculars and curled up behind a berm. He pushed a speed dial button and covered his eyes.

The flash of light was immense even with his hands covering his face. The blast originated from his North American Transportation and Logistics truck. Within roughly a one-mile radius, the explosion vaporized every living thing and turned objects to ash. Outside the radius, buildings were destroyed but still recognizable as buildings. Thermal radiation went out even farther and ensured that the space elevator complex would never be habitable again.

The blast also destroyed the lower half mile of the space elevator tether, severing it from the ground. Iran had become the first nation to use a nuclear weapon against a country with whom they were not at war.

Mokri took one last look at the mushroom cloud and jumped into his Jeep. *Time to get out of America.*

Chapter 47

Earth Orbit, Space Elevator

Building the space elevator was proving to be much more interesting than riding it. Once you got past the initial exhilaration of being in space, it felt more like a long cruise. Frank examined the comfortable but sparse environment. Perhaps more like a cruise ship in steerage class. As he built future elevators, he was going to have to class it up for the tourist industry.

The climber climbed the ribbon using a series of rollers. Ground-based lasers powered the rollers by shooting light into a receiver on the base of the climber. The receiver was a high tech solar panel with a man-made sun pointed at it. Close to the ground, the vehicle sped up the elevator at one hundred twenty-five miles per hour where the earth's gravity was strongest. As it moved farther away from the earth, gravity would pull on the climber less, and it would accelerate to nearly three hundred miles per hour. Power was only necessary to a height of twenty-two thousand miles. After that, centrifugal force would carry it to the end of the ribbon at the sixty-two-thousand-mile mark. Frank and his fellow passengers wouldn't be going that far. They would stop at a station twenty-two thousand miles above the earth's surface.

Frank decided to make the best of the long trip. He flipped open a tablet and pulled out a stylus. He opened up a spacesuit design he had been working on. His current design had the mobility of a thick wet suit. The insulating capabilities were sufficient to protect from the extremes of hot and cold in space.

However, he hadn't quite solved the pressurization problem yet. He had read about a prototype suit that used hundreds of wire tendrils to apply pressure directly to an astronaut's skin rather than creating a pressurized cocoon of air like a typical bulky suit.

Using this concept as a starting point, he extended it by integrating a series of computer-controlled servos that tightened and loosened the tendrils. Microsecond adjustments to the suit allowed the astronaut to move while ensuring that uniform pressure was applied to the skin. Unfortunately, his current algorithms weren't great. They kept the internal suit pressure high enough, but they impeded movement too much. He modified the code and sent the changes to the suit's design team.

He flipped through his e-mail and answered the critical ones. He moved on to answer the more trivial ones, but had to admit to himself that he was running out of things to do. As Frank settled in for the long boring ride, a warning sign flashed and the loudspeaker turned on. "Ladies and gentlemen, we have an emergency."

The passengers stared at the speaker, wide-eyed.

"We're going to slow the climber and bring you back to earth."

"What's the problem?" Frank asked.

"There are no issues with your climber. You're all completely safe. Frank, if you can pick up a headset, we would like to speak with you individually."

Frank placed the headset over his ears while the other passengers stared. "What's up?" Frank asked again.

"There's been an attack on the other elevator."

Frank's thoughts immediately turned to Tim and all his employees. He hesitated. "How many casualties?"

"The attack was nuclear. Homeland security and local teams are scrambling, but they expect no survivors at the base."

"My God. Who did this?"

"No one knows if it was foreign or domestic terrorists. It's too soon to know the details."

Frank paused, not wanting to ask the next question. "Any word on Tim?"

"That's why we need to speak to you. Their climber is at the same altitude as yours. He was outside the blast radius." Frank looked at the altimeter readout on the wall of his climber. Frank's elevator had stopped ninety miles above the earth.

"So that's good. Can you contact them?"

"We're trying, Frank. We want to patch you through so that we can walk them through options."

Frank cycled through the alternatives. The blast destroyed the ground-based laser, so the climber had no power. If the climber stayed attached to the ribbon, centrifugal force would drag it into space. Everything depended on the climber's height when the explosion occurred.

"Don't patch me through. It will just slow things down. I need to know the exact height they're at."

"One second." Frank heard shouting on the other end. "They're ninety miles up."

They could allow themselves to drift away from the earth. This would eventually pull them high enough that gravity wouldn't pull them back down to the surface. Ultimately, they would fly into outer space. "If we let them float out, can we get a rocket to intercept them?" Frank asked.

"No. It will take them days to float out of the gravitational pull of the earth. But that isn't enough time to scramble a rocket and train a crew to capture a runaway climber."

"Then they need to get into the escape vehicles before they hit the one-hundred-mile mark. Above that height, they will be in low earth orbit. They'll float away, and we'll never catch them."

"They'll go straight down into the middle of a radioactive wasteland."

"They may drift depending on atmospheric conditions. You need to make this happen now. And turn this thing around. Get me back down to earth."

***

Tim was still enjoying the novelty of the ride. The conversations with his fellow passengers were starting to die out as everyone focused on reading or watching movies on tablets. Tim was still disappointed that Lucy couldn't join him. She had work obligations that prevented it. She promised that she would jump on one of the next rides. It would have been a great story to tell their kids someday. Kids... he was probably getting a bit ahead of himself. The wedding plans weren't even finalized yet.

The emergency sign flashed, and the radio came on. "Everyone needs to get into the escape pods now."

All the passengers spoke at once. "What are you talking about? Nothing is wrong here."

"There's been an attack on the elevator base. No time to discuss. You have two minutes to eject or you'll die. Move. Now."

Everyone jumped up. The two escape pods held three passengers each. Tim had drilled on their use. Strap in. Wait for ground control to activate the eject button. Push the eject button. Float safely to the ground. He hoped.

The eject button in Tim's module turned green. He slapped it hard with his palm. At first, nothing happened. There was a slight downward movement as gravity pulled them back toward the earth. The radio in Tim's pod came on. "This is ground control. We need to know which of you are in this pod." They quickly walked through their names.

"Thank you. We need to walk through some quick instructions. The attack on the station severed the tether."

"I don't understand," Tim said. He felt his heart race as he looked at the other open-mouthed passengers. "We didn't feel anything."

"You wouldn't at first. Your inertia continued to move you upward. But you can't focus on that now. You need to be aware that you can't get out of your capsules when you hit the ground. You have enough air to wait until rescue crews arrive, so there will be no reason to exit. Do you understand?"

"We understand," Tim answered for all of them. "But why?"

"We don't know exactly where you will land."

"Why does that matter?"

"The attack on the space elevator was nuclear. If you land at the blast site, you must stay in the shielded escape pods until we can rescue you. You may drift out of the radioactive zone, but don't chance it. Stay in the pods."

Chapter 48

The Moon, Zhulong Base

Feng's ship came to a graceful stop on the lunar landing pad. The copilot double-checked the systems, and they suited up. The first order of business was to meet with Commander Chow. Colonel Feng bounced to the ore processing facility and entered the airlock. Once the pressure equalized, he removed his helmet. He ran his fingers through his hair, rank after the multi-day journey from earth.

He opened the other side of the airlock and entered the structure. Commander Chow was waiting for him and saluted. "Welcome, Colonel."

Colonel Feng returned the salute. "Commander Chow, you are relieved of duty. I will be taking over for you. I wished to tell you directly."

Commander Chow's arm collapsed from a sharp salute and hung at his side. "I don't know what to say. This is unexpected."

"It should not be. You are behind schedule. This failure happened on your watch."

"With respect, it happened under our watch. I have kept you apprised of all major decisions, and I have followed your orders in all cases."

"That is perhaps part of the problem. You rigidly follow my orders, but you have few ideas of your own."

"This is not true. I have struggled with broken equipment and limited supplies. Despite this, I started helium-3 production."

"Your team is demoralized, and the mission is suffering from a lack of leadership. The feeling from the Politburo is that the team is not being well utilized."

"In other words, someone must take the fall, and it cannot be the general secretary's son?" Commander Chow straightened his posture, set his jaw, and stared into Colonel Feng's eyes.

"Watch yourself. You can gracefully step out of your role and fade from view. Alternatively, I'm sure my father can contrive some means by which you have been derelict in your duty." Colonel Feng glared back at the commander, but he was grateful when the man finally looked away.

"I will make plans to return within two weeks."

"You will return now." The commander could have shown more leadership, but he did not deserve this. He was quite correct that this was a political decision. "You will use your remaining time to give me a tour of the facility."

***

At the conclusion of the tour, Commander Chow departed without saying good-bye to the larger team. Colonel Feng decided nothing good could come from it. The team must understand that important changes were afoot.

He walked from the processing facility to the living quarters. He waited for the airlock to pressurize then removed his helmet. As he opened the door to the crew quarters, a wave of stench hit him. It smelled like one of the open sewers in rural China. He surveyed the faces around him. No one smiled. Red-rimmed eyes stared back at him, likely the result of cold or flu. Seeing their distress firsthand was different from reading about it in a weekly report. Perhaps his father's order to come to the base himself was wise after all.

Feng debated how to handle the situation. Should he take a page from Chow's book and play the disciplinarian? Perhaps he should threaten and cajole? Inspire? Empathize? First things first.

"Can someone get me out of my suit?"

Two men rushed forward and helped him out of his cumbersome spacesuit. He walked around looking at their quarters. The lack of cleanliness was a risk. Flu or the common cold could spread throughout the entire team overnight. Germs propagated in a space environment even better than on their native earth.

The team was standing at attention. "Everyone please relax. Find a place to sit down." He smiled warmly and added, "If you can."

This drew no return smiles from the team. The tight quarters were not a joke to them.

"China has asked a lot from you. It is a great honor to be part of this effort. But I also know how difficult it is to leave behind loved ones and the comforts of earth. I left my family only three days ago, and I already miss them. I can only imagine what you must be feeling."

A couple of heads nodded in the audience.

"I have not supported you properly, despite all you have accomplished."

Eyes widened as they looked around the room at their fellow team members. Feng guessed they had expected a tongue-lashing, not an acknowledgment of their efforts to date.

"I have decided to remove Commander Chow from this mission. He will be returning to earth immediately."

Some in the audience nodded their heads in agreement, while others leaned back and folded their arms. Many likely blamed Chow for the deprivations they suffered. The more sophisticated among them likely knew that Chow hadn't made any rogue decisions.

"We must meet our helium-3 production goals, but this environment is not conducive to success."

The team nodded at this. People sat more upright. Arms unfolded.

"I need your ideas. What do we need to do to get back on schedule and improve morale?"

Silence, as he half expected. They were not used to complaining directly to superior officers. He pointed to one of the women in front. "You. Mae Lu, if you could make one improvement, what would it be?"

She jumped when she heard her name. He had memorized everyone's name, role, and family background in preparation for this trip. The extra effort had the desired effect. "Sir, thank you for asking. As I'm sure you know, we are supposed to have three separate crew quarters, and we only have this one. If we could even get one more operational it would help a great deal."

"Anything else?"

"Perhaps we could divide the living quarters into male and female? We have all been trained to live in close quarters with each other. However, some privacy between the sexes would be appreciated."

He turned to another team member. "Lieutenant Tan, I understand you were top of your class. You must have some good ideas for improvements."

"Yes, sir. We have focused all our efforts on keeping the mining vehicles going twenty-four hours a day. To do this, we have to repurpose personnel away from their primary duties to drive the trucks. Engineers that could be making improvements to the facilities are driving mining vehicles instead. An engineer unknowingly pushed a vehicle too hard through rocky terrain. It took us a week to fix it."

One of the men near the back turned red and looked at his feet. Feng assumed this must be the man in question. "You in the back." The man looked up from his feet but did not quite make eye contact. "There is no need to be embarrassed. Why were you driving a truck without adequate training?"

"Sir, Commander Chow re-tasked me. I am sorry about the vehicle. I was only trying to meet our quota for the day."

"I am sure you were doing your best to meet our goals. Clearly driving the mining vehicles is not your specialty." He smiled at the man to lighten the mood. "So tell me, what is?"

"I have responsibility for human support systems. Oxygen, water, et cetera."

"Then, why don't we put you in charge of getting a second habitation up and going."

The man finally made eye contact and smiled.

The meeting generated several other good ideas. After two hours, Colonel Feng retired to a cot in the back of the quarters. With some changes and hard work, they would develop an imposing lead over the Americans.

With any luck, their competitors would drop out of the race. Failing this, his father would expect him to use all the tools at his disposal. He tapped an application on his tablet, entered a security code, and reviewed the manual for arming the nuclear weapons.

Chapter 49

California Desert, The Salton Sea

The escape pod touched down in a desolate environment. Tim looked through one of the leaded glass portholes. He saw a blasted-out mobile home sitting on scorched earth. Beyond that sat the twisted, rusting wreckage of what must be the remains of the space elevator complex. The worst had happened. They had landed in the middle of the blast zone. Tim wondered how long before the radiation killed them. Irreversible cellular damage was likely already happening.

He heard an animal-like scratching outside the pod. How could anything survive in this desolation? As if in response to Tim's query, a young man's face appeared in one of the windows giving a thumbs-up sign. Tim fell back from the window.

A young EMT greeted them. "You folks OK? Anyone hurt?" The words were barely audible through the thick porthole.

"We're all fine, but what about the radiation? Don't you have any protective gear for us?" Tim shouted in response.

The EMT's eyes followed Tim's as he gestured at the desolate landscape. Understanding dawned in the man's eyes. "This is the Salton Sea. It looks like this all the time. You landed thirty miles north of the blast. You're safe."

Tim breathed out and opened the hatch. "What about the other escape pod?"

"Not good news I'm afraid. They landed in the middle of the blast zone. These capsules are shielded, so we assume they're alive for now. But no one is sure how long the shielding will protect them. It wasn't designed to withstand the radiation from a nuclear blast."

"Why doesn't someone go in and get them while there's still time?"

"It's too hot. We don't have any vehicles in the immediate area that can approach safely. It would be suicide to go in now. Specialized equipment is coming from Los Angeles, but it's going to take time."

Tim nodded. Just an hour ago, he was laughing and talking with them.

"Folks, we need to get out of here. We're safe now, but we're too close to the bombsite. Pile into the ambulance, and let's get out of here before the prevailing winds change. They're telling us to go north to escape the radiation. Once we're far enough away from the blast, we'll cut west over to the coast."

The small group climbed into the back of the ambulance and departed.

Tim called Lucy and his family repeatedly without success. He could get a signal, but he guessed the towers were full of traffic with people talking to loved ones across the country. One of his fellow passengers was able to get through on her network. When she was done, he asked to borrow her phone. On the second try, he got through to Lucy.

"Lucy, it's Tim."

Lucy didn't answer. "Are you there?" he asked.

"Is this a joke?" she replied.

"No, it's me. I'm OK."

"But I saw the news. The attack. I assumed you were dead."

"Half of us survived. We were able to escape in one of the pods." There was a brief uncomfortable pause. Tim thought for a moment that she might be crying, but then decided not.

"I can't believe it. I assumed you were lost. I'm so happy, honey. I'll fly out there immediately. I can probably get into LA or San Diego."

"Don't do that. I'll fly to DC. The airports will be a mess. I can have my dad get a corporate jet so that I can bypass the commercial traffic."

"That makes sense. I'm so glad you are safe." Another pause. "I love you."

"I love you, too. I can't wait to get out of here. Let me jump off. I need to make sure my parents know I'm OK."

He hung up and called his mom. He was able to get through after the third ring. "Mom?"

"We were so worried. Your Dad is still riding down the space elevator, and getting updates has been impossible. He said you were going to be OK, but I wasn't sure."

"I'm fine. We made it, but the other half of our party landed in the radiation zone. It could've been us."

"Those poor people. I'll pray for them. When are you coming home?"

"Mom, I should go see Lucy in DC. She assumed I was dead."

His mom paused before answering. "Yes. You're right. Of course. I wasn't thinking. You should go to your fiancée. Afterward, perhaps you can both come down to Austin. I'll work with your father's assistant to get you on one of his planes."

"Thanks for understanding, Mom. We'll be down in a few days. I need to jump off this phone so others can use it. Give my love to Dad and Sam."

***

Tim felt a hand on his shoulder and woke with a start. "Sir, we're arriving at Reagan National. If you don't mind, can you fasten your seatbelt?" the pretty young flight attendant asked.

He missed Lucy more than ever after his brush with death. When they landed, he almost knocked the flight attendant over in his excitement to get off the plane. He gave her a sheepish grin and jumped down the short stairway to greet Lucy.

He took her in his arms and they held each other quietly for a moment, tears in their eyes.

"I thought I'd lost you, honey," Lucy said.

Tim wiped his eyes and laughed it off. "We Sawyers are pretty tough, but I was scared. I was sure we had landed in the radiation zone at first. I'll leave the test flights to Dad from now on. Media relations suits me better."

They jumped into the car and put it on auto so that they could talk.

"I was terrified. I didn't know what had happened to you," Lucy said.

"You should've called my parents. My Mom said she left a number of messages on your phone."

Lucy glanced away and said, "I know. It's just…"

"What? You can tell me."

"I guess I wanted to lick my wounds in private."

Tim tilted his head to reestablish eye contact with her. "That wasn't very convincing. What's really wrong?"

"I guess I'm still not sure that I'm welcome in your family. I guess it would be different if we were married, but I'm in that in-between status. Fiancée isn't quite the same thing, you know?"

Tim wrinkled his brow. "This isn't still about Sam's initial reaction to you, is it?"

Lucy looked away. "I don't feel like I'm part of the family yet. Technically, I'm not."

"I told you that everyone is excited about the wedding. Sam apologized, and she meant it. I promise you. I know my sister."

"You're right. I need to get over it."

"Besides, if it's really bothering you, I know how to fix it. Let's move the date up. Let's get married next month."

"But your mom. She's planning this huge wedding. I don't want to mess things up."

"My mom will get it. Chalk it up to coming so close to losing each other. She'll move heaven and earth to get everyone lined up with a different date."

"Let's talk about it inside. We're almost home."

The car parked itself, and they went into Tim's house. He pulled her close in the entryway and motioned to the bedroom. "Shall we?"

Lucy put a hand on his chest and pushed him gently away. "We should celebrate. Let me pour you a drink. You've earned it." "I don't know. I've been doing so well. I hate to mess up my perfect track record."

"An occasional drink isn't going to hurt you. You're through the worst of it, and I don't see you sliding back into drug use any time soon. You've got new things in your life now. You have me." She kissed him and walked into the kitchen to fix their drinks.

She returned and handed him a cocktail. "Here you go, honey. What should we drink to? Close calls and narrow escapes?"

They drank, and Tim asked, "What about a new date? We should move it up. My Mom will take it as a personal challenge to get everything adjusted."

"Are you sure?"

"She's a master at this stuff."

Lucy cocked her head and watched him for a full minute.

"Honey?" Tim said.

"Sure, whatever you say."

"If we do it earlier, we can avoid all the pomp and circumstance." He yawned. The stress of the last couple of days must be getting to him.

"Let's talk about it tomorrow."

"That sounds great." He put his hand over his mouth and yawned again.

"Tired?"

"I slept on the plane, but I guess the stress must be getting to me. I'm wiped."

"You should lie down."

The room spun. "I feel strange. You better call…" He dropped his drink, and his head collapsed onto the back of the couch.

Lucy retrieved a rarely used mobile phone from a hidden pocket in her purse. She dialed a number from memory. "I have Frank Sawyer's boy."

Chapter 50

Austin, Automated Technology Labs

"I was saddened to hear of the loss of life at the space elevator complex," Dr. Yang said.

"Thank you, doctor. Thousands died in the blast. I lost a number of my own people. Hundreds more will likely die from radiation."

"At least your son survived. Thank God for that."

"Yes, I suppose it could have been even worse," Frank said. He was still too angry to discuss the tragedy. Many of the deceased were his people. People he had known for years. He changed the subject. "Let me introduce you to my daughter and get you settled."

Frank walked Dr. Yang to the labs where they met Samantha. She held out her hand to Dr. Yang. "How are you settling in?"

Lisa and Frank had invited the Yangs to stay in their guesthouse. They were still waiting on the immigration situation to work itself out. Dr. Yang had applied for political asylum from China under the auspices of religious persecution. While this would probably not have worked with any other Chinese citizen, the United States government was more than happy to bend the rules in this case.

"Our quarters are comfortable and spacious. I am amazed at how much room there is in America. Your mother tells me everything is big in Texas."

Sam laughed. "So they say. Has my father shown you around the ranch?"

"Yes, he took me out to the edge of the ranch to shoot shotguns. I did quite well considering I have never shot a gun in my life. In China we have lots of guns but not for citizens."

Frank looked away and studied something on his phone.

"Daddy," Sam scoffed, "Did he outshoot you?"

"Your father is a good teacher," Dr. Yang said.

"Just not good with a shotgun. Dad, a man who has never shot a gun in his life did better than you on the skeet range."

"Sorry. Perhaps I should not have mentioned the shotguns?" Dr. Yang asked.

"I was having a bad day, Dr. Yang. Normally, I'm second or third when we have our contests."

"Liar," Sam scoffed. "It is a running family joke that Dad is an awful shot."

"I'm not awful with guns, I'm awful with shotguns. It's not the same thing." Frank changed the subject again. "Dr. Yang, I wanted you to sit with Sam and get a sense of where we are with fusion. Your help has been invaluable, but I am guessing we can do even better."

Dr. Yang sat down in front of a terminal and reviewed their designs. "This is most impressive work. I know how much you needed to fill in based on the data I sent you. To accomplish all this in such a limited time is quite amazing."

Sam smiled and said, "The output stunned us. The helium-3 we return from the moon will generate energy for five thousand years."

"Using current energy demands, I assume?" Dr. Yang asked

She nodded.

"Then the number should be closer to ten thousand years. As I look at your designs, I think we can roughly double the energy output. Also, our fusion reactors are much smaller. We expect a commercial reactor will be the size of a house. A Chinese house, not a Texan house," he joked.

"We're lucky to have you on our team. I know you had to give up a great deal to leave China." He looked away for a moment before answering. "We will make a home here." He paused again. "We left many family and friends behind, but we get a daughter in return. Perhaps she will be a great scientist like you."

"Like her father," Sam answered with a smile.

"I'm curious, Dr. Yang. We used current energy consumption levels to do those calculations, and it sounds like you did the same. Did you ever discuss potentially large increases in energy demand?" Frank asked.

"So much of our focus was on finding a clean energy source to power our large manufacturing base. Just matching those energy needs with a cleaner alternative was viewed as a huge success."

"Of course, but think bigger." Frank spread his arms expansively. "Over time, we'll get better at harvesting helium-3, and you'll figure out ways to create an even more efficient fusion process. In fifty years energy will be so cheap it might as well be free. Think of the implications of free energy."

"As an example, clean water becomes limitless?" Dr. Yang asked.

"A perfect example. The planet already has infinite water in our oceans. Desalinization plants are expensive to operate. But the main reason they are expensive is the high cost of energy."

"If you had the desire, you could turn the Sahara desert into a tropical paradise or an agricultural hub."

"In our modern society, energy is a proxy for life. If you have infinite energy, you have infinite water and limitless food. Living spaces in deserts can be cooled. Homes in frigid regions can be warmed. Free energy will lead to limitless abundance, at least for material things."

"What about the downside of all this material abundance?"

Frank raised an eyebrow and tilted his head. "You seem like an optimistic man. I'm surprised that you can find a downside in all this."

"I am from China. We live on top of each other. While hyper-abundant food and water are a blessing, what will it do to the world population? Humans will expand to take over every habitable inch of the planet."

Frank shook his head. "I believe mankind has a different destiny. If my space elevator is successful and energy approaches a zero cost, we'll leave the planet in droves. It will be slow at first. We won't see more than a few thousand people on the moon in our lifetime. But that will change. Within a century, I can see millions on the moon, cities on Mars, and mining operations in the asteroid belts."

Chapter 51
Rural Pennsylvania, Farm House

Tim opened his eyes and attempted to make sense of his environment. A cheap light bulb illuminated the chipped and dirty concrete floor. The air smelled like dirt, as if he was underground. As he took in his surroundings, he noticed a bearded thirty-something man with large one-inch rings in his earlobes. The man flipped through the pages of a vegetarian cooking magazine.

Tim struggled to move his arms and legs, but they were tied to a stout wooden chair. The reality of his situation hit him. He screamed, "Where am I? What's happening? Who the hell are you?"

The bearded guy jumped up and dropped his magazine. He ran up the stairs two treads at a time. Tim shouted, until the man returned with Lucy in tow.

Tim shouted to Lucy, "What the hell is going on? Who is that guy?"

"You haven't put it together yet? Must be the drugs, though I would've assumed you could handle them better given your history."

"What are you talking about?"

"I've kidnapped you."

"What do you mean? Is this some kind of sick joke? It's a bit much after what I just went through in California."

"It's not a joke. You are an unfortunate pawn that I will use to get to your father."

"My father? What does this have to do with him?"

"Your father is going to stop his efforts with the space elevator and helium-3 fusion. You're going to make him do that."

"Is this a misguided environmental protest? Did you have something to do with the rocket attack on the other elevator? What's up with Sasquatch here?"

"Excuse us for a moment, would you?" Lucy asked. Sasquatch climbed the stairs and shut the door behind him.

She leaned back against a table and folded her arms. "At your core, you are a naïve child spending your parents' money and hanging out with your protest buddies. The stakes are bigger. This is about who will dominate the world economically and militarily for the next century."

"You're working for the Chinese?"

"Your father stole our technology. We know it. One of our chief scientists defected to the United States and is living in open view on your father's ranch. The sheer audacity of your father is stunning. The U.S. government is going along with it under the guise of religious asylum."

Tim shook his head in protest. "No, that's not right. Sam discovered fusion in parallel with the Chinese. My sister perfected fusion before Dr. Yang and his family defected. It was only natural that a fusion scientist of his caliber would want to work for my dad once he got here."

Lucy wrinkled her nose. It was an expression that Tim would have deemed cute a day ago. She continued, "You really believe that? How do you think your sister made such quick progress? It took us years to accomplish the same thing."

His father had no love for the Chinese government. They had stolen his intellectual property. They persecuted their own people. It wasn't beyond his father to retaliate.

"I'm going to need your help if you are going to survive this. You're going to record a video for your father. On the video, you will say that environmental terrorists have kidnapped you. You will tell your father that you will be tortured and killed if he doesn't shut down his operations."

"But that's not even true. You've already told me that you're with the Chinese government."

"Get with the program. We can't send a video to your father saying that the Chinese government kidnapped a U.S. citizen. What would your government do? What do you think the world community would do?"

Tim digested this for a second. "But that means you can never let me go."

Lucy stared back at him.

"You're going to kill me? Over money?"

"We're not animals. There are options."

He scanned the dusty cellar, the broken furniture, the cobwebs. "Like what? I stay chained up in a basement for the next ten years?"

"You could defect. Confess to the world that your father stole our technology. People would believe you."

"I don't even believe he stole the technology."

"I thought you might say that."

"And you can't possibly think my dad is in a position to stop things. The government is too invested at this point."

"Then we go with option two. The Chinese government will contact your father through separate channels. They'll tell him they have infiltrated an environmental terrorist group with their spies. My government will offer to help find you in return for an open admission by your father that he has stolen Chinese technology. If the U.S. government continues without him, they will cause an international incident. Besides, they don't have anyone who can make it all come together with your dad out of the picture."

Tim struggled against the ropes, nearly knocking his chair over. "He'll never agree."

"Why do you think I've spent so much time turning you into a model citizen? Your dad isn't going to let anything happen to you. You're literally the prodigal son returning to his father's farm after squandering your inheritance."

"On whores."

"What?"

"The prodigal son squandered his money on whores. You're correct. It's an apt comparison."

She snarled and pulled back her hand to slap him, but then her expression softened.

"This gives me no pleasure." She picked up a baton from a nearby workbench. "The only thing left to do is make sure that your dad knows we're serious." As Tim slipped into unconsciousness, he saw tears streaming down Lucy's face.

Chapter 52

Earth Orbit, Space Elevator

Frank sat in the nearly completed terminus station at the end of the elevator. After the chaos of his first ride, he was finally here. The environment was stark, but certainly not as stark as previous generation space stations. Centrifugal force created artificial gravity. Food and other material comforts were relatively cheap to bring to the top of the elevator, so they were more readily available. Occupants still needed to monitor things like excess water use, but overall it was a comfortable environment to work in.

Everything had worked seamlessly. He marveled at the fact that he had made the entire trip in jeans. No spacesuit or helmet required. Even though the concept was his brainchild, it amazed him that an untrained civilian could be sixty-two thousand miles into space.

A number of his best engineers accompanied him. Their goal was to deploy their mining equipment to the surface of the moon. The Chinese opted for a strategy that relied heavily on human operators and traditional rockets. Frank's operations relied on his semi-automated robotic technology and the space elevator.

Frank's team would give high-level instructions to the big machines. After that, they would operate with minimal oversight. The years of experience building similar systems on earth would propel them ahead of the Chinese team. The strategy had to work. His team was months behind the Chinese, and they were now down to a single space elevator.

One of the NASA astronauts spoke up. "Frank, the last load of cargo touched down."

Frank nodded. "Thanks for your expertise on this one. We have solid engineers on the team, but it's great to have some real rocket scientists around."

Frank turned to his engineers. "It's our turn, boys. Let's get these machines unpacked."

They all sat down in front of their respective consoles and sent commands to the machines. The metal boxes that protected the equipment during landing exploded outward. They came to life and rolled onto the surface of the moon.

"I have the coolest job on or off the planet," said one of the engineers.

They focused on the big helium-3 harvesting machines first. Unlike the Chinese trucks, Frank had modeled his mining operations off the big crop sprinklers in his native Texas. Long arms radiated out from a central point where the helium-3 collected in huge storage tanks. The mile-long arms would strip-mine a circle two miles across before moving to the next location.

Unlike the Chinese machines, Frank's did not use solar or hydrogen energy. He had considered this design. The Chinese vehicles had the advantage of being able to harvest helium-3 immediately using solar power, albeit at a slower pace. He had opted instead to build a small helium-3 reactor on the moon powered by his last remaining stores from earth. Once the fusion reactor was up and going, they would have more than enough energy to run the system for years. It would take Frank longer to mine his first batch of helium-3. However, completing his fusion reactor would solve his lunar energy needs permanently.

He turned to one of his engineers. "How does the boring machine look?"

"Everything is showing green."

"Fire it up, and let's see how it performs." The boring machine was not technically necessary for harvesting helium-3. It would dig tunnels under the moon's surface. Frank's goal was to build a series of underground rooms that could eventually serve as habitable chambers for people. They would eventually need to seal the tunnels to prevent air from leaking into space, but they could start drilling now.

The meters of rock and earth above the tunnels would protect against solar radiation and the massive temperature swings on the surface. On earth, the typical difference between daytime and nighttime temperatures might be as large as fifty degrees Fahrenheit. On the moon with no atmosphere, the temperature varied four hundred degrees. Depending on the time of day, a human would alternate between freezing and boiling to death without appropriate protection.

"The boring machine is up and going."

"Remind me again how long before we have to change the cutting blades."

"We're estimating two weeks. We don't know what's under the surface. We have some good guesses based on previous NASA research, but we won't know until we drill."

"Keep me up to date on the daily progress. This approach should be better than building structures on the surface like the Chinese, but only time will tell. Hopefully, I guessed right."

"You usually do. It's a smart approach."

Frank sat back and grinned at the team. "You did it, guys. If we get a run of good luck, we can catch up with the Chinese."

He got out of his chair and slapped the NASA astronaut on the back. "I have to catch a ride down to complete my astronaut training. I'm getting pretty good."

"It's not that hard in the new suits. You'll pick it up quickly," the astronaut assured him.

Frank gathered his gear for the multi-day trip back down the space elevator. As he was settling into his seat, an e-mail arrived on his tablet from Lucy. He tapped the screen and a video opened with a close up of her face.

"I'm a member of the Mother Earth Militia. I've kidnapped Tim. Cease your mining operations on the moon immediately if you want to see him again. The Mother Earth Militia won't allow the capitalist pigs who have destroyed Mother Earth to destroy her daughter, the moon."

The camera panned away from Lucy's face to show a bound Tim. One eye was swollen shut and his face was a mass of bruises. He was barely recognizable, he was so beaten and bloody. Tim spoke through cracked lips. "Dad, I'm sorry. This isn't a joke. Lucy is with the eco-terrorists."

"Pig," she shouted. A fist came in from outside the camera view and caught Tim in the cheek, opening a fresh cut. Blood trickled down his face to his chin where it dripped onto the floor. "Don't you dare call us the terrorists."

"You and your team will return to earth now, or we will send Tim back to you in pieces."

Frank froze. Tim had come so far, and now this. He had actively encouraged Tim's relationship with Lucy. How could he be so wrong? Now Tim's life was in danger again. He had no choice.

Frank walked back into the control room where his engineers were hard at work. "Gentlemen, stop what you're doing. Now. We need to return to the earth's surface."

Chapter 53

Austin, Automated Technology Headquarters

Samantha and Stephen grabbed lunch together in Frank's office for the third time this week. As they chatted over the space elevator and the fusion program, Sam's mobile phone rang. She considered ignoring it, but it was her father.

She answered the phone. "Dad?"

"Sam, Lucy kidnapped Tim. I need you to drop everything and help me find him. I'm stuck coming down the space elevator, and I can't do anything. Track down Stephen to assist you."

"He's right here. I'll put him on speaker."

Frank said, "Lucy sent a video telling me to halt my operations or she will hurt him. He's in rough shape."

"Oh my God," Sam said. "How bad is it?"

"He's black and blue, but he was coherent on the video."

"Can you send it to me?" Stephen asked. "Maybe there is something on it that we can use."

"Yes, but don't start there. Sam, I need you to break into the AutoDrive databases and see if you can figure out where she has taken Tim."

Sam shook her head. "That's a federal crime. The government will shut us down before we even begin."

"I have a backdoor to the system that I've never used. If you're careful, it will be untraceable. I can also give you a time range when Lucy kidnapped him. Get a pen and paper, and I'll give you the details. I don't want to send it through my phone."

Sam grabbed a pen from her father's desk and wrote the information down.

"Honey, you were right. I should've dug deeper into Lucy's background," Frank said. "Let me get out of your hair. Find him."

Sam raced through the halls to find another computer. She couldn't use Frank's corporate workstation to hack a federal system. They went to an isolated set of computers in a different wing of the building. She used these computers for those rare occasions when she needed to do something covert.

"How are you going to do this?" Stephen asked.

"I have information on every car that ever jacks into the highway system, even if it's being driven manually. I can also tell the owner of the car. The only thing I can't track is the rare vehicle that doesn't have our technology on board."

"So you know who is driving?"

"Not quite. I can make assumptions, but I won't know for sure. We could cross-reference the driving times with the cameras on street signs or tollbooths, but that's a separate system. It isn't realistic to hack into it. The FBI or local police would need to get the appropriate warrants to access that information."

Stephen considered this for a moment before responding. "There's a gap in this logic. If they drove a car that doesn't have your company's technology on board, you wouldn't be able to track them."

"There are so few of them on the road, that using one would stick out like a sore thumb. We wouldn't have detailed information on the vehicle's movement, but it would be unlikely that someone would use such a car. That said, it's a potential issue."

She checked to see if Lucy or Tim's car had plugged into the system. The data indicated that both cars were still in front of Tim's house. Even so, Sam decided to play it safe. "Can you have your people check for Lucy's and Tim's cars in Georgetown? Here's make, model, and license information." Stephen called a series of people on his corporate security team to get things moving.

Sam next checked to see which cars had driven through Tim's neighborhood at odd hours. She assumed the kidnappers must have stopped near Tim's house. They couldn't risk parading Tim down the street even late at night.

This search narrowed her to a list of twenty. A number of these were taxis, pizza delivery cars from major restaurants, and other vehicles that were not likely candidates.

After removing these, her final list came to ten.

Stephen completed his calls and sat down next to her. "What now?"

"I have ten cars that are worth checking. All of them stayed on the eastern seaboard, but it's a big area. Five stayed in DC metro. Three went to New York City. The remaining two went to Pennsylvania and Kentucky."

"That's too much for us to cover. My security team doesn't have the manpower for that kind of search."

"Do what you can. My father will have to pull some strings with law enforcement eventually anyway."

Stephen put his hand on Sam's shoulder. "We should've listened to you. Your instincts were right."

Sam pulled Stephen closer and said, "Just find my brother."

Chapter 54

Washington, DC, The White House

"I am so sorry to hear about Tim. You will have the full power of the U.S. government behind you," President Brown said. "Thanks, Ellen," Frank replied. "I have some ideas that will require your administration's authority."

"How can I help?"

"As you know, Automated Technologies operates our nation's highway system, but much of the underlying data is intentionally obfuscated from us." Frank was scrupulous about ensuring that no one in his company tracked the whereabouts of individual citizens. He had terminated a number of employees in the past for breaking these rules. In one rare instance, he had turned one of his employees over to the courts for prosecution.

"I can give you the information you need under the auspices of national security. With only a single elevator standing, we can't have a fringe terrorist organization holding sway over you through your son."

"Perhaps you can predate the request?"

"Why?"

"Because I've already reviewed the data."

The president rubbed her temples. "You need to play by the rules if we're going to work together. I can't risk a political scandal. Don't do that again."

"Agreed," he said. "Have you considered that this may not be domestic terrorists?"

"We've both seen the video. They were quite clear as to their motives."

"But does it make any sense to you? Most of the greenies support our agenda, as you would expect. On one hand, I have 'don't pollute the moon' crazies picketing outside my offices in Texas right now—"

"There you have it."

"But these guys are the fringe of the fringe. They're also not that bright, even when they aren't stoned. I'm not sure they have the wherewithal to conduct sophisticated terrorists attacks on their own."

"What alternative explanation would you suggest?"

"These groups are rabidly socialistic. I'm wondering if they might have ties to China? At least the Chinese have a reason to want to destroy my work."

She scoffed despite the severity of the situation. "No offense, but this sounds like conspiracy theory nonsense."

"Bear with me. I was told that the Chinese rocket used to attack my space elevator was sold to the Mother Earth Militia by a Chinese American woman."

"And you didn't tell us? What were you thinking?"

"I preferred to handle it myself at the time," Frank said.

"That's idiotic. We have a thousand times the resources you do. Why would you..." She paused and Frank watched the recognition spread across her face. She didn't complete the obvious thought.

"I was trying not to alienate my son. I screwed up," Frank said.

"That was irresponsible, but I understand your reasoning."

"Lucy aside, the Chinese do have the strongest motivation to shut me down."

"They wouldn't risk it. Can you imagine the international consequences?"

"Consider the stakes. You still don't understand the far-reaching consequences of losing this race. The winner will be the dominant superpower for the next century."

"I get it. Let me get you the data you need to find your son. You can psychoanalyze the motivations after you get Tim back."

Frank nodded and asked, "Any progress on the California blast?"

"Minimal. We do have some video immediately before the explosion."

"From satellites?"

"Better than that. From the ground."

"The video wasn't destroyed?"

"Apparently copies of all video feeds were simultaneously made on-site as well as offsite. We can tell that the blast came from the delivery docks."

"Your people are assuming it's one of your suppliers?"

"It's our initial focus. Several were on site when the explosion went off."

"How can I help?" Frank asked.

"We need a replacement elevator."

"Agreed, but for now our focus should be on protecting the existing one. My attention is stretched too thin at the moment to build another. Once things stabilize, we can certainly contract to build a replacement for you."

"By that time, it will be Gladwell you're building it for."

"You must know something the pollsters don't. It will be President Whitman who inks that deal."

A secretary opened the door. "Vice President Gladwell is here to see you, Madam President."

"Speak of the Devil," President Brown said. "Frank, you'll have to excuse me."

***

"Did you order him to restart his mining operations?" Gladwell asked.

"I did not."

"That wasn't what we discussed. We had an agreement. America doesn't bow to terrorists. It will end badly." Gladwell couldn't understand how this incompetent weakling had ended up at the top of the ticket. And by extension, how he had ended up at the bottom.

"Frank's company isn't America. It's Frank's company. We owe him some time to figure this out."

"This is a strategic national asset. Privately owned or not, we can't lose this race to the Chinese over one man's feelings for his son."

President Brown slapped the table. "I'm still president. It's not your call, Thomas."

"The election is a month away." *Insolent bitch.*

"And the inauguration is two months after that. If you are lucky enough to be elected, then it will be your decision."

"Lucky enough?"

"Yes, lucky enough. You're losing. The party is disappointed in your results to date. Your problem, Thomas, is that people can sense who you are. You're the kind of guy that would get a man's son killed to further your own political interests."

"You mean America's political interests?" Gladwell asked.

"It's sad that you can't distinguish between the two."

Chapter 55

Phoenix

Colonel Mokri parked down the street from a national car rental chain in downtown Phoenix. He met one of his American truck drivers outside the office. "Thank you for driving to Dallas to drop off this package for me. It's a rush order, and there isn't time to use our trucks or FedEx."

"Of course, Mr. Martinez. I'm always happy to help out the boss."

"I'll rent the car in my name so that you don't have to use your credit card."

"I was hoping you would offer, sir. My credit isn't all that good."

Mokri walked inside and rented a mid-range Jaguar for the man. He put the car in his name and added his employee as a second driver. When he came out, he tossed the keys to the man and pointed to the Jaguar.

"I appreciate the last-minute assistance. I thought you might enjoy a nicer vehicle."

The man's eyes lit up. Mokri guessed he had never been in a Jaguar before. "I only request that you not speed. Also, here is five hundred dollars to cover hotel and food. Keep anything you don't use."

"Yes, sir," the man responded as he walked off to get in the car. Mokri waved at him as he drove off.

The first small step in his escape plan was complete. He hoped it would take the Americans some time to determine the source of the attack, but you could never be sure. The Americans always moved quickly during disasters. He assumed that they would identify his truck as the source of the explosion, perhaps using satellites. The blast should have destroyed any video footage.

If the Americans did identify his truck, they would do a search and determine that he was in the United States. They may assume he died in the blast, or they may not. They might assume he was alive and making a run for it. If so, they would find the car rental and assume he was going to Dallas. They would even be able to track him the entire way using their AutoDrive system. He had purchased airline tickets from Dallas to Tijuana to complete the ruse.

Meanwhile, he would drive to Houston. There, he would book a ticket to Honduras using one of his assumed identities. From there, he would drive back into Mexico and make the long road trip back to Tijuana. With any luck, he would be home in three days.

***

Five days later, an exhausted Colonel Mokri arrived in front of his home. He had turned on his radio periodically during the long drive to see if he could catch any news on America's search efforts. So far, there was nothing.

He fumbled for the keys to his door and walked in. He threw his travel bag in the foyer and walked into the living room. He flipped on the television and turned up the volume so he could hear his favorite telenovela in the kitchen. *Very good. I only missed one episode.* His favorite character, Jorge, was still pursuing the young daughter of a wealthy Mexican senator.

He looked in his empty refrigerator. He threw some moldy leftovers into the trash. He decided to break with his religious traditions and grabbed a Dos Equis. He popped the top and took a large swallow. He remembered some frozen burritos in the freezer and microwaved them. As the timer dinged, he heard a breaking news segment on the television. Apparently, the Americans were progressing.

He sat down in front of the television with his food and beer. The report was light on details. The police detained a person of interest outside Dallas. Mokri knew this was a possible outcome, and he had a plan ready. Relations between Mexico and America were not strong, particularly if you knew the right Mexican officials. Mokri did. He muted the television and picked up his mobile phone to dial one of his contacts in the federal police. Everyone in Mexico believed he was a native, and he could likely gum up extradition procedures indefinitely. If things became too difficult, he could always slip out of the country. He took another drink of beer and congratulated himself on the thoroughness of his plan.

Too late, he heard a noise behind him. Two bullets hit him in the back of the head. His brains sprayed all over his widescreen just as the newsbreak concluded and his soap opera restarted. His last coherent thought was, *Will Jorge get the girl?*

Chapter 56

Pacific Ocean, Oil Rig

"Update?" Frank asked. He and his team were discussing where things stood with the news of Tim's kidnapping.

"We're effectively frozen at your request."

Frank had ordered any work that would be visible from earth halted while he figured out the situation with Tim. "Is there anything we can do that won't endanger Tim's life?" he asked his engineers.

"Mining efforts have stopped. They are too easily observed from earth."

"What about ancillary systems? Were you able to test the railgun?"

"Yes, but the system had significant aiming and trajectory problems."

"A gun that doesn't shoot straight. How not straight?"

"There is a good chance we'll miss any cargo that is launched back to the station. There's even a chance that we'll hit the elevator with a projectile moving at five kilometers per second."

Frank rubbed his temples. "Let's avoid that."

"We're pushing the envelope on everything. Why not use rockets to return the helium-3 for now? Fix the railgun issues later."

Frank controlled his frustration. He knew his team was trying to help, and he didn't want to shut down the brainstorming process. "Our advantage over the Chinese is that we innovate. A 'me-too' approach isn't going to cut it. We have to think differently about every aspect of the problem."

"We're trying, Frank. All our work is through remotely controlled robots with a multi-second delay due to the distances involved. It's not as if we can walk up to the railgun with a screwdriver and fix it."

Frank held up his index finger. "Let's come back to that. Where are we on the drilling operations?"

"That part of the operation is proceeding beautifully. It's not observable from earth. We've diverted more energy to building out the tunnel system than anything else."

Frank smiled at this small piece of good news. "How are the strata?"

"The underlying rock is harder and more stable than we estimated. The rooms will require less support than we thought. It won't take too long to make it habitable. We have temporary inflatable structures that can be setup in a matter of hours."

"It doesn't do much for near-term helium-3 harvesting, but at least it's something. What about my motorcycles?" Frank had contracted with Kawasaki Heavy Industries to build him a set of lunar motorcycles. He was partial to their dirt bikes and used them to get around on his ranch. He figured they could probably build some amazing moon vehicles. He didn't want something that would use solar power to go eight miles per hour. He wanted something that would go closer to fifty.

"They're ahead of schedule, and they're fast."

Frank's eyes lit up. "How fast?"

"Seventy-five miles per hour on earth with a run time of nearly five hours using hydrogen cells."

When Frank needed to clear his head, he fired up his dirt bike and raced around his homebuilt track at the ranch. Lisa hated seeing him riding at speeds approaching a hundred miles per hour. Despite the fact that he geared up every time, he would rarely go a year without cracking a rib or breaking a wrist. Lisa thought it was juvenile, but the diversion kept him sane. He could only imagine what a similar bike might do in the moon's reduced gravity.

"All right. Some good news and some bad news. Do what you can to move things forward, but do absolutely nothing that can be monitored from the ground. Tim's safety comes first."

"Everyone shares your same priority. No one wants anything to happen to Timmy." Frank smiled at the juvenile nickname. Many of these men had known Tim since he was a toddler.

"When we find Tim, we need to move fast. I will need to get to the surface of the moon with a team of our best engineers to get things fixed."

"What? You've said you want everything done remotely and via automation. Now you want to go there personally."

"Rules were meant to be broken. I want that railgun fixed, and I can fix it. I want enough of a habitat that we don't suffocate or starve to death. And I want those motorcycles. Let's definitely get the motorcycles up there," Frank said.

"You're the boss. We'll make it happen," the man replied.

Another engineer rushed in, breathless. "We've lost contact with all systems on the ground. Everything's dark."

"Get the telescope image on the screen," Frank said.

"We have, but the dust is too thick to see anything."

"Rewind the video footage."

The engineer tapped a keyboard. He rewound, then pushed slow-motion play. "Here you go."

Everything was fine until a dust cloud enveloped the entire base. "Rewind and step through it frame by frame." It made no sense. They had already harvested some oxygen, but not enough that it could cause an explosion of that size.

They watched a frame-by-frame progression of the video. A brief streak from the south entered the frame right before the explosion.

Frank removed his hat and scratched his head. "Was that a missile?"

Chapter 57

Boston, Harvard University

Benjamin Whitman and Thomas Gladwell strode to the middle of the stage and shook hands. They were a study in opposites. Benjamin stood four inches taller than the vice president and carried fifty extra pounds of muscle. Benjamin's tight black curls were cut as close to his head as they had been in his West Point days. Shrapnel scars marred his black skin in places.

Gladwell's stylists had molded his hair into the perfect power haircut. His lean features and light skin marked him as an old money East Coast patrician.

The men separated and walked back to their respective podiums. Benjamin gripped the side of his, then remembered that his handlers had recommended against it. After his first primary debate win, he had warmed to the process. The format of the debates allowed him to be himself. He spoke from his heart throughout the primary debates.

But his handlers told him repeatedly that tonight's presidential debates would be different. He would need to stay to the right of Gladwell to avoid losing his base. However, if he were to win the all-important independent vote, he would need to pivot to the center. If he failed to temper his statements, he would lose. Never quite a lie, the handlers pointed out. However, he would need different messages for different audiences.

The moderator explained the ground rules. "You have a minute to respond to the questions I ask you. Your opponent will then have a minute to respond. You will have a final thirty seconds to rebut your opponent's answer. Please avoid interrupting each other. The first question was randomly chosen and goes to Vice President Gladwell.

"Sir, you have been at the center of one of the greatest public/private technological innovations of modern history. Most vice presidents sit in the background. Why has your vice presidency been so different from many of your predecessors?"

Benjamin cringed inside and hoped it didn't show on his face. He knew this was a layup for Gladwell. He also knew he wouldn't get the same easy questions. He would just have to be sharper than the vice president. *That shouldn't be too hard.*

Gladwell warmed to the question. "American companies are the greatest and most competitive in the world. However, there are some things that are too big to be done by the private sector. I'm proud of the faith that President Brown put in me to build this space elevator. Our enemies fear its construction. We will find the ones responsible for the attack and bring them to justice."

"Mr. Whitman, do you have a follow-up?" the moderator asked.

"I do. While I am no longer working at Automated Technologies, when I was there we were thankful for U.S. government participation. But let me be clear—we invited the government to the table, not the other way around. Innovation will always come from the ingenuity of American business, not government. Furthermore—"

Breaking the rules, Gladwell interrupted. "Benjamin, I have to ask why you're running for president of the United States of America. You have so little regard for public servants and public service."

Rather than interrupting to reinforce the debate rules, the moderator turned to Benjamin with an expectant look on his face.

There were one or two good answers to this question and a hundred bad ones. "Mr. Vice President, I feel that there is a place for the public sector. There are basic things the government should do. For example, national defense."

"Yes, yes. National defense. Republicans always go to national defense as the only clear case of where the U.S. government plays a natural role in our lives. But come now, Benjamin. You must be able to come up with another example in which government has a role. By extension, where you should play a role?"

Apparently, the moderator was going to sit this debate out.

"Not so fast. Let's stay on national defense, Mr. Vice President," Benjamin said. "It is the most critical thing that the government provides. I'd say the U.S. government failed miserably under your leadership by allowing a nuclear attack on our soil."

At this, the moderator awoke. "Surely, Mr. Whitman, you can't blame the vice president for the attack on the California space elevator."

Gladwell raised his eyebrows and stared at Benjamin, apparently content to let the moderator do his work for him.

"I do indeed blame the vice president. We told him not to build the elevator on U.S. soil due to potential terrorist attacks. There are only a handful of nations with a navy sophisticated enough to attack an ocean-based platform. He chose to build it where he did specifically to dole out political goodies to his constituency."

"You call jobs for the people of California political goodies?" Gladwell shot back.

"First, you didn't create those jobs. Private industry did. Second, the families of the deceased would have preferred that you focused on national defense. Or do you think they want your focus to be on taking undeserved credit for job creation?"

"You son of a bitch. How dare you!"

The audience made a collective gasp.

The moderator stepped in to save Gladwell from himself. "Gentleman, this has been a spirited debate. However, let me remind you that we have a series of rules governing these discussions for a reason."

"Mr. Whitman, the next question goes to you. The American economy has been languishing for decades, in large part due to sluggish job creation. In your role as CEO of Automated

Technologies, your innovations have made our lives easier and more pleasant. But the focus on automation has eliminated as many jobs as it has created. How do you respond to the charge that you have personally destroyed American jobs?"

Benjamin felt the blood in his temples pulse. As the only job creator currently on the stage, he found the question offensive.

"We've created hundreds of thousands of good-paying jobs at Automated Technologies. Honestly, we've even created jobs for so-called public servants who manage and monitor the highway systems we've designed."

Benjamin winced. *I need to dial it back.* Federal, state, and local governments employed thirty-five percent of U.S. workers. Benjamin did not need to alienate this constituency.

"But I have the statistics right here," the moderator continued. "You've created perhaps two hundred thousand jobs, but millions of truck drivers and cab drivers are unemployed as a result."

"I have no idea where you got your numbers. Your two hundred thousand number excludes our larger network of suppliers. That number is closer to one million."

"Fine, but my question remains. What about good-paying, middle-class jobs that have gone away? What about those truck drivers?"

"As a business person, you can't look at it that way. If a machine can do a job better, cheaper, faster, and safer, then that job is busywork. The unshackling of American business creates new, higher-paying jobs. Government must get out of the way."

"Mr. Vice President, your response?" the moderator asked.

"You see how he breezed over the loss of middle-class jobs. We public servants have to build the social safety net to catch these people. We've invested in job training to get these displaced workers back into the workforce. Benjamin isn't concerned with the human toll left by so-called progress."

Benjamin couldn't handle the naivety of the response. "We've been sitting at ten percent unemployment for nearly two decades. How is your job training working out for everyone?"

"At least we're trying," Gladwell responded.

"Trying and failing. The private sector wouldn't allow that level of failure. You would go out of business. Your boss would fire you. The great thing about our republic is we have a built-in system for firing failures every four years."

Gladwell pounded the podium. "Ben, I would ask that you show a little respect for the office."

"Mr. Vice President, I didn't know that we were close enough that you would be comfortable addressing me by my first name. It's great to see that I've earned your friendship. Or perhaps there is something else driving your disrespectful tone and your easy familiarity with me?"

The audience's eyes searched the room for something to look at other than Gladwell. The large hall was totally silent. The moderator's mouth hung open. Benjamin Whitman had played the race card on a liberal, and it appeared to be warranted.

Benjamin shook his head dismissively at Gladwell and turned to the audience. "Let's get back to jobs. I promise you I will have unemployment under five percent by the end of my first four years. I will do this by working with the private industry to rebirth the energy sector and open space exploration to humanity."

He paused to let the promise sink in.

"If you believe me, hire me. If I don't deliver, fire me in four years. But you won't, because I always deliver on my promises to my employers. And let me be clear, you are my employers."

Chapter 58

Washington, DC, The White House

"You know Vice President Gladwell. Director Roberts leads the FBI," President Brown said to Frank.

Frank turned to face the director. "Thanks for your assistance with my son's kidnapping."

"We have some good news. Your daughter provided us with solid leads using data from the AutoDrive databases. When we combined this with traffic cam data, we were able to isolate your son's location."

"Where and when can we act? I have people ready, willing, and able to assist with my son's extraction."

Director Roberts glanced at the president who said, "Frank, this is an FBI investigation. We can't have private citizens seeking vengeance. The director can allow one of your people to come along as an observer."

"I have people in my employ I trust who can help with this. You have to understand, this is my son—"

"I know it's your son, and that's a large part of the reason you won't be driving this. We don't need a father's emotions getting in the way. You can trust us. I'm not giving you a choice."

"I suppose I don't. Please don't screw this up."

"You have my word."

"Director Roberts, I have another question while you're here," Frank said. "I lost a number of men and women in that California blast. They were serving as consultants for the final stages of the elevator construction. I'd like to know if you're making any progress on that front."

This time the director looked at the vice president who cautiously nodded his head.

"We've tracked one of the trucks back to a Mexican transportation and logistics company. We believe that the owner was a deep-cover Iranian based on information provided to us by the CIA."

"Was?"

"He was found murdered in his home."

"That seems like pretty compelling evidence to me of Iranian involvement. Who do you think killed him and why?"

Director Roberts looked at the floor. No one responded.

Frank looked back and forth at their faces. "How about the bomb blast? You have to be able to tell something from the size of the blast and the associated energy signature."

No one answered the question.

Frank nodded slowly. "You've already evaluated the bomb blast. And you assume this spy was killed by his own government to create plausible deniability. You know damn well it's the Iranians. What are you doing about it?"

"Think about the international community. We can't accuse Iran of attacking us. As soon as we do, we need a response, or we look weak," President Brown said.

Frank pounded the table. "Look weak? You are afraid to act because of what other countries will think of you? You don't look weak; you are weak."

"You're not in my position. I'm not going to risk yet another war in the Middle East. Our country doesn't have the stomach for it. You're not a politician, but you have to at least understand that."

"I understand that if you are too afraid to act, I will," Frank said.

"That's a little extreme even for you," the vice president said.

"I guarantee that Iranian mullah and his lapdog president are dead in a month if you don't act."

"You're under stress because of Tim. You've lost all perspective since Benjamin went on the campaign trail," the vice president said waving his hand as if to dismiss the statement.

"I have to agree with Thomas in this case. You can't attack a foreign country's leaders. It's a crime. I forbid it," said President Brown.

"You forbid it? If you don't have the intestinal fortitude to deal with Iran, you surely don't have the courage to deal with me."

"If you do this, I will prosecute you to the fullest extent of the law. You're admitting in front of the president of the United States that you're planning an assassination," the president said.

"I agree. This will span administrations. You won't box this country into a war with Iran to satisfy your need for revenge. You won't box me in," the vice president said.

"If you think I'm dumb enough to leave evidence behind, you've misjudged me. And Gladwell, I'll trust Benjamin to handle things when he's sitting in this office. Those Iranian boys are dead."

Chapter 59

Boston, Gladwell's Personal Residence

Gladwell was taking a rare mini-vacation away from the campaign trail to regroup. He poured a glass of Macallan from a Waterford crystal decanter and surveyed his tastefully appointed office. The mahogany desk, expensive first-edition collector's books, the pictures of him with various presidents of both parties from the earliest age. He even had one with President Reagan after his retirement from political life. The presidency was in his DNA. He was bred for it. The expensive private schools, the connections. His siblings had all gone into leadership roles in New York financial houses or Boston law firms. He had devoted his entire adult life to public service. He had earned this.

He was idly watching one of his favorite cable news channels, waiting for the presidential polls to arrive. These polls were recent enough to have the results of the Harvard University presidential debates included. He was nine points behind Whitman, well outside the margin of error. He flipped through to the other cable news channel. They had him at more than thirteen points behind Whitman.

It was all so unfair. Whitman should never have been able to steal credit for the space elevator. He had deftly turned the California fiasco into Gladwell's fault. *It's not as if I could have foreseen a nuclear attack.*

On top of that, racism charges were flying in both left and right circles. He should have listened to his political consultants.

They warned him that talking down to Whitman could backfire. The nerve of that private sector leech implying that a liberal with his credentials could be a racist. That black son of a bitch would pay.

Once he was in the White House, he would punish Frank Sawyer for his treachery. He would cut off existing government contracts and tangle him up in the courts. Perhaps he would nationalize the technology behind the highway system. He might even remove the government protection from the space elevator in the Pacific. *How will Sawyer fare without the navy to back him up?*

And that childish rant on Iran. Not even Frank could possibly be stupid enough to assassinate the leaders of another country. With even a little bit of evidence, Frank would be convicted in the court of public opinion. With a little luck, maybe even a court of law. In either case, Frank's operations would be vulnerable. Public opinion would certainly support the use of eminent domain laws against a war criminal.

Gladwell pondered other options. As president, he could easily come to a deal with the Chinese that would benefit both countries. He was a master dealmaker from his years in the Senate. He could aid the Chinese with their international court case against Sawyer for the theft of their fusion technology. He might even push the U.S. courts to allow them to sue in America.

Removing private industry from the equation opened entirely new windows of opportunity. He could share the intellectual property rights for the space elevator with the Chinese. In return, he could negotiate the rights for fusion on behalf of the U.S. government. The two countries would control global energy production. They would divide the world into East/West axes of power, and he would control half of it. He would have more power than any previous U.S. president.

Gladwell poured another Scotch. This was starting to make sense. Any right-minded individual could see that a private citizen couldn't be allowed to have this much power. For that matter, Frank Sawyer would be dangerously close to controlling space in the coming decades. Who knew what he was shipping up the space elevator.

Yes, Gladwell could deal with the Chinese. They would see the logic behind dividing the world into hemispheres of influence. He was all about compromise. There was more than enough money and power to go around for him and this General Secretary Feng fellow.

Of course, all this assumed that he was in the White House. He contemplated his chances. The state of his current bid for the presidency was a travesty of justice. Justice aside, he was losing. Badly. He drained his Scotch in a single swallow. It gave him the courage to dial the phone.

A calm, emotionless man answered.

"You told me I should call if I needed extra insurance to win the election," Gladwell said.

"I did, indeed. I take it you've seen the most recent polls?"

"I have. To be clear, it's a temporary dip. I have no doubt I'll recover."

"Of course, Thomas. No doubt whatsoever."

The hair on the back of his neck stood up at the use of his first name. He had used the same technique in the debate to assert his power over Benjamin Whitman. It hadn't worked, but this time it did. "I'm glad you agree. That said, it's better to be safe than sorry."

"It is better to be safe than sorry. Are you asking for our help, Thomas?"

"I am."

Chapter 60
The Moon, Zhulong Base

Colonel Feng's two months on the moon were productive ones. He would soon be in a position to return two tons of helium-3 to earth. It had been an arduous time working with the team to correct Commander Chow's mistakes, but it was working.

By getting people reoriented on their core roles, the right expertise was focused on the right problems. Listening to the team's concerns about their living environment had been one of the most impactful changes. Productivity increased dramatically as soon as they opened the second living quarters. Men and women were now able to live in separate areas. People were getting adequate rest between their shifts.

They still couldn't produce enough food, but he had also temporarily fixed that problem by overinvesting in expensive launches from earth. People not only had enough food, they had good food. The brief outbreak of influenza ran its course without sickening the entire team.

Morale was up. Productivity was up. Feng could sense the team's elation at being part of something successful. They were still mildly behind schedule, but not enough to matter.

It helped that the Americans were now woefully behind. Colonel Feng grinned at this. He had destroyed his enemy's ability to compete without killing a single person. The American efforts were frozen. They didn't even have anyone on the moon to do the forensic work to determine why their operations were in ruins. The

American's technology-based approach was proving to be worthless compared to the will of the Chinese workers.

Colonel Feng put on his headset to deliver his weekly report to his father. The general secretary's face appeared on the small screen.

"Progress?" Secretary Feng asked.

"We will be ready to ship our first two tons of helium-3 back to China in one month."

"Your team's morale?

"Exceptional, Father. Improving living conditions made a large difference. I appreciate the support from the Politburo to expand our budget. I realize we have spent billions more than planned."

"Bah… it is nothing. This is a strategic investment that will change China's destiny forever."

"How is the broader political environment?"

"For a change, you show an interest in politics?" the general secretary laughed. "The Americans suspect we destroyed their base, but they cannot prove it."

"They are not pressing for international courts to intervene?"

"With what evidence? Besides, the world community would not hear of slowing down our efforts. We have successfully rallied support in the United Nations much more effectively than the American government."

"That is wonderful news."

The general secretary's broad grin filled the small screen. "I have more good news. I want you to return with the first shipment of helium-3. As the conquering hero, you will take your rightful place in the Chinese political leadership. We have much to do."

"My family will be happy to hear it."

"You have earned the hero's welcome, son. A thousand years from now, historians will speak of your role in establishing the Feng Dynasty."

Chapter 61

Rural Pennsylvania, Farm House

"We're getting ready to go in, Frank. I know you're worried, but we've got this. The FBI is sure Tim's inside. They'll get him back. I'll call you when he's safe," Stephen said.

He turned his mobile phone off and put it back in his jacket pocket. Too many missions were blown by lack of attention to small details like unsecured mobile phone ringers and watch alarms.

He replaced his earpiece with one of the operation's radio earbuds. Stephen wouldn't be participating directly in this operation. He was here to observe only. The FBI rescue team had trained as a unit for years. The addition of another team member, no matter how skilled, would present a distraction. That said, he preferred to be prepared. He checked his vest again and zipped up his jacket. He chambered a round in his 9mm and rechecked the magazine.

They were going in under cover of darkness. The night was clear with only minimal moonlight. The operation should be routine.

To Stephen, the FBI team appeared both confident and competent. They were trained professionals going up against a bunch of eco-terrorists playing soldier. The terrorists likely had some of the assault rifles that their ilk railed against so much. However, Stephen knew the difference between buying an assault rifle and knowing how to use it under pressure. Weekend trips to the local shooting range weren't going to cut it.

The FBI team donned their night-vision goggles. Their targets had turned off the house lights hours ago. They hadn't seen any movement inside for at least two hours. A team of four crouched and ran forward toward the house. They moved in a zigzag pattern, staying in the shadows. A two-person sniper team remained behind in cover at the edge of a cornfield to provide additional support if it came to that. Stephen settled in to watch the action through his low-light binoculars.

***

Tim stretched his aching neck and back as far as the ropes allowed. His body hurt after days of sitting upright in the hard chair. He could no longer tell the passage of time. The cellar had no window wells to let in natural light, so it was impossible to chart the course of the sun. The single dim lightbulb in the ceiling was always on. Tim sensed a pattern in the guard rotation. Three guards per day on eight-hour cycles or similar. He did the math and guessed he had been in captivity for a week. It could also have been a month.

The current guard slept against the far wall, his chair propped up on two legs. Tim smelled the telltale stench of marijuana on the man. The man had devoured an entire bag of potato chips and three cans of soda before passing out.

It was time to work on the ropes again. Tim tested the bonds for the hundredth time. The zip ties cut painfully into his wrists, but he felt more movement in the ropes. He wiggled the long end of the zip tie into the knot that held his wrists to the chair. It slid through. Tim sawed the zip tie back and forth. The rope loosened.

He worked the knot some more. His blood made it slippery. His heart raced as the rope fell to the ground. Tim snapped his neck back to look at the guard, but the slight rustling had not disturbed the sleeping man.

Good. Now my feet. I can do this. He pulled his right arm over the high-backed chair. It felt like someone was driving a nail into his shoulder after the days of inactivity. He was almost there. His right shoulder popped and Tim's vision went temporarily black from the pain. His arms were over the chair. He ignored his shoulder and bent to untie his feet.

As he struggled with the knot on his left foot, he cobbled together a quick plan. *Kick the guard in the face. Hard. Not so hard his chair falls. Cut the zip ties. Escape. Warn Dad.*

The basement door snapped open. Lucy slunk down the stairs with a silenced pistol in her hand. She absorbed the scene then shook her head in obvious disgust at the guard. She motioned with the gun, and Tim leaned back in his chair. Lucy glared again at the guard. She pointed the gun at him, then paused appearing to consider the situation. She tucked the gun into her belt and went to Tim.

"We're leaving now," Lucy whispered in his ear.

Tim glanced at the guard and tried to say, "What about him?" Lucy raised an eyebrow quizzically and Tim pulled the gag off his mouth. "What about him?" Tim repeated.

Lucy ignored the question. "The police are here. If you do exactly what I say, we'll both get out of this alive. Remember that you still have options. We still have options." She put her hand back on the grip of her pistol. "But I need to know you understand me."

Tim glanced at the sleeping guard again. His mind raced. He could wake up the guard which would wreck Lucy's plans. If he refused to move, she might shoot him. He couldn't know if Lucy would kill him or not. As if in response to this unasked question, Lucy pulled her pistol part way out of its holster. His turned a steady gaze back to Lucy. "I understand."

"Untie your feet and put your hands behind your back," Lucy said. Tim freed his feet, then stepped over his bound hands with his feet to get his hands behind his back again. He winced as he felt his shoulder pop and shift. Lucy glanced at the guard one more time, then pushed Tim up the stairs.

They slid out the back door, and Lucy guided him toward a row of cornfields behind the house. He stumbled in the dark but caught himself. She reached out to steady him and said, "Sssshh… we'll push through the field until we reach that line of trees."

Lucy donned a pair of night-vision goggles from her bag and helped Tim with his. She pulled out a detonator. "Shut your eyes."

***

Stephen was mildly allergic to something on the farm. He was far enough back that his sneezing wouldn't jeopardize the mission, but he had professional pride to consider. You didn't want to be the guy who sneezed right in the middle of a covert op.

As he closed his eyes to suppress a sneeze, the night sky glowed like midday. "Holy shit," he heard the team's leader say. "Team One are you OK? Call in your status."

A faint groan came through their radios. "Team One is down. We require medical assistance."

The agent in charge turned to Stephen and said, "Stay here. This is not your mission." Stephen nodded. Every ounce of his being wanted to get involved, but he knew he would get in the way. He needed to let the FBI work. He stepped back from cover into the forest to give them room to operate. He turned on his phone and waited for it to find a signal. He wanted to be ready to give Frank an update once they had something concrete.

As he crouched at the edge of the forest, he noticed movement in the trees to his left. He peered through his binoculars and saw a man and a woman walking together. They both wore night vision goggles. The man's hands were secured behind his back. That had to be Tim.

He looked back at the FBI agents and made a snap decision. He drew his 9mm and raced toward the couple.

***

Tim heard a twig snap and stopped. Someone was running toward them with a gun drawn. Lucy pulled Tim closer and put the gun to his head. "Freeze or I'll kill him." The cop froze and held his own weapon up in the air. She pushed the pistol against Tim's neck harder and said, "Drop it."

The man hesitated.

"I'm not saying it again. Drop the gun." The man threw his pistol into the bushes.

She pulled her night vision goggles down to look at him. Her eyes widened. "Stephen Clark. The man that stole fusion from us." She let go of Tim's shoulder and grabbed the gun with both hands. "This is all your fault."

She pulled the trigger two times in rapid succession, and Stephen went down hard.

Tim screamed into the night, "Damn you, Lucy."

***

The FBI team suffered multiple casualties, but no deaths. Everyone was going to live. The spotter for the sniper team turned to give Stephen an update, but he was gone. The agent saw two flashes in the night off to his left and heard a distant shout. He slapped his shooter on the shoulder and said, "We're being flanked."

They pivoted and the sniper focused his scope on the area in question. He saw two silhouettes, both with night vision goggles. He didn't see Stephen, but he knew he only had binoculars. The rest of his team was in the forward position near the house. "Two bad guys. I'm taking the shots."

***

The bullets knocked the wind out of Stephen. He gasped for air as he heard the chatter over the radio in his ear. He managed to sit upright and shout, "Tim, get down." He coughed into the microphone. "Don't shoot... hostage."

He couldn't tell if Tim or the snipers heard him, but Lucy did. She jumped in front of Tim and threw her arms wide as if defending him. She shouted, "No!"

A shot rang out and Lucy's chest exploded. She fell backward on top of Tim, and Stephen lost sight of them in the undergrowth.

"Stop shooting. Stop shooting. It's a hostage situation," Stephen barked into his microphone as his adrenalin rushed and he found his voice.

"Copy. Weapons secure."

Stephen crawled to his knees and found his gun. He felt his way through the darkness to Tim and Lucy. Lucy's chest was a mess of blood and gore. He holstered his gun and rolled her dead body off Tim. Tim's hand flapped like a dying fish as he struggled to speak. "Lucy... Dad... I'm sorry..."

Stephen pulled up Tim's bloody shirt to check the wound. The bullet had passed straight through Lucy into Tim's chest. Tim's hand stopped flapping. Stephen had seen enough deaths on the battlefield to know that Tim was gone.

He hung his head. After a moment, he pulled out his phone. It rang only once before Frank picked up. "Boss, I have bad news..."

Chapter 62
Austin, Sawyer Family Ranch

Frank sat on the edge of the bed, watching the growing crowd gather in front of his house for Tim's funeral service. A window was open to let in air. The curtains lapped at the windowsill, alternately concealing and hiding the bright-blue sky and the nearly full moon. The view echoed the thoughts in his head. Was any of this worth it?

He had flashbacks of Tim. Throwing a football with him when he was a young boy. Buying him his first car and the chaos of teaching him to drive. Some bad years too, where Tim meandered directionless, wasting his talents on addiction and fun. All punctuated by his hard work this last year to get clean and the tangible value he had added to the family business. Ultimately betrayed by the first woman he truly loved.

The wave of emotions left Frank frozen. He wanted to sit on the edge of the bed forever and avoid the well-wishers below.

Lisa came in and put an arm around him. "Are you ready? We have to go down. Your friends are here to support you. Ben will be here soon."

"I killed him," Frank mumbled.

"What did you say?" Lisa asked.

"I killed him," Frank repeated. "My drive to get this done at all costs blinded me to the dangers to our family."

She pulled her right hand back and slapped him in the face as hard as she could.

"Don't you ever say that again," she said, grabbing his left arm so fiercely that her finger nails drew blood.

Frank stared at her, dumbfounded.

"Some communist piece of trash murdered my son. You don't get to curl up in a ball and give up. You punish them. Take everything from them. Make them pay for this."

"We don't even know who did this for sure."

She gripped his arm even harder. A red stain grew on his shirt where one of her fingernails dug into his skin.

"This isn't a court of law. You know damn well pothead eco-terrorists didn't do this alone. This was the Chinese government. I won't let Timmy's death be in vain. You punish them for this."

She released his arm and walked into the bathroom to dab the tears from her makeup. She came back out and looked at him again. "You better change your shirt," she said. "You're bleeding."

Frank looked at the red stain on his shirt. "I'll keep it on." He looked into the bedroom mirror, put on his suit jacket, and manned up.

***

The Secret Service agent turned over his shoulder and spoke to Benjamin. "Sir, there's a crowd of protestors at the gate. We don't expect trouble, but I wanted to make you aware." As the Republican front-runner, Benjamin had Secret Service protection for the rest of the campaign.

The small motorcade of Suburbans and Benjamin's limousine worked its way through the crowd. Benjamin gritted his teeth as he glimpsed one of the signs. "Tim Sawyer got what he deserved! Save Daughter Moon!" These animals couldn't let it go for even a day.

A rock hit the bulletproof glass, and the agent said, "Hold on, sir." The driver gunned the engine and plowed through the protestors. A couple of them bounced harmlessly off the front edge of the car. Benjamin glanced over his shoulder to see if anyone was hurt. The agent saw his concern and said, "Sir, don't worry about this. We'll follow back around once you are safely inside to make sure no one is hurt."

"Thanks, agent. Take it easy, though. I don't need video of protestors being run over by my motorcade."

The vehicles drove down the mile-long road to Frank's sprawling house. Benjamin got out of his car and walked over to Frank and Lisa. Benjamin's wife Beth had already arrived to help Lisa with last-minute preparations. Benjamin hugged Lisa and pulled Frank aside to talk. "How's it going, buddy?"

"I'm hanging in there." Frank rubbed his bleeding arm under the suit. "Lisa gave me a pep talk."

"Feeling sorry for yourself, I take it?" Benjamin asked.

"A bit. She encouraged me to refocus my energy on more positive things like punishing the people that did this. By the way, thanks for doing the eulogy for me. I wasn't feeling up to it."

"I'm honored. Tim pulled himself together over these last several months. You have a lot to be proud of."

Frank's steely eyes grew watery for a second as he looked into the distance. Thankfully, the family minister gave them the nod that they were ready to begin. "Let's not talk about that now. Let's grab our seats."

The minister read some Bible verses that Lisa had selected. Benjamin listened with one ear as he mentally rehearsed his remarks regarding his only godson. He had always loved Tim as if he was his own. His relationship with the boy remained strong even when things were strained between Frank and Tim. Benjamin had always seen the possibilities in the boy. He was so happy for his friend that these possibilities finally manifested themselves in the final months of Tim's life.

The minister cued Benjamin that it was his turn to speak. The Secret Service agents moved to stay close to him but thankfully avoided making a show of themselves. Benjamin didn't want this to be about him today. He looked down at the surviving members of his best friend's family: Frank, Lisa, and Sam. A tear came, and he wiped it quickly away.

"When Frank asked me to be the godfather of his firstborn child, I was deeply honored. My wife and I never had children, so Tim was like a surrogate son to me. I watched him grow into the man he was at the end of his—"

A gun shot sounded in the distance. Sam screamed and clutched at her arm. Blood sprayed across the stage in front of Benjamin's feet as he heard a bullet whistle by his head.

"Shooter, get down!" The Secret Service agents dove at Benjamin to push him to the ground and block the shooter's view.

Benjamin would have none of it. He may be old, but he still had the physique of that young running back from West Point so many years ago. He threw the agents off and dove at Sam. He would be damned if he would let another one of his friend's children die. Not like this.

He dove at her and knocked her to the ground. He checked her arm quickly, and he could see that the bullet had struck a glancing blow. She was going to be all right. And then everything went dark.

Chapter 63

Austin, Seton Medical Hospital

"Dad, I'm fine. Go check on Ben again," Sam said. Her wound bled profusely at first, but in the end, it required only ten stitches and some bandages.

Frank nodded and rode the elevator up to the intensive care unit. Benjamin was out of surgery, and the news was not good. The bullet had grazed his brain. He was in a coma in critical condition. If he lived, the doctors were not sure that he would ever wake up. And if he woke up, his mental capacities might be badly diminished. He would be a shadow of his former self.

He spoke to the nurse on duty and asked to see his friend. The intensive care unit rules only allowed a single visitor in the room at a time, and Beth Whitman was the obvious priority. At the nurse's prompting, Beth came out to meet Frank. "Go in and see him. I need to grab a cup of coffee anyway."

"Any news?"

"Nothing new. The doctors don't expect any change, good or bad, for a while." A tear rolled down her face.

Frank hugged her and walked into the room. His big friend slept quietly. His head was bandaged, but other than that, he looked like himself. Feeding tubes and other medical paraphernalia would come later, but for now, he looked like he was taking an afternoon nap.

"How you feeling, buddy?" Frank asked. He had heard somewhere that a little part of the brain in comatose patients could still hear their friends and loved ones. Between the head injury and the drugs he was on, Frank doubted it. At least it gave Frank a sense of comfort to try.

"You're a brave man and a great friend. I hope you know that you saved Sam's life today. You saved my little girl."

No response other than the beeping of the monitors and Ben's deep, measured breathing.

"It doesn't feel like the whole thing is worth it anymore. All my talk about changing mankind's destiny while my own life crumbles in ruins."

Nothing.

"Tim, now you. Sam too, but for the grace of God and your selflessness. I hope you know somewhere in that head of yours that you saved her life."

Ben's eyes fluttered.

Frank's heart jumped, and he put his hand on his friend's shoulder. Then he relaxed. The doctors said that he might move. The movie version of a frozen coma patient apparently had little to do with reality. Eyes could flutter. Facial expressions could change. None of which could be taken as a sign of improvement.

Frank looked at the wall clock. "My time's up. The docs are going to throw me out. I wanted to let you know that I'm going to stop. Nothing is worth this. I want to be here for you. Beth needs friends and family to get through this."

Ben's right eye opened. "Frank…"

"Ben!" Frank scrambled ready to bolt for the door to get Beth and the doctors.

"Frank… don't be a pussy."

"Buddy, what are you talking about?"

"We've never lost. Not playing football, not on the battlefield, not in business. Let's not start now. You've got to show these bastards what we're made of."

"Ben, I… let me get Beth." Ben flailed weakly and found Frank's arm.

"Promise me you won't let these bastards beat us." The grip tightened like steel. Wounded or not, he was a big man.

"I… I promise."

"I bought you something."

"Is now the time?"

"I bought you something when I thought I was going to win the election. It's an island."

Frank assumed the mention of the gift was the residual effects of the coma talking. "But you're back. You're going to win."

"Maybe four years from now. No one is going to vote for someone with a bullet in his head. I wouldn't. But the island. You must meet with the president of Kiribati.

Now Frank knew Ben wasn't lucid. He was making up imaginary places and people. *Better to play along.* "You bet, buddy. The president of Kiribati."

"Now get my wife before I fall asleep again."

Frank ran out of the room and shouted for Beth and the doctor. They ran back into the room. Lisa hugged Frank, tears in her eyes. "He's awake?"

"Barely."

"What did he say?"

"He told me not to be a pussy. He told me to win."

Lisa laughed out loud at this. "Sounds like both your wife and your best friend agree. You've come too far, and it has cost us too much for you to lose."

"Looks like I'm going to be out of town for a few days. I need to get to the moon after a short visit to the Middle East."

A team of doctors and nurses raced into Benjamin's room and closed the door. Frank walked toward the room and heard Beth scream something unintelligible. A nurse warned him off with a glance. He stepped back to Lisa and put his arm around her.

Five minutes later, a doctor with an ashen expression on his face stumbled out. "We lost him. A blood vessel ruptured in his brain. There was nothing we could do."

Frank put his head in his hands and wept.

Chapter 64

Tehran, Azadi Square

A flea-bitten mongrel slept in a ball in the corner of a dusty street. He had wandered into town two days ago. He would periodically wake up and do dog things. He played fetch with the neighborhood children for a while. He also did some decidedly non-dog-like things. When he tired of playing ball, he would lie down and fall asleep instantaneously. No matter how much the neighborhood kids prompted him, he would not wake up and play. Not even when they poked him with the occasional stick. He also lacked other characteristics of flea-bitten mongrels. His eyes never ran, and he never drooled. For that matter, he wasn't flea-bitten. A flea wouldn't find anything worth biting.

Frank would have to address these deficiencies when time allowed. He would add them to version two. He watched the image generated by the lens behind the dog's right eye. It provided a decent view of the Eid al-Adha festivities. The supreme leader and president were both in attendance today. It also looked like he had the Council of Guardians, several vice presidents, as well as a variety of legislators and judges. *Eeny, meeny, miny, moe.*

He added up his dead employees killed in the Arizona attack for the hundredth time. Forty eight of his own people dead, many of them close friends. Many more were dead that weren't on his team. A large part of him wanted to detonate the dog and take out the entire Iranian political regime at once. He knew in his heart that not all these men were corrupt or evil. A proportionate response would have to do.

He highlighted the supreme leader and the president. He noted with a sense of irony that an icon of a ball was still highlighted on the screen. The dog was still in fetch mode. The Iranian children had enjoyed playing with it. He would have his consumer division build a stripped down version at some point.

Playtime is over. His cursor hovered over a button with an icon of a skull and crossbones. Flyout text appeared above the icon. Terminate. He clicked the button. A message popped up on the screen. "Terminate? Are you sure? Yes/No." *Never more sure in my life.* He clicked. "Yes," and turned to watch a broadcast on Al Jazeera.

The supreme leader started his speech. Frank watched the translation at the bottom of the screen. The lunatic was two sentences into a religious speech, and he was already babbling about the nuclear annihilation of Israel. *Definitely never more sure in my life.*

Frank turned to watch the dog's monitor. It trotted toward the crowd. An angry soldier in a Revolutionary Guard uniform shouted something at the dog and tried to kick it. The dog dodged lightly out of the way without even acknowledging the near miss. It plowed into the crowd, accelerating through the sea of legs. It jostled people, but not hard. It made a rapid beeline for the stage.

It reached the ring of guards surrounding the raised dais and leapt ten feet in the air. It accelerated toward the supreme leader and ripped a chunk out of the man's leg. Frank grabbed the arms of his chair as the dog tangled itself in the man's robes. Another Revolutionary Guard raised a rifle in the direction of the supreme leader then thought better of it. He threw down his gun and rushed to grab the dog.

The mongrel freed itself from the robes just as the soldier arrived and leapt at the seated Iranian president. Without a bark or a growl, it ripped two of the man's fingers off his hand. The dog jumped off the stage and ran back through the crowd. It dodged through the legs and attempted kicks. As it reached the far side of the crowd, it accelerated to sixty miles an hour.

Frank turned back to the Al Jazeera broadcast. Someone had dragged the supreme leader off the stage, but the president was convulsing on the ground in front of his chair. Even at a distance, you could see flecks of foam and spittle flying from his lips. Then a hand covered the camera, and the broadcast went dead. An announcer apologized for the loss of the broadcast. Frank smiled and switched off the television.

He turned his attention back to the dog. It sprinted down empty streets free of any pursuers. As it reached the edge of the city, he dropped its pace to a low trot to avoid attracting attention. He confirmed the dog's predetermined path on the screen and grabbed his mouse. He hovered over a button with a bomb icon on it. Help text appeared: "Self Destruct." He clicked the icon and a second confirmation message appeared. "Self-Destruct: Yes/No." Frank clicked "Yes."

The dog walked for another five minutes to a drainage ditch far from prying eyes, then scurried inside a concrete pipe. The dog ignited, and all its fur burned off. It then exploded in a loud puff of smoke with a sound like a backfiring car. A nondescript pile of metal was all that remained.

***

Thirty minutes later, a dusty Land Cruiser pulled up near the drainage ditch. The driver jumped out of the running vehicle with a thick black canvas bag. He gathered as many of the small parts as he could find. Within twelve hours, they were on a series of flights that would ultimately take them to CIA headquarters in Langley, Virginia.

Chapter 65

The Moon, American Base

The dust from the explosion at the American base had settled quickly in the vacuum of space. The team at least knew that there would be a landing pad when they arrived, but the status of their equipment was unknown. As the lunar lander touched down, the team made last-minute preparations to get to work. The NASA astronaut piloting the craft stayed inside to do a final systems check. Frank, his four engineers, and one geologist suited up for their first real spacewalk.

The silence was eerie. You could barely hear your feet hit the ground as the sound traveled through the suit. If you stood still and there was no radio chatter, it was the quietest environment Frank had ever experienced. He found it beautiful on one hand. On another, he wondered what the long-term psychological effects would be if he needed to station more people on the moon on a semipermanent basis.

Frank broke out of his funk. As his team bounded onto the moon's surface to survey the damage, Frank stopped them. "Guys, we have time. Take a minute to relish where you are. How about a race?" Frank tore off into the distance hopping fifteen feet at a time. They looked at each other and raced after him. Half the men managed to keep their feet, while the rest tripped and crashed into each other.

After ten minutes of playing around, Frank called everyone back together. "We have to get this mine back online, but I didn't want to forget why we are really here."

One of the men said, "I don't get it. I thought the real reason we were here was for the helium-3."

Frank sighed. "It's so much more than that. Look around. This is the new frontier. We're Columbus discovering the new world. America was a wilderness when Europeans arrived. Look at it now."

"America might have been a wilderness, but this place is a vacuum," the engineer replied. "The comparison is a bit of a stretch."

"Let me give you a quick history lesson. America completed the transcontinental railroad in 1869, only four years after the Civil War. Within fifty years, America was the strongest country in the world. We just rode the transcontinental railroad of the modern era all the way to the moon. You helped build it."

He let his comments sink in for a moment, then got down to business. "Let's figure out where we are. I want to know what works and what doesn't. I need to know what's salvageable. And I want to know what happened here. Let's get to it."

One of the engineers took radiation readings to determine if the area was safe. He updated the team. "There are a couple of hot spots that you want to stay away from. I'll mark them on your map. The worst of the radiation is in an area fifty feet square. Your suits have radiation detectors on them, so pay attention."

Frank hopped over to the underground tunnels and lowered himself inside. The geologist joined him to look at the sides and the roof of the tunnel in more detail. The tunnels were deep enough that the blast appeared not to have damaged them. There was no telltale debris on the floor. They still had to inspect them manually to be sure. He left the geologist to his work and climbed to the surface.

His next stop was the railgun. They hadn't been able to fix it remotely, but he could fix it now that he was here. Of course, the usefulness of these modifications was debatable if they didn't harvest helium-3 soon.

After four hours of inspecting and testing, the team went back to their ship and climbed out of their suits. Frank asked for updates. "Bad news first, gentlemen."

His lead engineer responded, "The primary mining and processing system is destroyed. It's not going to be able to pull any helium-3 from the soil. It'll have to be replaced."

"What about the radiation? Do we have to pick up and move?"

"We don't. Once the mining system is repaired, we can use it to pull the contaminated soil and move it to a different part of the site. Against the overall background radiation of the moon in general, it will be a rounding error."

"What about the helium-3 we already processed?"

"Destroyed."

Frank frowned at this. The helium-3 wasn't a huge financial loss. They had just started mining when the attack occurred. However, he likened it to one of those first dollar bills you see behind the cash register of family-owned restaurants. It had some sentimental value. Someone had dropped a nuke on his first dollar bill.

"What about other materials we've pulled out of the soil: oxygen, hydrogen, and ice?"

"Good news. The tanks where we store the other elements are farther away, and they weren't impacted by the blast."

His geologist chimed in as well. "The tunnels are in good shape. I didn't see any structural damage. We made them deep enough that they can withstand reasonably sized incoming meteorites. They're pretty tough."

"Two more questions for everyone. First, how long before we're back to where we were before the attack?"

The team discussed the various issues for a couple of minutes. "Six months minimum."

"That won't work for me, boys. I want everything up and going in half that time. If the Chinese get six months ahead of us, we're done. I'm going to fix the railgun right now, and I want to be lobbing helium-3 back to earth in three months."

His team looked at him as if he was crazy. His lead engineer reiterated the number for all of them. "We wouldn't lowball you. It'll be six months with everyone giving it their all."

Frank looked away, but nodded his head in understanding. No amount of cajoling and pushing would change the date. He had to accept six months and figure out how to make it work. Perhaps he could slow the Chinese down in the court of public opinion. He wished Ben were alive to work the political angles.

"Second question. Who the hell blew up my mine?" Frank asked.

The lead engineer weighed in on this one. "It's obviously the Chinese, but I have no evidence for you. The explosion destroyed the missile. Our video footage of the blast isn't sufficient proof."

"I know it's the damn Chinese," Frank said. "I need that proof. Find me something that I can take to the United Nations."

Chapter 66

The Moon, Zhulong Base

Like most meteors in the solar system, this one formed by the collision of two asteroids in the belt between Mars and Jupiter. The meteor was only six feet across. In Earth's atmosphere, much of it would likely burn up before it hit the ground. However, this meteor was not destined for Earth.

When it hit the moon's surface, it was traveling forty thousand miles per hour. It detonated with a force equal to ten tons of TNT. The resulting explosion was equivalent to that caused by the largest conventional weapons in the U.S. military's arsenal. If it had landed directly on the Chinese moon base, it would have completely wiped any trace of the Chinese operations from the moon's surface. The resulting crater was one hundred feet across, but the blast explosion was much larger.

***

Colonel Feng had finally transported enough oxygen from earth that the team could survive for weeks. Helium-3 production was ahead of schedule. In a matter of days, they would ship their first load of helium-3 back to earth.

Feng was checking one of the external helium-3 storage tanks with one of his engineers when the world around him exploded. A blinding flash preceded a shower of debris that covered the entire moon base. A fist-sized rock flew by Feng's head and punched through the engineer's chest, exiting his back. Blood sprayed out of the man, freezing solid as it fell to the ground in a lazy arc.

The fire and explosion destroyed the main oxygen storage tanks. An automatic safety switch should have stopped the fire there. It failed. The fire traveled down another hose to the men's living quarters where a second automated switch failed to control the flash fire. Fifty men died instantly. A couple of hearty souls hung on long enough to suffocate a minute later. Unconsciousness thankfully came quickly as fourth-degree burns covered every inch of their bodies.

The third and final oxygen seal held. While the two living areas were daisy-chained together, the explosion did not make it to the women's quarters. They had enough oxygen to survive for a day if they were lucky.

Feng stared in disbelief. He signaled to the engineers near him to switch to their emergency channel. "Everyone report in." Less than a third of his team remained.

He listened and did a quick running tally in his head. Of the sixteen people working on the surface of the moon, only four had survived. The blast annihilated the men's living quarters. There would be no point in checking for survivors. The women's quarters looked intact, but he couldn't raise them on the radio.

He loped toward the women's living area. Faces stared back at him through the windows. He signaled to them to switch to their emergency channels. "Are you all right? Damage report."

He could hear crying and shouting in the background, but one of the women responded, "We are alive. We are cut off from the main oxygen stores, but the explosion did not reach us. How is the rest of the team?"

"Unknown. Stay on this channel and let me think."

He ran through a short list of his options. If he acted quickly, he could potentially get resupplies sent before the rest of his team died. He spoke to the women taikonaut again. "Call ground control immediately and let them know that we have an emergency. We need to be resupplied with oxygen."

"Yes, sir. One moment."

Feng waited a minute then shouted into the radio causing spit to fly onto his helmet's screen. "What is happening?"

"I can't raise the earth. All our long-range communications equipment is dead. We have short-range communications only."

Most of their oxygen was gone. The main hydrogen stores were likely gone as well. One living quarters destroyed. Long-range communications destroyed. Their unmanned rockets for returning helium-3 destroyed.

They had one living quarters with limited oxygen. They had two functioning mining vehicles. These also had some oxygen for the operators to breathe and a limited amount of hydrogen to power the big trucks. The drivers would suffocate within hours. The tanks in the team's suits contained some minimal oxygen. They had stores of helium-3 with no way to return them to earth. They had two tactical nuclear weapons left.

He wracked his brain thinking through the alternatives. What would his father do? His father would protect the investment in the mission at all costs. He would spare essential personnel and jettison the others into the vacuum of space. He would protect the helium-3 stores. He would figure out a way to spin this into a political success. Colonel Feng, the hero of the Chinese party, saves the fusion program by risking his life or similar nonsense.

Colonel Feng was not his father. He would not be party to the death of his entire team. He would save them and damn the mission. If that meant he besmirched the Feng family honor, so be it. "Raise the American team on the short-range channel, and tell them we require emergency assistance."

Chapter 67

The Moon, American Base

Frank fixed the railgun and was getting ready to test it when one of his engineers raised him on his short-range radio. "We have an incoming emergency call."

Frank's heart raced. "Is my family OK?" There had been so much death of late. His first thought was that something had happened to Lisa or Samantha.

"It's the Chinese."

"The Chinese are asking for our help?"

"Apparently there's been an explosion at their facilities. A Colonel Feng is asking to speak to you directly."

Feng had likely been complicit or at least aware of the nuclear attack in California. He may even have known about the plans to kidnap Tim. He had personally lobbed a tactical nuke onto Frank's base. *And he wants my help?*

"It will be a pleasure to personally tell that man to burn in hell. I'll be right in."

He reached the airlock and climbed out of his suit. "Give me some privacy will you?" he asked his engineer. He picked up the radio headset. "This is Frank Sawyer."

"This is Colonel Feng. We have not met, but I believe you know who I am?"

"You and your country are responsible for killing my son and a thousand of my countrymen. I understand you have called to beg for your life?"

"I am not a politician. I am a man of science. I am not so different from you."

"With the exception that I am not a murdering thug?"

"I wonder if the spouses and children of the former Iranian leadership feel the same way?"

Frank smiled to himself before pushing the transmit button. "I couldn't tell you how they feel. Allah must not have been smiling on their recent activities."

"I do not wish to argue, and I do not want to beg for my life. I am here to beg for the life of my team. They are engineers and technicians, not politicians or soldiers. They are all going to die."

"Why would I aid you or your countrymen?" Frank asked.

"You have a reputation as a moral man. I am not religious, but it is my understanding that your faith would lead you to spare no effort in saving my team."

This gave Frank pause. This piece of trash had found a weak spot. *Can I live with the deaths of the Chinese team on my conscience? No, but Feng doesn't need to know that.*

"What do you have to give me in return?"

"You have accused China of deceit and murder in private, but you have not done so in public. Knowing your reputation, I assume this is not out of a false sense of political correctness?"

Frank was silent. *Never negotiate against yourself.*

As expected, Feng continued, "I cannot comment on the attack on California or the death of your son. I would if I could, but I know nothing concrete about either. Anything I say would be pure conjecture and assumption."

Frank made no comment.

"Are you there? Is my signal still coming through?"

"Yes," Frank answered.

"I will admit to personally launching a nuclear attack on your facility at my government's direction. I will say in my defense that I knew without a doubt that your base was completely unmanned."

"China will deny it and say you were under duress."

"Not if I video tape the confession while showing you the two remaining nuclear missiles. The evidence against me will be inconvertible."

"If you do this, you can never return to China. I can't imagine that even your father's political ties would save you."

"You are correct. I will not return to my family. I will not return to China. I will not return to Earth. I will die here."

"You have a deal."

***

Frank and his team raced across the lunar surface on their Kawasakis. They were one-man vehicles, but Frank remembered seeing pictures of entire families on scooters in third world countries. They could squeeze enough people onto each bike with a bit of creativity. All the bikes carried extra oxygen on small trailers. Even with the extra oxygen, it would be difficult to get his team and the Chinese back to safety. He had considered bringing up one of his automated dogs to test it out on the moon. In retrospect, he wished he had. The automaton would have given them more oxygen-carrying capacity. He would prioritize it in one of the next cargo flights.

They crested a crater and saw what was left of the Chinese moon base. They stopped in front of what appeared to be the only habitable building still standing. He raised Colonel Feng on the radio. "Get your people out here."

Frank cobbled together a workable plan with Colonel Feng. They had enough hydrogen in one of the large Chinese mining trucks that they could make significant progress toward the American base carrying twenty of the Chinese team. The problem was that the truck was too slow, even with the hydrogen power. Anyone on the truck would suffocate before getting back to the safety of the American base.

Frank's team would carry as many of the Chinese team on their cycles as possible. They would make a second trip back to retrieve the people on the mining truck prior to their oxygen running out. Frank's calculations showed the plan worked. Barely.

"Move out, everyone. Colonel Feng, my team will take it from here. You have something to show me," Frank said.

Feng nodded and walked Frank toward one of the storage facilities in the complex. Frank turned on the recorder on his helmet and faced Feng. "You owe me a confession."

The colonel nodded. "My name is Colonel Fei Feng. I recently attacked the American moon base with a tactical nuclear weapon. My goal was to disrupt the progress of the American's helium-3 mining operations. As proof of this, I have agreed to show Mr. Frank Sawyer the two remaining tactical nuclear weapons." He paused to point at the missiles. "The decision to attack the American facility was made purely at my discretion and not at the urging of the Chinese government."

Frank tapped a button and paused the recording. "Hold on their, partner. That isn't what we agreed to."

"I don't know what you mean. I am only telling the truth. I will not lie about the Chinese government's involvement. I am not a traitor."

Frank turned off the video recorder. "So, you beg for my assistance to save your people, but you cheat on your part of the agreement? After everything you've done, I should kill you for this."

"If it gives you satisfaction, please do. I will not face my father or my countrymen. In fact, the nuclear weapons are set to go off in less than two hours. I will be here when they do."

"Predictable. I figured you might arm the nukes to prevent me from getting access to your helium-3."

"I have to know, would you have taken it?" the colonel asked.

"Of course. It would be just compensation for destroying my equipment. Perhaps I'll disable your nukes and take everything anyway."

"Not even you can dismantle a ticking time bomb in a cumbersome spacesuit reading Chinese characters you don't understand."

"You mean I can't just cut the red wire?"

"As you say, Mr. Sawyer."

They walked out of the storage facility back toward the living quarters. As expected, the truck and lunar cycles were gone. The team had moved fast to ensure their survival. As they got closer, Colonel Feng paused. Only three trailers remained with their extra stores of oxygen. Frank's cycle was gone.

"Where is your cycle? How will you return?"

In response, Frank pulled his cordless drill from its safety tether and slashed a hole in Feng's suit. Air rushed out of the gash. Frank's training taught him that people don't actually explode when exposed to vacuum. He also learned that it hurt like hell. Frank pushed Feng hard in the chest and knocked him to the ground.

Chapter 68

The Moon, American Base

Colonel Feng woke with a start. His head throbbed, and he could only see out of his right eye.

"Good morning, Colonel. May I say that you look like hammered dog shit. That's a Texas expression, but it suits you."

"Where am I? What have you done?"

"You told me you aren't a politician. You are a scientist and astronaut. Why don't you tell me what's happening, genius?"

He vaguely remembered Sawyer cutting his suit and staring gleefully into his face. His helmet was off, but he was still in his suit. He checked himself over and saw a patch where Frank had slashed him.

He assumed that Sawyer wanted the satisfaction of killing him rather than leaving it to the explosions. Perhaps he changed his mind at the last minute. Perhaps murdering him was too much for Frank to handle.

He looked around. Though blurry, he could see they were in one of the Chinese harvesters. The rescue team had ignored it, as the fuel cells did not have enough hydrogen to make it back to the base. It could run on solar energy, but its speed and range would not be enough. The oxygen would be gone long before the ponderous vehicle ground its way to the American base.

Then he remembered the spare oxygen tanks left by Sawyer's team. It was probably enough to provide oxygen for two back to the American base. But why? Why would Sawyer not leave him to his death and ride his cycle back to safety?

"You were right," Frank said.

"Right about what?"

"I'm not smart enough to disarm a nuclear weapon in a spacesuit while trying to translate Chinese symbols. You know what I am smart enough to do?"

"The bombs went off?"

"Of course the bombs went off, but you're getting sidetracked. You know what I am smart enough to do?"

"What... what are you talking about?" The colonel's speech was still slurred and unfocused.

"I am smart enough to call Dr. Jing Yang when I need help with helium-3 handling. I pumped two tons of helium-3 from your base's storage tanks into this truck. In case you're wondering, that's a little over two billion in U.S. dollars."

"You cannot get away with this theft. My team will know what happened. I know what happened." The colonel leaned forward as if to attack Frank, then collapsed back into his seat.

Frank shook his head at the colonel's half-hearted attempt to rally. Decompression didn't seem to agree with him. "I'll say it came from our operations. It gives us time to fix the damage you caused to our base. By the way, thanks for arming the nukes."

"What do you mean? Now you will not have access to any of the Chinese technology."

Frank scoffed at the notion. "Mine's better. I wanted your helium-3, which I now have. The only thing I struggled with was how to convince you to blow up your own facility. I needed to ensure you were back to ground zero."

"We can rebuild. It's only a matter of time before we catch up with you."

"Not with your confession. No rational country will let China provide energy to them at this point. You'll be a pariah. Ironically, you might be the only country that won't be running your industrial base on helium-3."

Colonel Feng vomited down the front of his suit.

Chapter 69

The Moon, American Base

The mining truck crunched to a halt at the remains of the American moon base. It was low on power and low on oxygen, but the plan worked. Frank and Colonel Feng were alive, though the Colonel was in bad shape.

Frank spoke into the short-range radio to one of his men. "What's everyone's status? How's the Chinese team holding up?"

"We're fine for now, but we don't have the facilities to support the additional people."

Frank did the math. Twenty-three taikonauts plus Feng. Eighteen of the women survived in their quarters. Most of the men died in the explosions. Five men working on the surface survived when the disaster struck. His team consisted of the NASA pilot and five others. Including himself, thirty-one people remained. He raised the NASA astronaut on the radio. "How many people can you fit in the ship for the return trip?"

"It has room for ten," the astronaut replied.

"In case you haven't noticed, we have a few more people than that now. What if you use a crowbar?"

"It's not safe, but we can carry fifteen. Not everyone would have a seat, but the life support systems could probably handle it."

"Probably?" Frank asked.

"Probably. There is no safety margin if we carry five additional crew members, but we should be OK barring emergencies."

That meant sixteen people had to stay behind in a base that was nowhere near operational. Worse, that would mean the second flight wouldn't even be able to take everyone back at once. One of the fifteen slots would need to be reserved for the captain. He played with the radio for a moment, and was able to get all the Americans on at once.

"Guys, I need to know how to keep sixteen people alive for the next week or two. Assume the spacecraft will be gone."

One of the engineers asked, "Can't we cram everyone into the return ship? We don't have a permanent place for people to live. We intended to bunk in the ship for the next few weeks."

"That's no longer an option," Frank said. "Our pilot informed me that we can fit fifteen maximum per flight. That means some people need to stay behind."

The geologist said, "We could deploy one of the temporary underground storage modules. We designed them to fit in the tunnels. We planned to use it for a limited time while we built more robust facilities. It was intended more for storing sensitive equipment than people."

"How long to install it?" Frank asked.

"No more than two hours to install it, but we planned on operating it for a week before putting anything in it. It's never been tested before."

"Get it setup. Unfortunately, we don't have a week."

"Who stays behind?"

It was unfair to ask his men to remain behind in a temporary enclosure. They had enough food, water, and oxygen to survive. However, the temporary enclosure was spartan. It had no cooking facilities, no lavatories, no beds, and no furniture. It would be a truly awful few weeks.

"Someone has to pilot the ship which leaves fourteen open slots. I'll stay behind. I need Colonel Feng on the first return flight. He's in bad shape, and I need him to survive. You guys can take five slots. We'll open the remaining eight to a lottery for the Chinese."

There was no response. Frank asked, "Did you guys hear me?"

After a moment, Frank's lead engineer spoke. "I don't want to speak for everyone here, but we knew this was going to be dangerous work. I would like to stay behind to see if we can make some progress. I know we don't have all the replacement parts we need, but let's not abandon the mission."

The geologist said, "I second that. I also don't feel quite right leaving the women taikonauts behind to live in squalor. I realize they're better trained than I am by a long shot, but it doesn't sit well with me."

The rest of the team agreed.

"It's an honor to work with you, gentlemen," Frank said. He spoke to his pilot. "Make the necessary preparations for the return trip. I'll let you work with the Chinese team to let them decide who they want to send back with you."

Frank turned to Colonel Feng. He looked awful, but he was still conscious. "Looks like you're on the next flight back to earth."

"I do not wish to return. I prefer to stay here and die. At least let me send my crew back on the first flight. I'll return on the second."

"You'll die if you stay here. It's not an option. I need you to stay alive so that we can debrief you before we return you to your father."

It was hard to read the Colonel's expression through the blood and vomit, but Frank guessed he wasn't happy. He would need to restrain him on the flight back to make sure he didn't hurt himself.

Chapter 70

The Moon, American Base

Frank bounced back from the railgun. He tapped commands into the tablet velcroed to the arm of his suit. The computer took over. At precisely the right time, it fired the railgun back toward earth. A blue arc flashed, and the empty capsule streaked into space.

He patched into the long-range radio and spoke to an engineer back at the terminus of the space elevator. "Cargo is away. How's my aim?"

At five thousand miles per hour, the capsule would take roughly thirty-five hours to reach the space elevator. The actual time would be slightly longer as the capsule would use reverse thrust to slow down as it neared its destination. Without decelerating to a more manageable speed, the capsule would obliterate the elevator. If the thrusters worked as planned, it should be an easy enough task.

"Right on target," the engineer said. While the journey wouldn't be done for over a day, he could already calculate the flight path. Assuming the cargo didn't hit anything in the void of space, it should be easy enough to catch.

"Excellent," Frank said. "Let's make sure that the capsule decelerates and that you're able to successfully catch it. If you can, the next capsule will have our first load of helium-3 in it."

Frank bounded to their temporary quarters and entered the airlock. He waited for the pressure to equalize, then removed his helmet. He braced for the inevitable stench and entered the makeshift living quarters.

Frank resisted the natural gag reflex in the back of his throat and struggled to maintain a leader-like demeanor. With no toilet facilities and no means to clean up, it felt like a third-world country. They had hung a blanket on the far side of the enclosure to provide limited privacy, but there was no plumbing. While they had plenty of food, water, and oxygen, it was a truly awful experience.

The Chinese were particularly miserable. Their mission was a failure, and they had no duties to distract them. Frank's team's morale was high despite the squalor. The extra time on the moon meant that much more of the equipment was back to fully operational status.

Despite the progress, Frank's lead engineer grabbed his sleeve and frowned. "I need to speak to you privately."

They walked to a quiet corner of the room and the engineer lowered his voice. "We have a problem. This enclosure is leaking oxygen."

"How bad is it? Can we hold out until the ship returns?"

"Barely," the engineer answered. He rubbed the back of his neck. "But we can't hold out any longer than that."

"In other words, we have fourteen slots available on the next ship and sixteen people that need to make it back to earth. Options?" Frank looked up and noticed one of the Chinese taikonauts walking toward them.

"Sir," she said. "I speak English, and I am a pilot. Can I help?"

Frank looked her up and down and considered the offer. "Can you pilot an American ship?"

"The principles are the same. If I had someone talking me through it, I'm sure I could get us back safely," the woman said.

Frank nodded. "We can ask the NASA pilot to stay behind and land the ship using automated controls. We've done it several times already to land equipment on the surface. The primary reason we have the pilot on board is as a backup when we're carrying people."

"That leaves one person without a ride home," the engineer said.

The woman looked back at her remaining crew. "It is only fair that one of us is left behind. We would all be dead without your assistance. We will work it out amongst ourselves."

"You give up too easily," Frank said. He turned to his engineer. "Tell our guys to get in here." He turned back to the Chinese pilot. "We need your people on this, too."

It took thirty minutes to get the entire team inside the shelter. Frank briefly outlined the problem. In closing, he said, "I need options. Leaving someone behind to die isn't one of them. Let's figure this out."

One of the Chinese team members raised his hand. "My English is not good. Translate?" he asked the Chinese pilot. She nodded, and they spoke rapidly back and forth for a moment.

"It is perhaps a serviceable idea," the Chinese pilot said. "Someone can stay behind in a suit attached to the primary oxygen tank. The suits carry some water. The person could stay in these quarters for additional protection from the surface temperature changes."

Frank shook his head. "It's a good idea, but there's not enough water in the suits. The longest a human can live without water is around five days. Less in this environment."

"What about the trucks?" one of Frank's engineers asked. "The trucks are oxygenated. You could remove your suit in the truck. You'd be able to eat, drink, et cetera."

Frank turned his nose up at the et cetera. The living conditions would be worse than their current predicament. Having your bed, dining room table, kitchen, and toilet all in the tight cab of a mining truck sounded truly awful. Awful, but survivable.

"That could work," Frank said.

Several of the Chinese looked back and forth at each other. Frank nodded to the Chinese pilot who rapidly translated the conversation. Several of the Chinese wrinkled their nose at the idea. However, the man who brought up the spacesuit idea spoke for several seconds.

"He wishes to volunteer to stay behind," the pilot said.

"Brave man," Frank said. He nodded to the man acknowledging his selflessness and hoped it translated. "Give me a moment to think through things."

It was a workable plan. The person would probably survive. However, he didn't completely trust the Chinese team. They were probably all honest men and women. They likely all viewed themselves as being in Frank's debt for saving their lives. However, if someone planned to stay behind and cause problems, they would be the one to volunteer. There was no good way to gauge their loyalties.

Frank also didn't feel right asking any of his men to stay behind. He knew any or all of them would volunteer in an instant, but it would have to be him. *Think, damn it.*

"The railgun," Frank said.

"What are you talking about?" his lead engineer asked.

"We can send someone back using the railgun. They'd get there faster than the ship."

"The capsules don't have life support, food, water, or even light. And anyone inside would be liquefied by the accelerations."

Frank tapped some calculations into his tablet. "I can make this a two-day trip if I slow the railgun acceleration to the upper limits of human survivability. My prototype suit consumes half as much oxygen as a normal suit, since it doesn't need to create a pressurized environment. Considering that, can you rig something up for me in one of the capsules that can give me enough oxygen? We can use flashlights so it isn't dark."

The engineer squinted his eyes and rubbed his chin. "Probably. But what about food and water?"

"The suit carries some water, but water isn't absolutely necessary for a two-day trip. Food certainly isn't."

"Who goes in the flying coffin?"

Frank smirked at the reference. "I guess it's me."

***

"Boss, are you ready?" an engineer asked.

Frank checked everything for the last time. Oxygen levels were good. He took a sip of water. He confirmed the makeshift harness was as tight as he could make it. The LED lights his engineers had duct taped in place were on. He crossed his arms over his chest and said, "Hit it."

"Roger."

There was a brief pause before the acceleration slammed Frank against the back of the capsule so hard he couldn't breathe. His head struck the back of his helmet, and he fluttered on the edge of consciousness. One of the LED lights blinked out. Then the second turned dark. And then Frank passed out.

***

He woke with a start. His head and neck throbbed.

"Can anyone hear me?" Frank asked.

His heart rate spiked as he struggled against his harness. He tried to sit up, but couldn't move.

"Anyone, can you hear me?"

And then he remembered that there was no one there to hear him. The short-range radio in his suit wouldn't reach the moon, the elevator, or earth. In the rush to launch him on the return flight to earth, there was no time to rig any long-range communication.

He was on his own, in the dark. The heads-up display on his helmet should have reported the time and oxygen levels. There was nothing. The launch must have damaged the suit somehow. There was no way to know how long he was unconscious or how much longer the trip would be.

He moved in his suit and felt liquid sloshing around. *Great. I pissed myself. This will make for a fine story.*

He put his mouth on the surgical tubing that fed him water. He sucked in. Nothing. He thought for a moment. The water in his suit was likely from the broken water bladder. He smiled to himself. *I don't have any water, but it's better than the alternative.*

He considered the last months. He had won, but at what cost? His son was dead. His best friend murdered. Trusted colleagues had died in the nuclear blast in California. The revenge he had taken on the Iranian leadership had done nothing to fill that ache. There were still widows and widowers. There were children who lost a mother or father.

Would I do it again? Never. The cost was too high. But that's not the way the world worked. You never knew the consequences of your actions until things played out.

A sound went off in his suit. He couldn't recall the exact meaning of this particular audible alarm. His addled brain struggled to make sense of things. Then he remembered—low oxygen. His new suit consumed less oxygen, but apparently it wasn't enough to get him all the way back to earth. He knew it would be close, but he had never really doubted that he would make it. He couldn't communicate, but he could at least record a message. He tapped a button to start recording.

"Lisa, honey, I'm sorry. You know how important this was to me, but I took one too many risks. I put too much faith in the technology I designed. I should have used my head and looked for a more conservative solution. Perhaps that isn't in my nature.

"I want you to know how much I love you. You've been with me since the earliest days. We raised two great children. We built a business empire that has improved the life of billions. We've set the stage for mankind to conquer space. I couldn't have done any of it without you. None of it would have meant anything to me without you at my side.

"But there is so much that remains incomplete. Please forge ahead. Sam's almost ready to run the company. I had hoped that Ben and I would be there for another twenty years to prepare her, but that's not in the cards. Help her make a go of it. Help her also see that there are other things in life. Don't let her push herself so hard that she misses out on family and all the great things we had."

The air was running out. It was getting hard to speak. Hard to think. He didn't need his final recorded words to his wife to be spoken in delirium. Lisa would hear his imminent death in his slurred speech if he didn't wrap up soon. She would sense the budding irrational fear. She couldn't be allowed to relive that for the rest of her life.

"As you well know, tiresome romantic soliloquies are not me. Suffice it to say that I love you. Tell Sam I love her. Take care of yourself, honey. Take care of Samantha."

He felt his heart rate rise again. He forced himself to be calm. No reason to go out in a cloud of fear and worry. He had done what he had set out to do. That would have to be enough. He collected his thoughts and gave thanks for the amazing life he had been granted.

And then the reverse thrusters kicked in. He was home.

Chapter 71

Washington, DC, Eisenhower Executive Office Building

"Gentlemen, I apologize for not being able to meet with you in the Oval Office. Time was of the essence, and this couldn't wait for another month," Gladwell said to the ambassadors of the United Kingdom and France.

"Congratulations on your election," said the British ambassador. "It is most deserved, and America will be well-served by its decision." The French ambassador acknowledged the statement with a slight nod.

Gladwell glanced at the open spot on his wall where the picture of President Brown had hung up until the recent election. He shrugged off the compliment and continued. "I have news of Frank Sawyer's recent adventures that I want to share with you. He has somehow managed to save the remainder of the Chinese lunar team from a meteor strike. He's secured helium-3 worth billions, and he will soon stabilize his own operations."

"Quite impressive," the British ambassador said. The French diplomat said nothing.

"Yes, it seems he will be returning to earth as a conquering hero with complete control of the helium-3 market for the foreseeable future. Incidentally, he has incontrovertible proof that the Chinese used nuclear weapons in space, a clear violation of international law. I've seen the video."

"More impressive yet," the British ambassador said.

The French ambassador opted to speak for the first time. "And yet, monsieur, you seem to be less than pleased with the outcome."

"It is a dangerous amount of power to have in one man's hands," Gladwell said. He turned to the British ambassador. "I am reminded of George Soros breaking the Bank of England through currency speculation in the 1990s. Private industry at this scale is a dangerous thing."

"I must say," the British ambassador continued, "I have heard that Frank Sawyer is extremely patriotic. I should think that you would be celebrating to have a man of his stature and political beliefs in your corner."

"Frank Sawyer is in Frank Sawyer's corner," Gladwell said. "He sees little value in what we in government provide our citizenry and the global community. I hesitate to call him a patriot."

"Regulate him into obedience," the British ambassador said. "This is how one must handle these situations."

"I wish it were that simple. He was careful to set up a corporate and legal structure that makes that difficult. Even his geographic location is a challenge. His space elevator is bobbing around in the middle of the Pacific Ocean."

"But surely he must value the protection the American fleet is giving him. Threaten to take it away," the British ambassador said.

"Yes, and if the platform is attacked, the remainder of my one-term presidency will be a write-off. The man is a hero. I can't withdraw protection from one of the single greatest scientific achievements of the last two hundred years." Gladwell shook his head in disgust. "I have something more drastic in mind. I plan to nationalize his company. I can muster the votes to do it."

"That, sir, is a bold move. However, you correctly point out that Mr. Sawyer is returning to earth as a conquering hero. I would not expect him to remain silent on the issue. And, for a time, his bully pulpit is at least as big as yours," the British ambassador said.

Gladwell's eyes narrowed at the unambassadorial comment.

"You make my point for me. Why should a single private citizen have the prestige of a sitting president of the United States? However, I will soon have information that will make Frank Sawyer fall in line."

The French ambassador chose this moment to engage in the conversation. "And you wish to know whether France will fall in line as well?"

Gladwell's eyes narrowed even more. "I wouldn't put it that way. We're allies. What is good for one of us is good for all of us."

"I agree completely," the British ambassador said. "But what is it that you could possibly hold over Mr. Sawyer's head that would make him agree to any of this?"

The French ambassador raised his eyebrows at this comment. "Surely, you must know with the reach of the vaunted MI-6?" The British ambassador frowned at the backhanded compliment, while the French ambassador continued. "Iran. He speaks of Iran. He intends to paint Monsieur Sawyer as a war criminal if he doesn't agree to the vice president's terms. Correct?"

Gladwell's narrowed eyes morphed into a broad smile. "Any comment on my part would be premature, but rest assured Frank Sawyer will do what his country asks of him. Of that I have no doubt."

A knock at the door interrupted the conversation. "Sir, your next appointment is here," a secretary announced.

"Gentlemen, duty calls."

"Mr. Vice President, I look forward to your inauguration," the British ambassador said. "You can rest easy that you will have the support of the British government behind you."

The French ambassador clasped hands with Gladwell and said, "Good afternoon, Mr. Vice President."

He attempted to pull back his hand but Gladwell held it firmly. "And France?"

"I will take this information to my superiors as is my duty." He extricated his hand.

Chapter 72

Austin, Automated Technologies Headquarters

Colonel Feng's video confession ended, and the lights brightened. Frank said, "As you can see, we have undeniable evidence of the Chinese breaking countless international laws. They launched a nuclear attack on an American private enterprise to say nothing of violating the prohibition against the arming of space. The international community can't trust China to control energy production. I will be addressing the United Nations, at their request, to discuss banning the Chinese from operating on the moon. I'll take questions."

"Does this mean your company will effectively have a monopoly on fusion energy production? How is this any better?" asked a reporter.

"For the time being, I have a monopoly. That's how new industries start. Then competitors move in," Frank said.

"But you are asking the United Nations to eliminate the only other viable competitor that you have. This seems like a shameless land grab."

"To be clear, it's my technology that will allow the world to get access to fusion at a reasonable price. I'm not ashamed to reap the financial benefits that come with my investments."

Another reporter chimed in. "How are you going to protect this investment? How are you going to prevent another California?"

At this, Frank turned to Gladwell, who had opted to join today's meeting. "I'll let President-elect Gladwell answer that."

"The American fleet will continue to protect the space elevator. We view it as a strategic asset not only to America but also to the world. In addition, we will be contracting with Mr. Sawyer's company to build a replacement elevator for the sole use of the American government."

The questions went on for another ten minutes at which point Frank's new press secretary wrapped things up.

Gladwell grabbed Frank's sleeve. "I need a moment of your time."

They walked back to Frank's office with the Secret Service in tow. With Benjamin Whitman's recent murder, they were on high alert. When they got to Frank's office, their leader asked to check it. Gladwell motioned for them to remain outside. "No need for all that." Gladwell and Frank went in and sat down.

"I was sorry to hear of Benjamin's death," Gladwell said.

Frank stared at Gladwell. Ben's death ensured that Gladwell would become the next president of the United States. However, Frank knew that not even this man would delight in his friend's passing. "Thanks, Thomas. I was already sad to lose him to the American people. His death came as a shock."

"I promise you I'll get a handle on these damn eco-terrorists when I'm president."

"What did you say?"

"I said I'll take care of these eco-terrorists. First your son's death and now Benjamin."

Frank saw no upside in sharing the connection between the eco-terrorists and the Chinese with the American government. After the government's refusal to move on the Iranians, Frank decided to file the information away. He couldn't depend on Gladwell to extract payback from the Chinese based on his handling of Iran. "I haven't heard any information connecting the eco-terrorists with Ben. Did the FBI find something?"

"Just an assumption. Who else would it be?"

Frank turned his chair away from Gladwell and looked out his office window.

Gladwell changed the subject. "I have a proposal for you." Gladwell came around to the other side of Frank's desk and sat on the edge.

Frank raised his eyebrows and moved his chair back, annoyed at Gladwell's invasion of his personal space.

"Not so much a proposal as a statement of how things will be."

Frank did not respond.

"I've spoken to some of my old colleagues in the House and Senate. They're proposing a bill to nationalize the space elevator and your base on the moon. It's too important to our national security to have it left in the hands of private industry."

Frank stared back at the vice president, unflinching.

"But it isn't all bad news. You will still have a strong hand in the management of the overall effort. We'll figure out a way for your company to make a reasonable profit on the investment."

Frank couldn't remain quiet any longer. "What's a reasonable profit?"

"Oh, I don't know—I'll tell you what. I'll establish a blue ribbon panel to answer that very question. I know some men and women from academia and government who should be on the panel. Some of the CEOs who contributed to my election undoubtedly have some insightful perspective."

"Undoubtedly."

Gladwell clapped his hands excitedly. "Also, we'll need to work with you to set production quotas. We need to decide which countries will be the first to receive fusion. I'll exclude several for strategic reasons. I'm sure you understand."

Frank leaned back in his chair and glowered at Gladwell before responding. "I won't be accepting any further contracts to build the replacement space elevator. Our deal was for one, not two. I'll go it alone in the Pacific. I'll figure out a way to protect the elevator without U.S. Navy involvement."

"You don't understand. You'll still have a role, but the technology is too important to leave in the hands of one man." The vice president put his hand on Frank's shoulder.

Frank stared at the hand, and Gladwell snapped it back to his lap. "I understand perfectly. You want me to work for you."

"Now, that is a glass-half-empty mentality. Think of it in the context of working for the American people. By extension, the world. Yes, you'll be living up to your obligations as a citizen of the world." Gladwell grinned, but his eyes had a savage sparkle.

"I'd be doing my duty as a public servant?"

"Now you've got it. A public servant. Having spent a lifetime in public service, I know there is no greater calling. I'll have my people write your speech for the United Nations. We should coordinate your comments to the international community with the public announcement of the bill."

"Get out."

Gladwell's jaw dropped. "How dare you? You can't kick the president-elect of the United States out of your office. I will be running this country in a month."

"Get out."

Gladwell's eyes gleamed with a religious fervor. "There is something else," he said. "You should've been more careful in Iran. You used the exact technology to assassinate the Iranian leaders that you demonstrated to me in Arizona. That was uncharacteristically foolish of you. You can play along, or I can put you in jail for the rest of your life for war crimes."

"Let me know what you find. Get out. Now."

"Come now, Frank. This is best for everyone. You'll still have some control over things. You'll still be a rich man."

Frank leaned forward on his desk. His eyes darted briefly down to the right-hand drawer then lighted on Gladwell. "Your boys should've checked my office. I would get out while you still can."

Gladwell's grin evaporated. Gladwell puffed up his chest, but then fight turned to flight and he scurried out the door.

Frank spun around and looked out the window. Gladwell. Did he really think Frank was unbalanced enough to keep a gun in his office and use it to threaten the president-elect? The man was a coward. A coward that was about to steal everything Frank had worked for, and Frank couldn't do anything to stop him.

As Frank stewed, the phone rang. His secretary knew to leave him alone if he didn't pick up after three rings. It rang a fourth time, then a fifth. He sighed and hit the speaker button. "What, Laney?"

"I'm sorry, but I have the general secretary of China on the phone."

He wasn't in the mood to revel over his victory over the Chinese right now. "Tell him I'm busy golfing." Frank's hate of golfing was legendary. That would let the man knew where he stood in Frank's estimation.

"He insists. He says he has information for you."

"Tell him to leave a message."

"He's the leader of the largest country in the world."

It would be small satisfaction compared to the loss of Tim, but he could at least muster the energy to gloat. He had beaten this madman at his own game. He couldn't muster the hate to kill the general secretary's son, but he had dishonored him. And by extension the father.

"Put him on."

"Yes, sir."

"This is Sawyer."

"Thank you for taking my call. We have much to discuss," Secretary Feng said.

"I don't see how. Unless you called to admit to killing my son."

The general secretary didn't respond.

"I may not be able to prove it in international court, but I know you killed Tim. I'll make sure you and your country pay for this for the next one hundred years."

"But I didn't kill your son. The FBI did."

"Semantics. Your agent kidnapped my son and put him in harm's way."

"You also have a daughter, I believe? She is quite renowned. She was able to discover helium-3 fusion with a small team in a tenth of the time it took us. You must be proud of her."

"Are you threatening my daughter now?" Frank gripped his hand into a fist.

"On the contrary, I'm merely pointing out a commonality between us. I also had a daughter."

"Great, we both have daughters."

"I said I had a daughter. She was recently killed. I was also proud of her accomplishments. Her death was a great loss. You would have liked her."

"Tough luck."

"Like your son, she was killed by an FBI sniper. You would have liked her a great deal. In fact, I would say you did like her from what I've been told."

"What are you talking about?"

"Marriage almost brought our families together. I understand the wedding was to be in three months. I of course would not have been able to attend for obvious reasons. Trust me when I say I meant your boy no harm. I play a much longer game than that."

"You're lying," Frank said through gritted teeth.

"I am admitting to a father that I ordered a kidnapping on United States soil that resulted in the death of his son. I can think of other lies that would be more… profitable."

Frank sat in stunned silence.

"As I said, you and I have much to talk about. I have information for you. I would like to meet face-to-face."

"Sure, I'll jump on a flight to China right now."

"I know you aren't bold enough to come to China, but I am bold enough to come to America. With the upcoming change in presidency, it is diplomatically appropriate that I make the visit. Perhaps I can visit your ranch and thank you personally for… saving my son. My daughter said your house is quite charming. Very Texan."

Meeting the general secretary on his home ground certainly gave him an advantage. Perhaps the man did have information worth knowing.

"Have your people coordinate with my secretary."

***

Gladwell walked out of Automated Technologies headquarters to his motorcade. He stepped into the back of his armored limousine. He saw a call from his secretary and answered.

"I have the director of the CIA on the phone for you, sir. He says he has urgent information for you."

"Put him on."

"Sir, we finished our analysis of the attack on the Iranian leadership," the CIA director said.

"And?"

"The robot was Chinese. There are Chinese characters and model numbers on many of the surviving parts."

Gladwell did not respond.

"Mr. Vice President? Are you there?"

"I'm here," Gladwell said.

"I thought you would be excited. This is clear proof that they assassinated the leaders of a sovereign nation that was supposedly an ally of theirs."

"Sit on this information for now. Thank you for your time, Director." Gladwell's phone shattered as he threw it against the side of the car.

Chapter 73

Austin, Sawyer Family Ranch

The general secretary's entourage finished scanning Frank's office for microphones and video surveillance devices. Frank would of course record the entire conversation. The Chinese found the devices they were supposed to find. They even found one of the devices that they were not supposed to find. They were thorough, but not thorough enough.

Frank opted to have Lisa and Samantha vacate the house. They were both aware of the connection between Tim's death and the Chinese. Frank could not in good conscience make them endure this conversation.

"Let's adjourn to my office," Frank said.

"The appropriate title of address is General Secretary Feng," one of the Chinese aides encouraged.

Frank's eyes narrowed, and he opened his mouth to retort, but the general secretary cut him off. "If I understand the Texan culture, formality is not overvalued. In my revolutionary days, my younger days, I was known only as Feng. Call me Feng. May I call you Frank, Mr. Sawyer?" The Chinese aides' eyes widened at this egregious breach of protocol.

"My office is in here." Frank pointed.

Feng stood motionless. "I understand you have a firing range on your property. Let's meet there. You know, when I was a young man, I was quite a good shot. I have heard from trusted sources that you are... adequate?"

Frank knew he was at least good enough with a shotgun to hit Feng in the chest at pointblank range. The firing range was a good choice.

The Chinese handlers and the Secret Service team eyed each other nervously. A Secret Service agent spoke first. "General Secretary, sir, that is not a good idea. We can't risk an international incident due to a gun range accident."

Feng turned to Frank. "Mr. Sawyer and I both have a military background." He turned to Frank and said, "Would you agree that it is highly unlikely that either of us will suffer any unfortunate accidents?"

"Assuming you don't shoot yourself in the foot."

Feng laughed heartily at this. "Take me to your range. Scan Mr. Sawyer and myself for listening devices. This conversation will be private. The rest of you will stay here."

A Chinese aid and a Secret Service agent spoke at the same time. "That is not a good idea, General Sec—"

"I have spoken," Feng said to his aid. He turned to the Secret Service agent. "Your concern is noted, but I am sure you do not wish to cause an international incident. Scan us now."

The agent and one of the Chinese security team scanned Frank and Secretary Feng, and they headed toward the range.

"I grieved when I heard of your son's fate. His death was never in the plans. The situation escalated out of control."

"If you mention Tim again, you may indeed have an unfortunate accident."

Feng ignored the threat. "I understand you are quite inadequate with shotguns. The shotgun is also not part of Chinese shooting culture. It is a gun for sportsmen who face combat with ducks on the weekend. The venerable AK-47 is much preferred."

"I have an AK-47. The Colt AR-15 is better."

The general secretary dismissed the statement with a laugh. "Not in the field."

"If one assumes that a soldier can be trusted to take care of his gear, it is better in the field. I suppose an AK-47 would be an appropriate choice for a less professional army."

"I propose a wager. We can see which is better."

"Let me see. If I win, you cede control of helium-3 production to me. If you win, I promise not to destroy every ship you send to the moon for the foreseeable future.

Feng laughed again. "My daughter warned me of your expansive sense of humor. It is proving to be true. However, we won't settle those matters here today. I propose a wager to exchange information."

"Why would I trust anything you say?"

"I haven't lied to you yet. I propose these rules. We shoot three shots each starting at fifty yards, then proceeding out from there. Whoever has the best three shots gets to ask a single question. The loser must answer truthfully. On their honor."

Frank would beat this old man with his parchment thin skin. While he lacked prowess with shotguns, he was exceptional with a rifle.

Frank unlocked the large barn where they stored guns and various off-road vehicles. He handed Feng the AK-47 and sat down to remove the scope from his own rifle. "That is unnecessary."

"If we're going to have a contest, let's at least make it a fair one. The AK doesn't have a scope."

"When I was a young soldier in the revolution, we did not use scopes. I am fine with iron sights. I know how much you Americans rely on your technology. Keep the scope on the gun. You will need it."

Frank set down the Allen wrench. "You get a lot of mileage out of the revolution. It must get on people's nerves."

The general secretary frowned. He sat in a nearby folding chair and sighted on one of the targets.

Frank raised his eyebrows and said, "We'll shoot standing... if you have the energy for it."

"Of course, of course. I was checking my weapon." He pushed the chair out of the way, nearly dropping his gun in the process.

Metal targets sat at fifty, seventy-five, one hundred, one fifty, and two hundred yards. Feng shot first. Three metal pings rang out in rapid succession as he drilled the target with ease. He turned to Frank and said, "Not bad for an aging soldier. Not even bad for a young soldier."

Frank fired next and likewise heard three metal pings.

"Tie. However, in the spirit of open communication, I will allow you to ask me a question."

After pausing, Frank asked, "Did you order the Iranians to launch a nuclear attack on the California space elevator?"

Feng drew his breath sharply through his teeth. "That is a poorly framed question."

Or you are purposely evading it, Frank thought.

Feng waited for an uncomfortably long time, even for Frank. "I see. You think I am being evasive."

Silence.

"I will answer the question you meant to ask."

Silence.

"We let certain allies that would be most harmed by oil's approaching decline know that they would still have a role in the world. In return, they were to thwart your space elevator plans. We were not in a position to deal with the situation directly. It would risk a war. Only the mad dog Iranians would go so far as to use a nuclear weapon against a civilian facility."

"You're admitting that you attacked and killed thousands of Americans."

"I am doing no such thing. I have answered your question, and I have given you more information than your question deserved. Seventy-five?"

Feng shot first again. Ping. Ping. Ping.

It was Frank's turn. Ping. Ping. Feng let out a terrific sneeze. Miss. Frank turned to him. "Is it going to be that kind of game?"

"I am an old man, and I am under the weather from all the travel. This Texas dust does not agree with me."

Frank merely stared.

"Come now. We are both ex-military men. We are used to bombs, the screams of the wounded. You are telling me that an old man sneezing is enough to distract you?" Without waiting for a response he said, "Here is my question. Did your daughter discover helium-3 by herself first, or did she only discover it after gaining access to our research?"

Not a bad question, Frank thought. If he said that she discovered it first, it would still implicitly indicate that they had subsequently gained access to the Chinese research. Should he mislead Feng or be honest. He owed this man nothing.

"You are taking too long. It makes me feel that perhaps you are formulating a story rather than answering my simple question."

Fair enough. Frank opted for honesty. It had the added benefit of allowing him to gloat.

"It's mainly your technology. Her own work was admirable, but we couldn't have done it without you." Frank tipped his hat at Feng. "Thanks for the help."

"That is quite all right. We've stolen technology from your company in the past. Turnabout is fair game."

"One hundred yards?" Frank said.

Feng nodded and blew his nose on a handkerchief. "I will try not to sneeze."

Feng shot. Ping. Ping. Nothing.

Frank eyed him then sighted his rifle. Not bad for an old man who was likely out of practice. Frank was impressed. He formulated his next question. Ping. Ping. Ping.

Feng grunted. "Your question?"

"Was Lucy Lee really your daughter?"

"I would not have wasted a question on something I already answered."

"I want to look you in the eye."

"You think looking into the eye of an aging politician who spent a decade in a prison being tortured is valuable? A man who has fought for ninety years to claw and scratch to the top position of the largest country in the world. My answers are truthful, or they are not. There is no looking into my eyes. There is no seeing into my soul."

"Answer."

"Mei Ying—Lucy Lee to you—was indeed my daughter, though not of my wife. Despite her heritage, she was important to me. She was a brilliant linguist and spy. None of my children have ever been allowed to lead the lazy uninspired lives of other politicians' children."

"And you didn't order her to kidnap and kill my son."

"As I told you, I did order her to kidnap your son. I miscalculated. The plan all along was to have a permanent spy embedded in the family of our chief competitor for fusion. I have spent a lifetime thinking strategically. In this rare instance, I let impatience overwhelm me. My carelessness, combined with bad luck, resulted in the death of our two children."

As Frank pondered this, the rage built inside him. He could not prove or disprove any of this right now. However, he would investigate and confirm it one way or the other. "One fifty."

"I will allow you to shoot first this time. The dust is getting to me again."

Frank nodded and took his first shot. Nothing. "Your American rifle with its expensive scope is not as good as you say it is." His anger at Feng was throwing him off. The man was getting in his head. As he turned to look at Feng, the rifle drifted over the secretary's feet.

Frank's eyes narrowed. The gun drifted higher on Feng's leg. If this man hadn't interfered, Tim would be alive. Feng turned away from him and looked downrange. "You still have two shots. How will you use them?"

Frank focused on how it would feel to squeeze two rounds into the back of the man's head. It would ruin everything he had worked for, but the man deserved it. Frank snapped the rifle back to the target and fired twice in rapid succession without pausing to site. He let his rage flow down the barrel. Ping. Ping.

"Impressive. My turn."

Feng squeezed off the first shot. Ping. Second shot. Nothing. He grunted and mumbled something to himself in Chinese.

He pointed the gun down to the ground and complained, "My eyes are not what they used to be. Perhaps I should not have chided you on your scope." He sighed and aimed his gun down range. Miss. "Your question?"

"Your supposed daughter was posing as an eco-terrorist. Eco-terrorists attacked my space elevator in the Pacific Ocean. Eco-terrorists picketed our property on the day Samantha and Benjamin were shot." Frank paused.

"What is your question?" Feng asked impatiently.

"Did you order the attack on the Pacific Ocean space elevator?"

"Of course. Why would we not take every opportunity to scuttle your efforts? I am quite proud of that attack. It had subtlety. No deaths to cause an international stir. Easy enough to pawn off on the eco-terrorists. They didn't even know that they were doing the bidding of the Chinese government."

The wind picked up. Hitting a target at two hundred yards would not be easy.

"You shoot first again. By the way, your government was kind enough to return my son to me. His political career is of course over. I suppose his wife will be happy that he gets to spend more time at home. Quite a noble act, considering your anger at me."

Frank didn't respond. Feng was trying to get under his skin. Frank sighted on the target and waited for the wind to die down. At this distance, the scope swayed back and forth over the target. The distance was too far to get a steady lock. Frank would have to pull the trigger just as the scope swayed across the target.

Ping. Miss. Ping. Two out of three. Not bad at this distance.

Feng picked up his rifle. The wind picked up again. Feng waited for it to die down, but it gave no indication that it would.

"You are stalling. This wind is trivial compared to the screams of the dying," Frank said sarcastically.

Ping. Miss. Miss.

"It appears that the Colt deserves its reputation. Your question?" Feng asked.

"Did the Chinese government assassinate Benjamin Whitman using eco-terrorists as a proxy?"

Feng set the rifle down on the table. "Now, the real game can begin." He continued, "We had nothing to do with Mr.

Whitman's death. Moreover, we have spent a great deal of time and energy infiltrating the left-leaning groups in your country. Particularly those with a green bent. We find that they have a religious zeal that approaches the fervor of the jihadists.

"I can therefore assure you that eco-terrorists had nothing to do with his death. We would know if they did," Feng said.

"So who did? A random shooter?" Frank asked.

"In my country, we incarcerate or kill our political enemies. It ensures progress and the common good. Is America that different?"

Frank digested this.

"Who was most threatened by Mr. Whitman's candidacy? The Chinese government? Why would we care? Neither of your political parties is particularly friendly with China at this point.

"I understand you are getting ready to address the United Nations. I understand that the United States will be nationalizing your space elevator and helium-3 production. The United States will of course attempt to edge out China with recent events."

Frank remained silent.

"Don't bother denying it. Any of it. We're quite confident of our sources," Feng said.

"You didn't have any legitimate questions to ask today, did you?" Frank asked.

"I would never ask a question to which I did not already know the answer. As I said, I came here to provide you with information. May I?" He motioned to the AK-47.

Frank nodded.

Feng checked the clip to see how many rounds he had left. He sighted on the two hundred yard target and pulled the trigger five times. Ping. Ping. Ping. Ping. Ping.

Feng stepped back and admired the rifle. "Still the best weapon after all these years."

Frank had been gamed. The question was whether any of the information was true.

"We will never be friends," Feng said. "But you have more dangerous enemies than us. We know that Mr. Whitman handled much of the business negotiations and politicking for your company. Perhaps you are out of your depth."

Frank missed Benjamin on so many different levels. This mess was indeed something that Benjamin would be adept at handling.

"If you come up with a plan that doesn't involve the American government dominating world energy production, perhaps I can help. There are many in the world who would rather not see control of the moon in the hands of your government. For the time being, our interests are aligned."

The general secretary turned on his heel and walked back to the house.

Chapter 74

Austin, Sawyer Family Ranch

At times, Frank swore he regretted the success of his space elevator. The endless parade of well-wishers from the corporate and governmental worlds distracted him from more pressing matters. He wanted to focus on increasing helium-3 production, building fusion reactors, and negotiating the endless contracts with various countries. This meeting would be particularly onerous. The ambassador of France had personally requested an opportunity to meet Frank to congratulate him on his accomplishment. Frank tried to duck the meeting, but the man was insistent. He even agreed to come to the Sawyer ranch to respect Frank's schedule.

The doorbell rang. Frank opened the door to see an unexpectedly tall and masculine looking Frenchmen with his beautiful wife. Aides followed behind carrying gift boxes.

"Bonjour, Monsieur Sawyer."

"Ambassador, ma'am, welcome to our home."

Frank brought them into the living room and introduced them to Lisa.

"May I first say how sorry I am to hear of Benjamin's passing," the ambassador said.

"You knew Ben?" Frank asked.

"He was a dear friend of ours," the ambassador's wife said. "As you know, the Whitmans spent a lot of time in Washington on behalf of your company. We are stopping by to see Beth during this trip to share our condolences, and we will be at his services."

Frank didn't know what to say. Ben ran in broad circles to be effective at his job so that Frank could focus on his. It made him miss him even more.

Lisa stepped in to fill the void. "We all miss him."

"Let's talk about happier things. We have gifts." The ambassador motioned to his entourage to put their boxes on the ground. They stepped outside to provide the couples with some privacy.

Frank said nothing, so Lisa chimed in. "You are so kind, Mr. Ambassador. Shall we open them now?"

"Of course, of course. I wish to see your reaction." He handed the two boxes to Frank and Lisa. The man rubbed his hands together and leaned forward with a grin.

Frank removed the wrapping paper and noted that the box inside was labeled Paul West, a maker of high-end custom cowboy boots. *Better than escargot and truffle oil.*

He opened the box and froze. While admittedly beautiful, the supple boots had a large red, white, and blue flag emblazoned on them. It was not the American flag. Frank stared at the tri-band French colors emblazoned on the top of the boot. He pursed his lips in an ironic half smile.

The French ambassador slapped his leg and let out a loud laugh more appropriate for a Texas honky-tonk than a Paris café. "You and Mrs. Sawyer will make a striking couple if you wear those to one of your local Austin bars."

"It might generate some conversation," Frank conceded.

Lisa frowned at Frank. "They're beautiful, and we'll definitely find ample opportunities to wear them."

"I am glad you like them, Madame. My family's wealth comes from cattle ranching in the south of France. While we appreciate a good pair of boots, I am not ignorant of France's reputation in Texas. Forgive my sense of humor."

Frank liked this Frenchman despite himself. He was not only a friend of Ben's, but a rancher as well.

"Perhaps you would like to see my property? We have some longhorn cattle you might like. They are different from the longhorns in the south of France," Frank said.

"I was hoping we could spend some time alone. Ladies, if you will excuse us."

Frank escorted the ambassador out to one of the ranch pickups. "Perhaps we could ride?" the ambassador asked. "I am never around horses in Washington. It would be a nice change of pace."

Frank nodded, and they diverted to the horse stalls. They each saddled their own horse. The ambassador made small talk as they rode the few dusty miles to where the longhorns grazed. They climbed off their horses and leaned against the wooden fence.

"Beautiful animals," the ambassador said, nodding at the longhorns. "Is this a working ranch, or are they for sentimental value?"

Frank raised his eyebrow at this. "Of course it's a working ranch. Lisa manages it, and it makes good money every year."

"Admirable. Our ranches are also still quite profitable. I wish I could spend more time there, but duty calls."

"Duty. You mentioned you wanted to speak to me alone. I assume this isn't purely a social call?"

"No. I have information for you."

One of the longhorns sidled up to the wood post fence, and the ambassador rubbed its nose affectionately despite the grime. He ignored the resulting dirt on his tailored European suit. The man's authenticity was pleasantly surprising.

"Benjamin told me you have a healthy disrespect for politics and government?" the ambassador asked.

"You could say that," Frank agreed.

"Aside from losing your closest friend, you must also miss the role he played on your team."

"Ben was definitely more inclined to entertain foreign ambassadors than I," Frank joked.

"And yet, politics has its place. Would you not agree?"

"National defense, public safety, a few other areas—"

"I don't mean such things. Everyone can agree to that. I am speaking of realpolitik. I assume you know the term?"

"I have a basic understanding."

"It is politics devoid of ideological notions. On its worst days, devoid of moral or ethical considerations. It values practical outcomes above anything else."

"Exactly the kind of thing I avoid."

"You know, or you will soon, that your company will be nationalized and your achievements taken from you?"

Frank frowned and looked at the horizon. The sharks were circling. Apparently, another one was getting ready to enter the already bloody water.

"What is it that you want?" the ambassador asked.

Frank walked down the edge of the dusty path. The ambassador followed him.

"The space elevator is the single greatest engineering achievement of the century. Helium-3 will soon provide unlimited energy to the entire globe. Both are stepping-stones to my real goal. One viable commercial operation in space will lead to another which will lead to another."

"But that will fall into place without you. You should return home and work with your wife to manage the ranch."

"I disagree. It must be free from men like General Secretary Feng. They would use the technology to control others rather than freeing them."

"Yes, yes. You have defeated the totalitarian Chinese with their massive economic muscle without firing a shot. A masterstroke. All the more reason to hang up your proverbial spurs and relax."

"I'm finding my own government is no better. And I can assume I've landed on the purpose of your visit?"

They walked down the trail in silence for another fifty yards.

"France and America are allies. We value the relationship," the ambassador said.

Frank did not reply.

"However, realpolitik dictates that there must be counterbalancing forces in the world. Too much power in the hands of America is not good for France and not good for the planet."

"With our current leadership, perhaps it isn't even good for America," Frank agreed.

"Allow me to be trite. Nature abhors a vacuum. If not China, and not America, then whom?"

"I hope you don't mean France. The boots were nice and all, but—"

The ambassador grew serious. "I am not joking anymore. Who will govern this new colony? You said yourself it will expand beyond helium-3 almost immediately."

"Let private industry do it."

"Impossible. Men with guns and missiles will insist they are more up to the task. Are you familiar with George Washington?"

"Of course."

"Why would a man that was already wealthy fight against the English? He would have prospered under American rule or British rule. By the time he was done being president, all he wanted to do was return to his farm in Virginia."

It was a thoughtful question for a French national. Washington put himself in harm's way. He did something that made little sense from a purely personal perspective. "Washington saw a gap that no one else could fill as well as he could. He stepped into the gap," Frank answered.

"You must fill this gap or someone will fill it for you. You shall have my government's assistance if you need it."

Chapter 75

Kiribati, Kanton Island

Heat rose off the asphalt of the six-thousand-foot-long runway adding to an already hot and humid day. The president of Kiribati waved expansively at the long stretch of asphalt and said, "Before Mr. Whitman struck this bargain, the jungle had reclaimed everything you see."

Frank guessed the recently refinished tarmac was long enough and good enough that most commercial airliners and cargo planes could land with ease. His intuition that Ben was hallucinating about a mythical island were wrong. *Ben had been busy. But to what end?*

"Tell me more about this agreement," Frank said.

"I am surprised that Mr. Whitman did not share the details with you."

"I was building the space elevator. He was running for president. Then he was murdered."

The president looked away. "I am sorry. I should have been more sensitive to your friend's passing."

"He'll be missed. But tell me, what did you agree to?"

"The agreement is simple, but the mechanics have been difficult. We were to refurbish the airport and cede this island to you. As I understand it, his intent was to meet with the United Nations to have it declared a new country in its own right. In return, we receive fifty million dollars and guaranteed employment for up to ten thousand of the residents of Kiribati."

The landing strip would make the logistical support of the ocean-going space elevator much easier. *But why go for country status?* The sound of a helicopter broke Frank's reverie as it raced to the far end of the island.

The president answered his mobile phone and spoke in a language that Frank didn't understand. He turned to Frank and said, "Come with me. The guests I've mentioned have arrived."

They climbed into the back of a Range Rover, and the driver took them around the outer loop of the island. The unpaved roads jostled the truck, but the roads had been recently redone. Someone had filled the potholes with gravel.

The driver stopped the truck in front of a beautiful white house reminiscent of something from the Texas plains. Frank commented, "The architecture of the house reminds me of home."

"As it should. That was the intent. This home was built for the future president of this country with no name."

Frank furrowed his brow, unclear on where this was going. He nodded to the helicopter. "Who are we meeting?"

"Come with me."

They walked up the gravel path to the front door and entered. An overweight bald man and the Chinese ambassador sat in the living room sipping bright blue island drinks with umbrellas. They looked up at Frank's entrance and grinned.

"Mr. Sawyer, it is good to see you again," the Chinese ambassador said.

Frank scowled at the man and made no comment.

"My welcome is genuine. Times change. We have much to discuss. Let me introduce you to my colleague, the Russian ambassador to America."

The large man stood and clasped Frank's hand with a grip that was more fat than muscle. The hand felt like a wet mitten. "It is good to finally meet you. Mr. Whitman was always quite insistent that any discussions between our nation and your company go through him."

"We divided and conquered to avoid blurring the lines of responsibility. Why are we here?"

The three politicians looked at each other and came to a silent agreement that the Chinese ambassador should explain.

"We are here because we cannot afford to let America have control of the moon and, by extension, world energy production. We are aware through our conversations with the French government that President Gladwell has put you in a most uncomfortable position."

Frank hid his irritation with the French ambassador for sharing a private conversation. More realpolitik nonsense. "I'm not going to betray my country to China and Russia. Your intelligence is accurate, but I prefer the devil I know."

The Russian pulled his huge lower lip over his top lip and shook his pudgy hands. "That goes without saying. We merely hope to give you the tools to prevent your President Gladwell from betraying you."

Frank leaned forward, put his elbows on his knees, and folded his hands. "You have a plan I take it?"

The Chinese ambassador said, "This plan was created by Mr. Whitman. Your friend the French ambassador has continued it in his absence."

"Wonderful, but what's the plan?"

"You have broad international support for the following. First, this island will become an independent country that you will lead. Second, the moon will become a temporary protectorate of the United Nations. You will be its governor. Third, you will resign from Automated Technologies."

"Why would I do any of that? No offense, but I hate politicians, and I don't want to be one. I love private industry, and I'm not going to give up the right to run my own business."

"Then you will lose it all. America will nationalize your company and your technology. You can go back to your lab and invent better mousetraps. But your involvement with the lunar efforts and the broader commercialization of space is done."

"Do you have something other than one of those umbrella drinks?"

The president said something to one of the attendants in the kitchen, and a Shiner Bock materialized in Frank's hand. Frank looked at the bottle approvingly. *They pulled out all the stops.*

"I have other senior leaders in my company that I trust. I would like to put them in the political roles and maintain control of the company."

"Impossible. We discussed that alternative with anyone that matters. Only you have the name recognition. The entire deal falls apart if you don't step into both roles."

Frank clanked the bottle on the coffee table. "I literally can't imagine a worse job than reporting to the United Nations. I can't see doing that for the rest of my life."

"I did say temporary protectorate. The moon's long-term status remains open to discussion. In the meantime, you will be the impartial arbiter of its development and of helium-3 production."

"And you would trust an American to be fair in his dealings."

"We would trust an American who has been cheated by his government. More than cheated. There is the matter of your friend's death. Do you believe eco-terrorists hired a professional sniper with the skills necessary to get past the American Secret Service?"

Again, the indirect reference to Gladwell's involvement in Ben's death. Unprovable, but not implausible. *What would Ben do?*

As if he could read Frank's thoughts, the Chinese ambassador continued. "You trusted Benjamin Whitman?"

"With my life."

"This plan was not created by a cabal of politicians. Your best friend and closest confidant developed this plan. We are merely executing it."

That was the rub. Ben had seen the freight train coming down the tracks, and he had developed a strategy to get me onto a different set of rails. As he always had.

"You've given me a great deal to consider. Take me back to my jet."

Chapter 76
New York, United Nations

Frank looked out at the faces of the United Nations delegates from around the world. There were two broad contingents. One briefed on a new world order in which America would lead mankind's journey into space. A world in which America would dominate world energy production in the coming decades. A world led by the beneficent United States that would decide who got what. A world led by a man that had likely murdered his best friend and stolen his life's work.

The other contingent had been briefed on... something else.

The teleprompter clicked on. Gladwell's political team had scoured the speech. Just the right amount of emotion and nuance. Frank would castigate China for its attacks on American property and its flagrant abuse of international law. He would celebrate the role of the American government in righting the situation. The politicians made sure that the focus rapidly switched to how this would help the world. There was no need for America to gloat.

Frank began, "Delegates of the United Nations, the American government prepared a speech for me today. A speech that would celebrate mankind's progress and world unity. A speech that would create a new world order with unlimited energy for all, controlled by the American government."

He walked over to the teleprompter. He shoved it off the stage onto the floor where it shattered.

The audience shifted in their seats and turned to look at each other.

"Ladies and gentleman, that won't be happening. We've seen governments clashing over the last year in a mad rush to control space. We've all seen the actions of the Chinese. The world community would be crazy to let a country with this flagrant disregard for law and order have a controlling interest in space."

There were fervent murmurs of agreement across the large room. Heads nodded throughout the audience.

"However, there is also no way that America can be allowed to control this market. America will work tirelessly to transition every responsible country from fossil fuels to fusion power. This will take time, but no one will have the option of staying on fossil fuel in the long run. How will their factories or cities compete with countries that have unlimited energy at a fraction of the cost? The answer—they won't.

"Once America has worked with these countries to get them switched over to fusion, fossil fuel will disappear as a viable energy alternative. Any country not doing America's bidding will see their helium-3 supplies dry up. And they will have no recourse."

More heads nodded in agreement.

"The only way that America can do this is by nationalizing... by stealing... my space elevator technology and preventing other countries from getting it. I propose a different solution entirely.

"I propose that the moon be setup as an independent protectorate of the United Nations for a period of three years. During that time, Automated Technologies will operate the only helium-3 mining operation on the moon. This will ensure economies of scale and the most rapid development of fusion for the earth.

"At the end of three years, the moon will be an independent entity with country status. It will have representation here at the United Nations. I will provide a proposal to you outlining how I will distribute fusion power around the world initially. It will also contain an outline of a proposal for the governance of the moon in the coming years.

"At the insistence of many in this room, I have agreed to be governor of the lunar protectorate. I will also serve as the first president of a newly independent country formed from Kanton Island in the Pacific Ocean.

"Finally, I have two requests for this body. First, that the lunar colony be named Timotheus after my son, Tim Sawyer. Second, that you fast track the approval of the new country of Whitman Island, named for Mr. Benjamin Whitman. Thank you for your time."

The audience sat quietly while they waited for the translation to finish. Two thirds of the room immediately jumped to their feet to give a standing ovation. The remaining one third rapidly followed. One man remained seated. As Frank locked eyes with him, President Gladwell stood with the rest of the chamber and stiffly clapped his hands. His expression matched that of every other politician in the room, but his eyes gleamed with hatred.

Chapter 77

Washington, DC, The White House

President Thomas Gladwell sat with his back to his desk staring out across the lawn. He held an untouched glass of scotch in his hand. Frank Sawyer had won. Even in death, that anti-government, unpatriotic oaf Whitman had outplayed him. Two men that hated politics had beaten him, the consummate politician. He mulled over all the alternatives available to him to make Sawyer and his family pay.

He considered making another phone call, but he knew it was too risky. Two men conveniently dying at just the right time would be a bit too much for anyone to swallow.

He had lost most of his allies in the United Nations. Three of the five permanent members of the U.N. Security Council had boxed him into the corner. There were even signs that merry old England wanted distance from his administration. *Cowards and fair-weather friends.*

There were no realistic military options available to him. Instead, the world community was extorting him to provide protection to Frank's business as part of an international fleet. Sawyer now had United States military protection without giving anything in return.

Samantha Sawyer, now the head of Automated Technologies, had quietly reincorporated in the nascent country of Whitman Island. He could certainly tax and hyper-regulate Automated Technologies' assets in America for a short time. But the company would move its operations to the new location. Any legal action on his part to nationalize assets of any kind would certainly play out in a public forum like the United Nations. The world community would paint him as a bully and a thug.

He had eight years to make the man pay, but for now, Frank Sawyer was out of his reach. All he could do for the time being was collect information and bide his time. He swallowed his scotch in a single swallow and poured another.

Chapter 78

Austin, Sawyer Family Ranch

Frank Sawyer sat on the wraparound porch reading and watching the Texas sunset. Lisa came out with a Shiner Bock for him and a glass of wine for her. She tilted his tablet up. "What are you reading?"

"I'm flipping through the Federalist Papers, the Bill of Rights, and John Locke's treatises on civil government."

"Fascinating."

Frank knew his wife well enough to know that meant the opposite. *Perhaps a conversation for another day.* He locked the screen and set the tablet aside.

"It's beautiful," Lisa said, glancing at the sunset.

"It is indeed. Have I told you recently how much I love y—?"

"One of your guys sent me your recording from that flying coffin."

"Oh. That was supposed to be deleted. Listen, I—"

"No need to say anything. It said what needed to be said. I feel the same way and more. I'll spare you the need to prepare a second 'romantic soliloquy.' I figure one is all you can handle per decade."

She smiled at him, and they were both silent for a while. "How are you feeling?" she asked.

Frank stared at the sunset and nursed his beer. "I accomplished everything I wanted."

"You always do."

"Our son and best friend are both dead because of it. I would give it all up to have them back."

"I know you would, but the world doesn't work that way. There's no way you could've known how this would play out."

"I'm settled with that. I know it's true in my heart, but I miss Tim. I miss Ben."

"Tell me about Ben's island again."

"It's the smallest sovereign nation in the world. No more than a few square miles of land."

"The point being?"

"Distance. When you lie down with thieves and killers, you become a thief and a killer."

"Fusion? Iran?"

"Both morally correct decisions on my part. Both were tempered responses to theft and mass murder. Still, neither decision represents the kind of person I want to be. Ben wanted to create some distance for me."

"The moon should help with that." Lisa laughed and held up a celebrity magazine she'd been reading. It featured Frank on the cover with the title King of the Moon.

Frank didn't return her smile at first. "I hope you're right."

He forced himself to get out of his funk and smiled at her. "Are you ready to go? It's a worthwhile place to visit. Given time, it might be a worthwhile place to live."

"I'm excited. And nervous. I would hate to give up this." She motioned at their ranch and the sunset.

"We need to come up with a title for you. First lady seems too mundane. Queen of the Moon?"

She laughed. "A bit too pretentious for my tastes. I would like to do something useful if I give up managing the ranch. We'll see." She continued, "How do you feel about taking a government role?"

"It's a necessary evil. The world can't let China control the moon, and I'll be damned if I'll let that bastard Gladwell have a hand in things." Frank fumed that he had no way to make him pay for Ben's murder. For now, not even a way to prove Gladwell's hand in things.

Lisa nodded but remained silent for a few minutes before continuing. "I understand why you can't be Chairman of Automated Technologies and take on the governorship of the moon. As it is, there is going to be a huge conflict of interest." She paused. "Is Sam ready?"

"She's young, but she can do it. She's learned from the best."

"She's learned from the best? Are the beer and the new role making someone feel a bit imperious tonight?"

His eye clouded over. "I meant Ben. She's up to it. She's got more passion for that side of the business than I ever did. And she certainly has my engineering skills."

"She has Stephen to help her, too."

"That would be awkward for them. She would be his boss. I've offered him a job heading security for Timotheus and Whitman Island. I expect he'll take it."

"You own the company. It's workable if we keep it in the family."

Frank sat bolt upright. "Isn't that a bit premature?"

"Perhaps. A mother's intuition would say it isn't all that premature." She patted his hand and he relaxed back into his chair.

As they watched the sun set in the western skies, the last rays silhouetted the full moon in an amber-red glow.

About the Author:

Jerry Kaczmarowski lives in Seattle with his family. His first book, Moon Rising, was released in June 2014. His second book, Sapient, is planned for release in late 2014. He writes techno-thrillers that explore the benefits and dangers of mankind's scientific advancement.

Made in the USA
Lexington, KY
08 August 2014